BRIDGES GOING NOWHERE

An action-packed thriller taking you

from the dusty deserts of the Middle East

to the snows of Sweden

*Part one of "***The Hart Trilogy***"*

Ilya Meyer

Bridges Going Nowhere

Second edition April 2015

This book is dedicated to my darling wife and our four wonderful children, the inspiration for everything I do

Prologue

45 seconds.

That's all it took to trigger a train of events intended to set a nation alight.

It all started as just so much routine.

It was a hot August day offering the regular Friday lunchtime performance. The scene was the same as usual – the rocky, windblown outskirts of town, where the sparse scrub sprouted wherever sufficient soil gathered in the cracks and crevices between boulders.

As usual the press were there with assurances of juicy footage, the Molotov cocktails were lined up ready for use, grip-friendly sharp rocks gathered and positioned in discreet piles at strategic locations leading from the western edge of the town all the way to the town's southern perimeter.

The stage was set for the day's theatre. A stage on which as usual every single movement had been carefully choreographed, in a show that had been repeated every single Friday afternoon for months and years. Shadowed as always by the media, ever hungry for that elusive angle that would once and for all prove the perfidy of the state apparatus in its violence against children. Children – a term that surprisingly often seemed to include muscular young men aged twenty-five, whose only crime was that they liked exercising their muscles by throwing rocks at people.

What was different was that on this particular Friday, all the action seemed to be focused on the outskirts of the town.

Cameramen sympathetic to the cause positioned in advance according to predetermined, carefully planned lines of sight and panoramic angles of vision, ready to catch the 'spontaneous' action. The youngest children given abundant supplies of rocks in their school satchels. A girl of 13 despatched in the vanguard to set alight the brush nearest the chain-link security fence. And heavily armed soldiers watching from a distance before grouping together to receive their orders.

And then the routine ebb and flow of rock-throwing and tear gas, a horde of press photographers waiting idly while first the children and gradually adults too started throwing stones, cameras switched on only after the soldiers started responding, and a sole soldier trying to catch as much of the action as she could from her vantage point atop a dusty Land-Rover; the army's usual inadequate attempt to prove, post-action, the justification of its innocence and its defensive response.

Under a barrage of rocks and Molotov cocktails the soldiers grouped, then gradually spread out and slowly forced the rioters away from the security fence and the western outskirts of the town down to the south, where the rocky fields gave way to dusty low houses lining narrow winding lanes.

Falling back on their previously prepared stockpiles of rocks the protesters kept the troops busy for over an hour.

But it didn't take an hour for the most important move to take place. Less than 45 seconds after the start of the rioting, as the action moved south, two men detached themselves from the crowd and moved silently away. Walking swiftly but without running, they made their way along the twisting streets till they came to a drab, nondescript two-storey house. Without knocking, they opened the faded blue front door and slipped quietly inside.

45 seconds to ensure the action would keep the cameras pointing the wrong way. The soldiers never saw them, never knew they had been there.

This was the scene that Friday afternoon – so typical of the scene every single Friday afternoon – in the Palestinian Arab town of Kafr Jibrin near Israel's security fence in that part of the world known to the Western world as the occupied West Bank, to the Palestinian Arabs as their nascent state of Palestine, and to Israel as the disputed Jewish provinces of Judea & Samaria.

Chapter 1

"Think caveman."

Adan Hamati and Haydar Murad had made their way safely away from the scene of the rioting, arrived at the blue door of the two-storey house and slipped inside. They dusted off their clothes and now sat on opposite sides of a small kitchen table in a sparsely furnished room.

A big man in his early forties, Adan Hamati perched somewhat awkwardly on the flimsy white plastic kitchen chair. He carried no outward signs of political or religious affiliation – not the *keffiyeh* that identified him as an adherent of the Palestinian Fatah party, nor the beard that was such a universal symbol of the religious fervour of Palestinian Hamas followers. He was tall, broad-shouldered yet not burly, had a thick head of dark brown hair and black eyes that glistened between long, almost effeminate upper and lower eyelashes.

But there was nothing in the least bit effeminate about Adan Hamati. He was a cool, level-headed and deliberate thinker – and an undisputed man of action. A strategist, a tactician – and a leading figure in the *Intifada*, the popular Palestinian Arab uprising against Israel that had seen so many people injured, maimed and killed on both sides of the Israeli-Palestinian divide.

Haydar Murad, sitting opposite him, was also his opposite in every imaginable respect. In his mid-twenties, small, wiry and seemingly bursting with restless energy in every movement, even in the way his eyes flickered around the room before coming to rest on Adan Hamati's calm face. Where Hamati was big, intimidating almost, Murad was small and agile. Where Hamati seemed to emanate a feeling of reassurance, radiating an aura of natural leadership, Murad was tense, coiled, ready to jump into the fray and do what was asked of him by his leader.

And yet, despite all the energy, the restlessness, the tension that made up Haydar Murad's personality, he was calmness and concentration personified when the time came for him to use his special set of skills, deploying a pair of rock-steady hands whenever he was asked to assemble the deadly mines and shrapnel bombs that were his signature.

Adan Hamati and Haydar Murad were a highly successful team in the ongoing battle for Palestinian freedom from what they saw as Israel's illegal occupation of their land. The land that stretched all the way east from the Mediterranean Sea to the Jordan River. The land from which they intended to expel every last Jew in their creation of the Arab state of Palestine.

Adan Hamati fixed his eyes firmly on the young man sitting opposite him.

Haydar Murad frowned and looked out the window. Or more correctly, he glanced at where the window should have been.

Bricked over. It seemed like he'd spent most of his life in airless boxes, windows either non-existent or bricked over. In the former case, in Israeli police or military cells; in the latter case staying constantly one step out of the reach of his Israeli pursuers.

"Think caveman?" Murad asked. "*This* is your grand master-plan? The Israelis have spent the past decades slowly returning us to cavemen conditions – we cannot drive where we want, we cannot work where we want, we cannot worship where we want – and you want me to embrace what they're doing to us?"

"Think," replied Hamati in measured tones. He looked at his companion. Haydar Murad had always been afflicted with a hot temper. A skilled fighter and a creative master in the art of bomb-making, Murad was nonetheless all too prone to rising to the bait – real or imaginary.

"Think," repeated Hamati. "What we have here is a project of truly momentous proportions. One that is so important we cannot do things by rote – we have to rewrite the rule book, play according to an entirely fresh set of rules."

Murad didn't seem to be particularly impressed. "Look," he said, glancing pointedly at the door, "it's about time you stopped talking in circles and got down to what it is you have in mind. The kids outside aren't going to last much longer before it's time for them to return home for their afternoon meal, and the press have to be given time to return to Israel to coordinate and file their footage. Why exactly are we here, what have you got planned?"

Adan Hamati stroked his chin, thought for a few seconds, then started speaking. "What is our biggest problem right now? No, don't go there – I know about your constant complaints that you can't get enough fertiliser and other materials for bombs. But I'm talking about something much, much bigger. Stop thinking micro, start thinking macro."

Haydar Murad looked puzzled, and not a little surly. Bombs were his specialty, and he didn't appreciate it when he thought someone was belittling the art at which he was such a master.

Hamati hastened to reassure him. "I want you to think on a larger, a *MUCH* larger scale. In fact, I want you to think about a map, a map of the world." He paused, choosing his words carefully before continuing. "Once again, what is our biggest problem right now? I'll tell you: we no longer have visionary leadership. We don't have a Yasser Arafat pulling the strings and telling the West what to think and what to do and when to do it. What we have is a leader who colludes with the West, one who doesn't dare test his own strength, our strength. It's time we demonstrated to him and to the world that we have strength. In abundance."

Murad was no longer looking impatiently at the door. His eyes were boring into every line, every pore of Adan Hamati's face. He waited expectantly.

"The fact is that Arafat knew how to stage-manage the world and court public opinion," continued Hamati. "But he didn't wait for opportunities to present themselves – he created them. He always managed to keep the Palestinian issue front and centre of the world's attention. He did a fantastic job persuading the world that the Zionist occupation of our lands is the prime cause of the conflict. The fact of the matter is that Chairman Arafat totally, utterly, occupied the minds, the agendas – even the finances – of the West for more than 3 decades. His occupation of the Western mind-set was far more successful than the Zionist occupation of our lands. He succeeded in wiping virtually all other issues off the table."

Haydar Murad's eyes were glistening. "You're right," his words fairly tumbled out. "This man," he spat out the name of the current President of the Palestinian Authority, "he's nothing but a shadow, he doesn't lead the Americans and the Europeans, he follows like a dog in their footsteps. But how are we going to convince him to try a different tack?" he asked.

"We aren't even going to try," replied Adan Hamati. "We're going to take the initiative. No," he held up his hand quickly to ward off the question he knew was coming. "No, we're not going to do away with him, we're not going to harm him.

In fact, we're not going to have anything to do with him – we'll let him continue his own race and we'll run ours, our very own private race that only you and I know about, for now."

Hamati walked to the tiny kitchen and opened a wall cabinet, found two glasses. He turned on the tap and let it run, waiting for the water to run cool. Filling the two glasses he returned to the table and placed one before his companion.

"Drink," he said. "We're going to be here a while as I explain what we're going to do."

And pausing only for an occasional sip of water, he explained to Haydar Murad how it came about that the Palestinian cause was currently stuck in the doldrums: it was all a matter of press coverage.

The world was simply focusing too much on irrelevant issues, such as the Taliban's increasing grip on Afghanistan, al-Shabab's increasingly daring actions in East Africa, the never-ending barrage of attacks by various al-Qaeda affiliates all across northern Africa, the domestic turmoil in the Lebanon, the increasingly brutal civil war in Syria, the horrendous Shia on Sunni carnage in Iraq. Not only that, now the Iranians were so close to their nuclear bomb, the West was almost totally preoccupied with the mullahs in Tehran. What the Palestinian cause needed was a major event, a 9/11 moment, one that would force the West's focus back on the Palestinian issue. Because it was the duty of the West to think only of the Palestinian issue. The West needed to stop frittering away its resources and time on irrelevant conflicts elsewhere. Palestine was the only game in town, period.

"Just get me the materials and I'll give the West something to think about," said Haydar Murad eagerly. "I'll set the entire Jewish occupation alight, from Eilat in the south to Kfar Blum in the north."

Hamati shook his head slowly. "No," he said. "We're not going to do anything so close to home, because that always ends up with our own children suffering. We're going abroad, my friend. Buy some warm woollies, we're going to Sweden."

Chapter 2

A world away from the small dusty town of Kafr Jibrin, but in reality barely more than a couple of hours south and west of the Palestinian Arab town, lies the Israeli city of Ashdod.

Even as recently as twenty years ago Ashdod, on Israel's sparkling Mediterranean coast, was pretty much a hidden gem. It had a small and stable population, but for some reason it had never developed into a fashionable tourist destination like Tel Aviv up along the coast or Netanya further north.

Ashdod had grown in recent years, but it still had pretty much of a small-town feel to it. And although plenty of gleaming white modern apartment buildings had sprung up over the years, it nonetheless managed to maintain the cosiness of a provincial backwater.

Which was a good thing, according to its residents. No-one felt this more strongly that the Hart family. They lived in a modest three-bedroom house one block away from the sea – in fact their upstairs TV room and one upstairs bedroom both afforded a magnificent view of the blue waters of the Mediterranean. No doubt some multinational corporation would eventually come along and block out their beloved view of the ocean by erecting a highly-priced, tall and ugly monstrosity of a hotel right in their line of sight, but that hadn't happened as yet.

With two children growing up in the household, it was always to be expected that the youngsters would bicker day and night over who would be favoured with the sea-view room.

But the Harts seemed to live by a different code. In fact, everything about them was different. Israel is and always has been a melting-pot of cultures, ethnicities, languages, cuisines, skin colours. And nowhere was this more starkly exemplified than with the Harts.

The father, Dov, had been born in Sweden of Jewish parents who came from Byelorussia, and after high school he and his parents emigrated to Israel and Kibbutz Yagur just south of Haifa. A huge bear of a man with an eminently apt name – Dov means bear in Hebrew – he was an amiable, once-blond but now balding, quiet-spoken engineer who had recently retired from a lifetime of designing and overseeing the building of key mechanical components for Israel's expanding navy fleet of fast surface attack craft. Years spent out on the Mediterranean testing his components had tanned his skin to a leathery brown complexion.

Sarah, his wife, was everything her husband was not: petite, fair, freckled with a fiery shock of unruly red hair framing her face and a pair of piercing green eyes. Born in Scotland of Jewish parents whose ancestors had lived in Scotland for as long as anyone could remember, she had come to Israel – oh, a lifetime ago – for a summer of picking oranges on a kibbutz before returning to her architectural studies in Edinburgh. In a tale that echoed so many others in the burgeoning Jewish state, Dov and Sarah decided that physical disparity notwithstanding, they were made for each other.

Sarah, however, decided that kibbutz life in Israel was not for her, while Dov was equally adamant that he (literally) couldn't stomach Scotland. A country where deep-fried chocolate bars seemed to be regarded as the very pinnacle of culinary delight and where everyone seemed somehow very reluctant to name the ingredients in Scotland's famed national dish, haggis.

Sarah and Dov compromised by moving somewhere neither of them had ever been before: Ashdod. Further south than Kibbutz Yagur, close to the Gaza Strip and the northern Negev Desert, and hotter than either really wanted, they nevertheless built a life and a home of their own.

What they lacked was the patter of little feet. Try as they might, and despite all the treatments available at the time, they had no success in producing children. At about the same time, the Jewish state launched a massive project to bring Ethiopia's Jews to Israel. And they came in waves. In 1985 alone Operation Moses brought almost six and a half thousand Ethiopian Jews to Israel by way of refugee camps in Sudan and various intermediary countries – they came on foot, by plane, in boats.

The very last flight out in Operation Moses brought a young heavily pregnant woman travelling alone. Her husband had died in the refugee camp in Sudan – and within one month of her arrival in the Jewish state of Israel she died in childbirth at Haifa's Rambam Hospital – but not before giving birth to a healthy baby girl. At the Atlit absorption centre where many of the Ethiopian arrivals were initially housed awaiting permanent accommodation, the staff scrambled to find a suitable family for adoption.

Sarah and Dov, on a visit to Dov's parents at nearby Kibbutz Yagur, heard about the baby and applied for adoption. In Israel, bureaucracy is not the simplest obstacle in the world but after a lot of table-thumping and teary appeals – and countless visits to their home by Social Services – the baby was theirs.

That longed-for baby. Amira. The name literally meant "treetop" but for Sarah and Dov the symbolism of the name was in the way their lives had suddenly bloomed with Amira's arrival – just like the way the crown of leaves at the very top of a tree flourished. A black-eyed, dark-skinned beauty with a ready smile and easy-going temperament. By the age of two she was developing into a thoughtful, patient and always happy child, an unparalleled joy to her parents. Amira was their world.

Which is why it came as a shock to Sarah and Dov to find that their world was about to expand. With the stress of conceiving out of the way following the arrival of Amira, Sarah became pregnant and two weeks after Amira's second birthday, Sarah gave birth to a son, Benny. His full name was Benjamin, in memory of King Saul of the ancient Israelite tribe of Benjamin. Saul was the king who united the Israelites under a strong monarchy at a particularly difficult time in the nation's history.

In keeping with the disparate physical attributes of the Hart family, Benny too looked nothing like the other three members of his family. Sarah was fair, Dov had a permanent deep suntan and Amira's complexion was glossy black. Benny however favoured his mother's light skin and soon grew a mat of light-blond curls to crown his features.

Not for nothing did the neighbours' kids refer to the Harts as the Crayolas – a none-too-oblique reference to the full palette of colours the parents and children presented. It wasn't meant to be cruel, but the normally shy Amira took umbrage and it wasn't uncommon for fists to fly as she defended the Hart family honour, and in particular her little brother Benny. The two children may have been a total contrast in terms of appearance, but they grew up inseparable as kids and totally dedicated to one another through their teenage years, twin souls in everything except age, looks, colour, temperament and genealogy…

Time flew by as the children grew. Before they knew it, Sarah and Dov were spending busy weekends washing army uniforms as first Amira and then Benny were called up for their compulsory army service. The IDF – Israel Defense Forces – calls up all 18 year olds, girls and boys alike, for military service after they graduate from high school. Girls serve two years, boys three. Both can also volunteer for additional years of service in what is known as "*Keva*" or the standing army, and many do.

Both Amira and Benny did.

Chapter 3

In what became a smooth-running operation of deception and carefully orchestrated 'spontaneous outrage', every successive Friday saw Adan Hamati and Haydar Murad meet behind the cover provided by the children of what many touted as the next intifada-in-the-making.

They met in various towns and cities across what the Palestinians referred to as the Occupied State of Palestine, the outside world referred to as the West Bank following Jordan's occupation of the territory along the west bank of the River Jordan from 1948 to 1967, and Israel referred to as the Disputed Territories – the Jewish provinces of Judea and Samaria that the Palestinian Arabs wanted for their nascent state.

And with each successive meeting Adan Hamati revealed more and more details of his plan. Careful to a fault, he wanted to be sure Haydar Murad was not shooting his mouth off and had tasked no fewer than three people to thoroughly monitor his movements, his phone calls, his home computer, even the market where he did his shopping. He did not explain the reason for the surveillance, just that it needed to be done.

So far nothing had happened to raise concern, so Hamati continued filling out the details of his plan.

Murad kept returning to one single question: "Why Sweden? What's there for us? Here we are at home, we know every inch of the ground, why on earth would we be interested in a place so cold even the cows wear coats in the winter – I've seen pictures on the Internet."

Hamati sighed and started explaining.

Chapter 4

"You know as well as I do that what you do here catches the headlines locally, it even makes the news in Europe and the US. But its effect is here today, gone tomorrow," said Adan Hamati, choosing his words carefully. He needed to navigate a minefield of emotions if he was to pitch his plan successfully – Haydar Murad's emotions, not his own – and Murad was the expert when it came to mines, both figurative and real.

"Your work is vital," he went on. "It not only keeps the Zionist occupiers off-balance, it gives our own people a good example to emulate, it gives them a much-needed sense of achievement and self-worth. It helps in our recruitment.

"But," he continued, watching his friend's face intently, "we need a bigger canvas. That is something that Chairman Arafat understood very well. To truly capture the imagination of millions, you need to address millions. So we have to work further afield. The way Arafat succeeded in doing."

Haydar Murad listened raptly. Here, it seemed, was someone who acted on a larger stage, someone who appreciated the limitations of their current situation and who wanted to rekindle the greatness of Yasser Arafat, the only true leader the Palestinians had ever had apart from the sainted Grand Mufti of Jerusalem early in the previous century, Hajj Amin al-Husseini – a man who fully understood and appreciated the brilliance of Adolf Hitler and his master plan. Perhaps Hamati was a man worth listening to, after all.

“Go on,” he said, leaning forward. They were sitting in yet another of those dusty, nondescript rooms without windows, this time in the city of Ramallah – the current seat of the Palestinian Arab government. Until they liberated Al Quds, which the Jews and Christians persisted in calling Jerusalem.

Hamati explained. “You want to know why Sweden? Several reasons. For one thing, like I said, what you do here is local. You do it so well, and you do so much of it, that it has become a victim of its own success – over the years it has become mere background noise, chatter, the sort of thing that ‘always happens over there’. We need to grab the world’s attention. Chairman Arafat always succeeded in pulling this off; whenever the world’s attention became distracted from Palestine, or whenever he sensed that the world was sinking into routine acceptance of the situation, he pulled off a coup that refocused everyone.

“So: why specifically Sweden, you ask? Firstly, because Sweden is ripe for the plucking. The Swedes pride themselves on being open-minded, more than just about any other people on earth. The Swedish mind-set of live and let live, their unofficial religion of political correctness cost what it may, their policy of positive discrimination to enforce equality of minorities – all this means the Swedes are the ideal target.”

"Target?" burst out Murad. "You intend hitting the Swedes? What have they ever done against us? Come on, if it weren't for Sweden we'd never have gained a foothold in Europe. Not just Olof Palme, but all their other politicians and intellectuals – they all made it possible for us to gain a voice in Europe. Come on, this isn't the right way to go."

Adan Hamati held up his hand, warding off his friend's protests. "There you are," he said wearily. "Just goes to show you how run-of-the-mill our movement has become. Even I am guilty of slipping into the rut of routine – in my case routine language. My mistake, I used totally the wrong word. Not 'target' in the sense you and I usually mean. Quite the contrary – we're going to use Sweden as the stage, but we're going to get the Swedes on our side as we carry out an action on Swedish soil against the Zionist occupation here at home."

Murad looked puzzled. "How are we going to hit the Jews with an operation in Sweden? And on top of that expect the Swedes to like us for it?" he asked.

"A very justified question, my friend," replied Hamati. "And I'll explain: you know, Jews have been living in Sweden for about 300 years, and there are about 18,000 of them living there. We Muslims have been living there for less than 40 years, and we already number almost half a million. And of the Muslims, our Palestinian brothers and sisters are the ones who are most successfully driving our agenda. And yes, before you can say it – I include our Christian Palestinian brethren because when it comes to liberating the homeland, they are Palestinian nation-builders first, Christians second; they're with us – in Stockholm, Gothenburg, Malmö, and a hundred other smaller towns and cities all over the country. We've been working for four decades to persuade the Swedes of the righteousness of our cause. And we've been so successful at it that virtually the entire Swedish media are on our side – and they don't even pretend to hide their sympathies. Our friends in Sweden tell us that if you open any Swedish newspaper, there's a 90 percent chance that on any given day there'll be a pro-Palestinian article in it.

"And much more to the point," continued Hamati, his eyes glittering with the fire of his convictions, "open any Swedish newspaper and there's a 90 percent chance that on any given day there'll be an anti-Israel or even anti-Jewish article on one of its pages. Sweden – the country, the society, the people – they're ripe for this move, I tell you."

Haydar Murad leaned his chair back on its two rear legs, rocking gently back and forth, considering what this meant for him. And asked exactly that: "OK, let's say I buy this scenario you've drawn up. What does this mean for me? I'm here, where I know how to lay my hands on the necessary materials for whatever plan of action we happen to have at any given time. How am I to get anything done in a country where I don't speak the language, can't even read the labels on the materials I need to buy, where I don't have the necessary local currency – heck, where I don't even have anywhere to live or know who I can trust to keep me safe?

Look, I get your point, but this sounds like it's something that's out of our league, it's an operation that needs a whole different sort of resource, a whole different sort of planning – nothing you or I can manage without making fools of ourselves or, worse still, exposing ourselves to the wrong sort of attention." He passed his hand through his thick wave of dark brown hair and wrinkled his forehead, setting his chair back down on four legs.

"You're right, and you're wrong," replied Hamati. "You're right, of course, because this isn't something you and I could do unassisted, so far from home. But you're wrong because we have all the assistance we want, locally, on the spot – and we're shielded from outside interference because the Swedes' famous tolerance of minorities means they have neither the will nor the means to penetrate our circles. They mean well, they want us Palestinians to feel that we, like all other minorities in Sweden, are free to live our lives as we want. Which means that they don't have much insight into how we live, what we want, what we do with our time. Want to hear an open secret? In the whole of Sweden there aren't even a dozen border control or police officials who even understand or read Arabic, and of those, fewer than half are familiar with the Palestinian dialect that sets us apart from our other Arab brothers.

"You understand what I'm saying?" he went on. "For one thing, they actually *want* us to live our lives separately because they feel it is colonialist and condescending to interfere with us, and for another, they don't have the means to penetrate our group even if they wanted to – they simply don't have the linguistic or cultural skills, or the manpower. Which means we're free to do as we want.

"And there's more," he went on. "We have to be selective, of course, in who we speak to, how we approach this. Very selective. But the fact is that Sweden has a huge and sympathetic Muslim community outside Palestinian circles as well: Somalis, Pakistanis, Iraqis, Lebanese, Egyptians – even Iranians, although we have to be really careful with the Shia scum."

"Wait a minute! I know what the mullahs and their Hezbollah lackeys did to our Sunni brothers and sisters – children even – in Lebanon and Syria. I want nothing to do with those dogs, those incestuous sons of apes. They can all go to hell, in fact I'd be really pleased to help them get there with my own bare hands, the murderous bastards." Haydar Murad's face was black with pent-up rage and frustration.

It wasn't an unusual reaction among Sunni Muslims, not by any means. The Sunni and Shia Muslims had been battling one another across a variety of arenas for almost as long as Islam had existed, for the most part spending more resources and draining more blood in internecine fighting than in dealing with what they regarded as their common enemy, Jews in general and the Jewish state of Israel in particular. While the Jews continued strengthening their ring of houses on the hills around Jerusalem – even the UN rightfully termed them illegal settlements, thought Murad wrathfully –

the Sunni and Shia groups continued to ignore this threat to one of Islam's holiest places, preferring instead to battle each other across a whole swathe of countries that included Turkey, the Lebanon, Syria, Iraq, Pakistan, Egypt. It was a crying shame, what a waste.

Adan Hamati placed a gentle hand on Murad's left arm. "Don't worry," he reassured him. "We know who we can trust and who we can't. Believe it or not, there are Iranians who are intelligent enough to put these differences aside for the greater good, for the glory of the Palestinian struggle and liberation of Al Quds from the unbelievers. Leave the Persians aside, they're not of interest here.

"Let me make you some coffee and I'll explain my plan," he continued as he walked over to a small gas stove and started pulling out a coffee pot, aromatic finely ground black coffee, sugar and cardamom. "Sit back and I'll draw you a future you never dreamed about in your life."

Chapter 5

An island of vibrant democracy, human rights and religious tolerance in a sea of volatile autocratic regimes, the embattled Jewish state of Israel virtually pioneered the inclusion of women in the regular military. Not just as a nod to gender equality, but born out of necessity. Back in 1948 when the collective world community under the United Nations first ratified and then officially approved the rebirth of the Jewish state in its former homeland in a carefully delineated part of the geographic area called Mandate Palestine, Israel had a total population of just 720,000 Jews and 156,000 Arabs. The idea was that the Palestinian Jews would get their own state, Israel, in 23 percent of Mandate Palestine, while the Palestinian Arabs – Muslims and Christians alike – would get their own state, Palestine, in the remaining 77 percent of the territory. Israel would have to accept a large minority of Palestinian Arabs in its population, making up 22 percent of the total, while Arab Palestine would not have a single Jew living within its territory. Under the leadership of David Ben-Gurion, who went on to become Israel's first Prime Minister, the Palestinian Jews agreed. The Palestinian Arabs did not.

The world's Arab and Muslim nations refused to accept the existence of the new Jewish state which emerged out of the colonial mandate in the geographic area of British Palestine. At the same time, however, those same Arab and Muslim nations eagerly embraced the existence of the new Muslim state of Pakistan which emerged out of the colonial mandate in the geographic area of British India.

This glaringly illogical imbalance notwithstanding, five Arab armies joined forces with local Palestinian Arab *fedayeen* to attack Israel and, in the words of the their religious and political leaders, 'drive the Jews into the sea' and rid the region of the 'Zionist plague'.

They failed. Instead, against all odds and with their backs to the Mediterranean, the Jews of Israel fought back their numerically and logistically far superior attackers, won some additional territories and lost others. One of the areas the Jews lost was the east of Jerusalem and large swathes of Judea and Samaria, two Jewish provinces that the Hashemite Islamic Kingdom of Jordan invaded, annexed and illegally occupied from 1948 until 1967, ethnically cleansing every single Jew from the territory and turning every Jewish synagogue and cemetery into rubble, even using Jewish gravestones to line latrines in an act of defilement that the UN chose to ignore. The only country that recognised Jordan's illegal occupation of the two Jewish provinces, which the Jordanians dubbed "The West Bank" because the provinces were located on the west bank of the River Jordan, was Pakistan.

Israel, of course, would not have survived without pressing its women into the war effort. Not just in back-room jobs but on the front lines. Very much on the front lines, shouldering old bolt-action rifles side by side with their men, using domestically handcrafted Sten machine guns with equally deadly force as Lebanese, Syrian, Iraqi, Jordanian and Egyptian regular forces carried out their invasion as per the instructions of their primarily British military commanders. All this in addition to constant attacks by local Palestinian Arab rioters and terrorists.

That ethos of Israeli women fighting for their country's security side by side with their men-folk lives on to this very day. In fact, there is one combat battalion in the IDF where young women – girls really, having just graduated from high school, and consisting of Israeli Jews, Arabs and Druze – make up 70 percent of the fighting force. And it is a true frontline fighting force. The elite Caracal (Desert Lynx) combat unit of the IDF reflects the virtues of its namesake – strength and stealth – serving with distinction on the Jewish state's Gaza, Egypt and Jordan borders.

Having completed her statutory two-year stint in the IDF with the grade of *Samal Rishon* or Staff Sergeant, Amira Hart signed on for 3 years of *keva* and after the first year had worked her way up to the rank of *Sgan Mishne*, Platoon Leader. Fluent in Amharic, which Dov and Sarah insisted she should learn throughout her school years so she wouldn't grow up rootless, and having an ear keenly attuned to the subtle nuances and gently flowing rhythms of the Palestinian dialect of Arabic, Amira developed through her teens into something of a multi-linguist, adding English learned at home with Sarah and in school to her Hebrew mother-tongue and the Swedish that her father Dov insisted on teaching both children. In the cosmopolitan melting-pot that is Israel, being multi-lingual is fairly commonplace and many people speak three languages or more, but it was Amira's particular combination of language skills that drew her to the attention of a Mossad recruitment officer on the lookout for unusual and useful skill sets.

So much has been written about Israel's legendary Mossad, the Institute for Intelligence and Special Operations, that most of it brings a smile of gratitude to the lips of the service's top brass. The sheer PR value is hard to match – and it's all free. That's good for recruitment – and for deterrent purposes. There's no getting away from the fact that the Mossad's reputation is richly deserved. Not just for the daring and bravery of its operations on the ground, but also for the massive and efficiently harnessed intelligence infrastructure on which it relies to feed its officers with necessary information.

Amira Hart was courted – at a distance – by the Mossad recruiter. She was vetted, her home background checked, her school grades verified, her army records pored over. She was a fighter, and highly intelligent. Came from a stable home background – yet a background that few others had in Israel. She had the gift of a couple of potentially very useful languages. And she was a looker. More than that – this girl was absolutely stunning, but in an understated kind of way. Pass her in the street and you wouldn't turn round for a second look at her, you may not even notice her. But sit down opposite her – or study her photo up close as the recruiter was now doing – and your jaw would drop.

The recruiter pored over photographs of Amira in uniform, in civvies, at the beach, sitting at a café with her friends. This girl had no right to be wasting her time in drab green fatigues on some dusty infantry base down in Israel's southern Negev desert, and truth be told she shouldn't really be let anywhere near "The Pile", the Mossad's brand-new, state-of-the-art training facility on the remote southern outskirts of Beersheba. By rights she should be gracing the front cover of every fashion magazine the world over, he thought – yet every shot of her seemed to show a naturalness bordering on diffidence. She wasn't a boastful beauty, she simply had massive presence. But first you had to register that she was even there.

Amira Hart was going to be a highly valuable Mossad asset.

And so her training began.

Chapter 6

Like many other Israeli families, the Harts had more than one child in the army at the same time. In many families in Israel, it is not uncommon for parents to welcome not just their own uniformed offspring home for the occasional weekend of food, more food and still more food, interspersed with manic bouts of uniform laundering and patching up of kit; as often as not, unpredictable numbers of their children's comrades-in-arms may also turn up for a weekend of rest and recreation, if their own homes are too far away for a short weekend off base.

Like his older sister, Benny too was in a combat unit, serving three years with the *Tsankhanim* or Paratroopers before following in his sister's footsteps and signing up for three years of *keva*.

If the Harts were in luck, both children would occasionally have the same weekend off base, returning home for some wholesome cooking and a clean bed. Although Benny towered over his sister and was about fifty percent broader across the shoulders, Amira never failed to put him in his place. "Bunny," she said, a smile teasing across her face. "You may be this macho paratrooper who jumps out of aeroplanes when most normal people take the stairs after the aircraft has landed, but you know what? In my Caracal unit, we do admittedly have guys too, not just girls – but the girls do the fighting and the guys do what we tell them, which is usually cooking and fixing our vehicles."

For all that he could have lifted Amira and all her kit high in the air with just one hand, leaving her dangling from a branch of the pecan tree flowering outside their modest home, Benny would always smile self-deprecatingly. 'Bunny' had stuck with him ever since childhood, when Sarah's hard-of-hearing aunt came on her one and only visit to Israel and, hearing what she thought was the boy's name, decided she had heard 'Bunny'. Her spontaneous comment back then had sent Sarah and Dov – and Amira – into stitches: "What sort of a name is 'Bunny'? Rabbits are cute – but this boy looks more like a poached egg than a cute bunny-rabbit. Where's his neck?"

The name 'Bunny' had stuck, and nowadays it was only Amira who used it – and only when she wanted to mercilessly tease her kid brother or when she had something really serious to discuss. But only within the confines of their home, never outside.

Like many youngsters approaching the end of their regular three-year stint in a combat unit, Benny was asked if he wanted to apply for a position with Israel's famed *Shabak* or *Shin Bet* internal security agency. And just like so many other young men just leaving the army, he declined. He hadn't yet made up his mind what to do after the army – whether to go travelling around the world for a year, or go straight to university. But after three years of running around in uniform he didn't feel all that crazy about running around the world, and he hadn't yet decided what he wanted to study or what he would like to spend the rest of his life working with.

So on one of his increasingly infrequent weekend furloughs he discussed the issue with his sister and parents. Amira was already "over there" – the Israeli youths' euphemism for Israel's overseas security agency – and she advised him to think hard about his future: Benny had languages in his favour, as well as an instinctive grasp of the constantly developing electronic and digital world – assets she reckoned would stand him in good stead in a position with the Shin Bet and that wouldn't require him to run around fields in a green uniform for the duration of his service, should he choose to sign up with them.

Benny gave the matter a lot of thought and decided it might be worth looking into. He loved the army, he enjoyed the camaraderie, he understood he was doing something vital for his country and his people. But then, everyone and their uncle did army service in Israel, and if he wanted to do anything out of the ordinary perhaps this was the way to go. Still doing a useful job, but not in uniform. Anything to get out of the humdrum routine of repetitious training, night ops along and beyond Israel's security barrier with the Palestinian Authority territory or bordering the increasingly volatile border with Syria, and the most dangerous operation of all: sitting in the middle of a field or atop a rocky outcrop trying to eat his field rations faster than the local ants ate him.

With his quick intelligence, his ability to think outside the box, his blond blue-eyed looks, and the fact that he legally had three nationalities and an equal number of legitimate passports – Swedish thanks to his father, British thanks to his mother and Israeli thanks to the country of his birth – he was a highly useful asset.

And so his training began.

Chapter 7

Haydar Murad let out a low, long whistle.

"Seriously?!? You reckon this could work?"

He didn't mean to sound disparaging. In fact, he felt anything but. He felt elated, he could almost hear the blood coursing in his veins, he was acutely aware of every beat of his heart as he leaned back, staring at Adan Hamati, a slow smile widening across his face as the scope, the sheer potential, of the plan dawned on him.

"Tell me again, you really think this could work?" he asked eagerly. He wasn't really expecting an answer. Adan Hamati wasn't in the habit of engaging in unnecessary talk. He wasn't going to repeat something he'd already said once – just a minute or two ago, in fact. And he certainly wasn't going to respond to something that anyone else might have misinterpreted as lack of faith in his, Hamati's, plan.

Hamati knew that Murad was impressed. No, he wasn't impressed, he was bowled over. His weren't words of doubt, they were a plea for confirmation that this really had a chance of working.

Hamati smiled back. He was tired. He'd done more talking than he could remember in many a year. He had spent long periods of time in solitary confinement in Israeli prisons and was thoroughly familiar with many of the cells in Ramle security prison. He'd been picked up for a variety of what the Zionist occupiers called 'security offences' which as far as he was concerned was just a way of saying 'for the crime of being a Palestinian Arab', and thrown into solitary confinement on a range of charges. Even he had to admit that sometimes his solitary confinement was justified. If you attacked a prison warden, or tried to strangle another Palestinian security prisoner who everyone knew, just *knew*, was an informer for the Zionists, well, even he reckoned that retribution was coming.

And that retribution usually took the form of solitary confinement. These Jews were crazy, with their idiotic 'human rights' and 'equality before the law'. Make no mistake, he was grateful for the care, in fact on more than one occasion he owed his life to the fact that the Zionist prison officers sent him to solitary instead of taking matters into their own hands and doing what any red-blooded Arab man worth his family name would have done. In the Palestine Hamati envisioned, there'd be no room for this kind of mollycoddling. You obeyed the law, and you thrived. You disobeyed the law and you'd pay. Brutally. Palestine was going to emulate the Zionist state in many ways, because as the Arab Spring degenerated into manic bloodletting along religious, tribal and sectarian lines, Adan Hamati saw that there were similar tensions among the Jews of Occupied Palestine – Ashkenazi against Sephardi, rich against poor, religiously observant against secular – but that the Jews somehow always managed to keep these things in check.

But one feature of the Zionist state that his Palestine was never going to copy was its ridiculous, time-wasting and resource-sapping preoccupation with 'human rights'. Human rights were for people who behaved like human beings, who toed the line, who did their bit for the furtherance of Palestine and of the Jihad. Step out of line and you forfeited those rights.

All these thoughts went through his mind as he surveyed his friend in silence. Silence. Silence that had accompanied his life for so many years during his various incarcerations in Israeli prisons that it had become second nature to him.

So he maintained his silence, knew that his friend did not doubt him, that Haydar Murad was just asking a rhetorical question. Hamati's smile was all the answer that Murad needed.

But someone had to break the silence.

"Yes," he breathed. "Yes, this is going to work. It's going to work because it is brave, it is audacious, it is completely different, and it will put us on centre stage. Where we need to be if we are to occupy our rightful place in the hearts and minds of people outside Palestine."

He glanced at his watch. Time to move on. "We'll meet in the apartment in Nablus next Thursday, at 6 pm."

They got up, grasped each other's hands in farewell, and went to the door. Opening it a crack, Murad looked out, up and down the street, then held up 3 fingers to his friend and slipped quietly away in the gathering gloom.

Three minutes before he too departed. Adan Hamati glanced down at his watch. Undid the strap, took the watch in his left hand and started winding the knurled knob with the thumb and forefinger of his right hand.

Adan Hamati did not possess a single item of any description that contained a battery or electronic circuit.

Chapter 8

Living in what is undoubtedly a rough neck of the woods, Israel has had to develop an acute security-consciousness that is probably second to none. But nothing is ever so secure that it cannot have loopholes. And nothing is ever so tightly controlled that somewhere along the line, it all comes down to human frailties, human needs, human characteristics.

A police force is only as good as the people wearing its uniform. Israel is no exception. With all the computers at its service, with all the human intelligence at its disposal, with all the officers patrolling the country's streets day and night, it still was no surprise that the human factor meant nobody made the connection.

With its stunning beaches and rich eco-diversity, Israel is a tourist paradise. It's also an archaeological treasure-chest, a high-tech magnet and home to many of the world's foremost computer software developers, medical research labs, experimental agricultural projects, weapons development centres and world-class academic institutions with a lively overseas exchange of both students and teaching staff. So there is always a steady stream of foreign visitors to the Jewish state.

And as in any destination that attracts a lot of overseas visitors, there are always thieves, pickpockets, burglars and opportunist grab-and-run artistes. It sort of goes with the turf. Which is why nobody at Israel Police noticed anything at first. Hotel break-ins happen all the time, in any city in the world. People dining out are often the target of skilled bag-snatchers when they leave their handbags, purses or other valuables unattended for that vital instant that the thief seizes. Pickpockets are rife from Rio to Rome, from London to Lisbon, from Tokyo to Tel Aviv.

Which is why nobody put two and together in Tel Aviv for many, many months. Or indeed in Jerusalem, Petach Tikva, Haifa, Ashdod, Herzliya, Ashkelon, Beersheba, Eilat or anywhere else across the length and breadth of Israel. The gradual rise in thefts, burglaries, break-ins. The imperceptible increase in the number of incidents reported to local, often small, police stations. The under-the-breath mutterings of individual hotel managers desperate to stop the thefts, but at the same time even more desperate to keep them from becoming public knowledge.

Eventually, however, the critical point was reached and the trend became apparent. Not because of any particular detection breakthrough by the police. But because two hotel guests at Hotel ScenicMed in Nahariya both reported the theft of significant amounts of cash from their hotel rooms in the same week. One an American retiree who kept all his valuables under his pillow because he reckoned he could keep an eye on his first-storey beachfront hotel room from the inviting golden sands right outside his balcony door, and the second a middle-aged Danish mother of two who had just deposited her handbag in her room for a few moments while she went to the hotel lobby to fetch some brochures about a coach trip up the coast to the caves at Rosh Hanikra followed by a visit to the famous Golan Heights Winery over to the east.

Desk Sergeant Ron Amichai snorted in exasperation as he dealt with the Danish tourist. She looked up at him sharply, assuming he didn't want to waste his time with petty thefts when there were other, bigger fish to fry.

Noticing her look of anger he smiled deprecatingly. "The problem is, you're not the first this week to report a theft from that hotel," he said. We've already had one this week, and..." he scrolled down the screen of his computer, "... it looks like three thefts were reported from two other hotels in Nahariya and nearby Akko just last week. Sorry if I gave the impression I wasn't taking your report seriously, we'll put someone onto this just as soon as I've completed taking down your details and logged the incident. You're booked to stay at the ScenicMed for another, let me see, 5 days, you're leaving on Wednesday, right?"

She nodded assent.

"OK, if you don't hear from us by Tuesday morning, get in touch with us at this number and we'll bring you up to date and confirm that your contact details and travel plans haven't changed so we can notify you should there be any developments, OK? Here's the signed form that you will need for your insurance claim."

She nodded once again, sighed, picked up the paper, took her two children by the hands and walked out.

Ron Amichai scratched his head, stuck a pen in his mouth and sucked hard. This idiotic ban on smoking in the workplace – it was going to kill him way before the nicotine ever did. He pulled the pen out of his mouth, rolled it thoughtfully between his thumb and forefinger as he stared at the screen.

"I wonder," he said to no one in particular, since at that particular moment he was blissfully alone in the otherwise busy and noisy station front room.

He reached for the mouse and started clicking and searching.

Chapter 9

Adan Hamati and Haydar Murad walked down the silent street two minutes apart. Bayt Sarona was a sleepy little town that didn't seem to have changed a whole lot over the centuries. The Jews had come to this barren land more than three millennia ago and fanned to other parts of Judea and Samaria, the Romans had arrived, outstayed their welcome and been driven back to the Roman Empire's heartland, and over the centuries Crusaders from England, Germany and France had been followed by a succession of Muslim rulers, most recently the Ottoman Turks, then the British, for a few short months the Jews once again, then the Jordanians had occupied and annexed the land on which the town – back then just a small village – was built, and then in 1967 the Jews had returned, kicked the Jordanians back across the Jordan River and Bayt Sarona flourished. It was still occupied – by the Zionists, may their best efforts turn to dust, but there was no denying that under the Jews, health had improved beyond belief, live births had more than quadrupled, all children went to school – including girls – and there was electricity, proper drainage, even paved roads.

But still no jobs. The Jews had built their so-called 'security fence' not far from the town, so the grazing land and the olive groves were not exactly cut off, but they were way too difficult to get to without time-consuming security checkpoints, traffic holdups, the whims of the IDF officer in charge on any given day. And there was no local industry to compensate. True, Israeli footwear manufacturer TalShoe had a highly successful factory in Maale Adumim, half an hour's drive away, and the company was really good to their employees – half the workforce was Palestinian Arab, the other half made up equally of Israeli Jews, Israeli Arabs and Israeli Druze. Practical coexistence 101, with everyone a winner – but the local Fatah leadership didn't like it. They wanted total separation of the Palestinians from the Zionist state – but they didn't offer an alternative. And without jobs, the youngsters turned to violence, political and religious radicalisation, drugs and women. Fatah didn't seem to understand this – or they didn't care. Either way, the local Fatah commander had successfully banned the people of Bayt Sarona from working in the Jewish-owned factory.

The result was a town that was stagnating, that was not yet in decline but that would tip over the edge unless something were done pretty soon. It was along a narrow, quiet street in Bayt Sarona that first Adan Hamati and then Haydar Murad walked purposefully but without hurrying that evening.

Each approached the same green metal door and, without looking around or knocking, opened it and slipped through in one swift, fluid motion. There was no lamp on in the hallway to light up their features as they entered. Two seemingly ordinary men, tired after a long day at work, returning home for an evening meal.

But there was no meal waiting for them. Indeed, both had been careful to eat before arriving because they both knew they had a long evening ahead of them.

Once again, it was going to be just the two of them.

And once again, they were meeting in a room devoid of any adornments, no phone, no television set, not even a radio. There was the ubiquitous gas cooker and a few simple utensils for making and drinking coffee, a small laminate-surfaced kitchen table and four mismatched chairs. A single light bulb hanging from the ceiling fixture, no lampshade. No windows, just the door leading in and out. Once upon a time, many decades ago, this room had probably been used by the owner of the large house for storage purposes. Today, it was empty – and ideal.

“Ground rules from now on,” announced Adan Hamati. “No more electrical, electronic or digital equipment. At all. No mobile phones, no digital cameras, no radios, not even a debit or credit card. No phone card. From now on you meet me in your skin, your underclothes, trousers, shirt, socks and shoes. A cap if you want, sunglasses if you must. Nothing else. Understand?”

Looking puzzled and somewhat affronted at the tone of Hamati’s voice, Haydar Murad nodded. “OK, so how about you tell me what this is about? You gave me the broad plan, but what’s with all these strange instructions?”

"Traceability, my dear friend, traceability. From now on, it's back to basics for us. We're going back to the Cold War era of human and analogue contacts. For security's sake. The Zionists pride themselves on their superb electronic surveillance capabilities. Well, let them follow our electronic trail as much as they like – there simply won't be one."

"But they can listen in on us," protested Murad. "They don't even have to be near us to point their long-range, remote-controlled microphones at us."

"True," agreed Hamati. "But first they'll have to know that we exist. They'll have to have a reason for picking up on us. And we won't give them one. From now on, my friend, we're going to be model citizens – nobody will have a single reason to give us a second glance, and we'll make sure the Jews are kept plenty busy elsewhere. You want to know something? They'll be pleased they don't have to bother with us – a couple of has-beens who've finally been beaten into submission."

There was unmitigated rage flashing in Haydar Murad's eyes. Like many proud Arab men, in particular those in the West Bank, he resented being portrayed as weak and submissive.

"You do realise this is a tool, don't you?" said Hamati. "We have to vanish off their radar, they'll be only too pleased to see the back of us, two fewer troublemakers for them to deal with. That's the way we want it to be. And in order to ensure that they don't decide to pick up on us, for any reason at all, we cut ourselves off from the electronic world. We simply don't make it easy for them to keep tabs on us. Don't get me wrong: they'll still know everything about our past – we haven't exactly led the lives of innocent boy-scouts after all. We just won't give them any reason to give us a second thought ever again. Starting now."

Haydar Murad nodded. He saw the point, it made sense. But he didn't like bowing down like a scared slave. He was a proud Arab, and he had every reason to be proud. His people had lived on this land for almost a century, and that gave him the right to walk tall – he didn't appreciate being told to adopt an attitude of servitude, whatever the tactical benefits.

Murad looked Adan Hamati in the eye. "OK," he said, "no problem. From now on, even my own shadow won't recognise the new, docile me. Mind you, I'll probably need a Valium prescription to keep my calm..."

Hamati smiled at his friend's joke. They embraced, then Hamati took a step back, placed a hand on each of Murad's shoulders and said: "So our next meeting is in Tulkarem on Tuesday two weeks from now. That's when you'll get to meet a few other people who are part of this project. And remember your own words: from now on, you are a shadow, you lead a blameless life – you become a model citizen whom nobody will look at twice – neither the soft-bellied fools in Ramallah nor the Jews in Tel Aviv."

And with that they sat down to a long series of detailed discussions. Almost three hours later they parted, exiting the house via the green metal door exactly as they had arrived, quietly, efficiently, unnoticed.

Chapter 10

Desk Sergeant Ron Amichai didn't really have time for this – he was way too busy dealing with the regular flow of cases that always seemed to be dumped on his desk. Burglaries, shoplifting, drug peddlers, people parking their cars all over the place while the new access road to the main bus station was being built. Every single case had to be documented, logged and filed away. And it all took time.

OK, he felt sorry for the tourists who'd come to Israel looking for a relaxing holiday in the sun and sand of Nahariya's pristine beaches, and if truth be told he really wouldn't have minded being able to tell that rather yummy Danish tourist that he'd found her stolen money, solved the case, been promoted, and then been rewarded by her with an evening at a beachside restaurant – without her kids of course.

But enough daydreaming. There was something that was bugging him.

A vague pattern. Or more to the point, a shadowy hint that there was a pattern that was evading him. It was there, he just couldn't work it out.

Research. He was going to have to go back over the police records. But first a cup of coffee. He walked along to the cluttered little pantry that housed the usually unwashed cups and scattered half-opened packs of coffee. How difficult was it really to finish one lot of coffee before opening a new one? Honestly, some people needed a kick in the shins.

He walked into the pantry, surveyed the usual mess and reached for an almost clean cup and a packet of his usual poison – strong, bitter Turkish coffee that, made right, poked the backs of your eyeballs and caused your hair to stand upright for the rest of the day. A nice, strong brew that saw you through the morning until lunchtime.

As his hand went to the domestic Elite brand coffee, his eye took in the other three half-used containers of coffee. One was instant coffee, in a glass jar. One was a fancy Belgian filter-in-a-cup thing that probably used up more scarce resources in its disposable plastic filter than was good for the environment, and the third was something he'd never seen before, a red foil packet with a label that read "Gevalia".

He picked it up. Swedish. Smelled good, to be honest, but a quick glance at the text on the package revealed a language that didn't resemble anything spoken by civilised human beings – what were all those strange dots and squiggles above some of the vowels? He didn't even know how to make this stuff – was it to be slow-boiled together with sugar and a pinch of cardamom like his favourite Elite Turkish coffee, or was it supposed to be filtered like the Belgian stuff, or just poured into a mug and mixed with hot water like instant coffee?

No point in chancing it – he'd stick with what he knew. When all was said and done, there was nothing to beat good old Elite Turkish coffee.

And that's when it hit him. That elusive crime pattern that he hadn't seen – because it wasn't where he was looking for it. Like his morning brew, he'd been looking for what he expected to find, where he expected to find it. And just like this morning's mess of different coffee varieties, it was exactly that that was the missing clue: similarity, but with variation.

He needed to look for similar incidents, but in varied locations.

Hastily brewing up his coffee and for once leaving a mess behind him for someone else to clear up, Ron Amichai returned to his desk and started searching the national police register for incidents of alleged pick-pocketing, burglaries, bag-snatching. He had expected to find a local epidemic, a gang of young thugs, either Jewish kids bored during their school holidays and looking for something to feed their voracious need for the very latest mobile phones or design sneakers, or Arab youngsters out to grab what they could from the foreigners who could be guaranteed to arrive loaded to the gills with lots of ready cash.

Which is precisely what he didn't find, of course. There were the incidents reported from Hotel ScenicMed this week, and a couple of other incidents from the other local hotels and shopping malls. But more to the point, there seemed to be a rash – if anything, a plague of epic proportions – of similar incidents the length and breadth of Israel. And there didn't seem to be any markers in the national police register to indicate that someone, somewhere, had noticed this pattern.

He let out a slow whistle as a clear picture began to emerge. All over Israel, at hotels, restaurants, shopping malls, conference centres and the country's many beautiful beaches, it appeared that thieves were hard at work. Thieves with a very particular taste: cash. Cash. Preferably foreign currency but also Israeli shekels. And jewellery.

Taking money was understandable – it was versatile, it was untraceable, it was universal. Jewellery was almost as good, especially if it was fenced overseas, or broken down and remade into new pieces. But what was most interesting was not what was being taken, but what was *not* being taken. Not mobile phones, not laptops, not credit cards or ATM cards.

In a sense, Ron Amichai could even understand the thieves' reluctance to take phones and laptops. They did admittedly command a good price in a marketplace where no questions were asked and money and goods changed hands in dark alleyways and dimly lit rooms, but they were traceable and could bring trouble from the law.

But who ever heard of thieves not taking credit cards?

What was the common factor here, what wasn't he seeing? Was it what they were taking, or what they were not taking?

And if it was what they were not taking, were they not taking phones, tablets and laptops because they were relatively bulky? Seriously, how bulky was an iPhone or Blackberry? Unless these were particularly lightweight thieves, who couldn't carry the weight of a laptop or phone. What, so suddenly the local butterflies and bees were turning to a life of looting and thievery? There had to be something else, a red thread that was so fine he wasn't seeing it.

Electronics. Digital technology. Anything with a chip in it. That had to be it. What possible other explanation could there be? This had to be it.

Sergeant Ron Amichai leaned back in his chair, sipped his by now stone-cold coffee and curled his lip in distaste at the inky black liquid. He'd earned a fresh cup of coffee, and this time he was going to sit back and enjoy it while it was fresh and hot.

As he started to get out of his chair to head to the pantry, he paused. Sat down again.

There were people who were paid to monitor this sort of thing. He wouldn't mind getting the salary of the computer whizz-kids recruited straight from college whose job it was to check out these things. Kids who knew nothing about police work but who were fast-tracked into cushy and well-paid desk jobs – but who seemed not to know what was going on under their very noses. Still, maybe there'd be a commendation in it for him, always something.

He reached for the phone and called his station commander.

Chapter 11

Amira Hart was turning out to be everything Israel's shadowy Mossad security service was looking for. A gifted linguist, she also had stunning good looks and a warm, winning smile that put people at ease and made them want to talk about themselves.

Like its various sister organisations the world over – the CIA in America, MI6 in the UK, Australia's ASIS, Canada's CSIS and so on – the Mossad is not all glamour and James Bond panache. A lot of its work is dull, humdrum, routine, cold, wet – and never surfaces in the public consciousness.

Amira Hart was trained to monitor the flow of money to radical jihadi organisations hell-bent on the destruction of the West, the Jewish state and Jews in general. Nominally part of the Mossad's counter-terrorism unit, she specialised in tracing funding via computers and electronically logged bank balances. Fluent in Arabic and with the more guttural Amharic intonation always available to disguise the exact origins of her particular strain of Arabic, she could make phone calls to various Arab banks the world over on the pretext of chasing up purported delays in payment to her bosses' accounts – it was amazing just how easy it was to gain access to privileged information simply by sounding like a lowly clerk employed by a moneyed and powerful Arab.

With her dark, distinctly African looks, Amira Hart could go where anyone else would stand out like a sore thumb. She could dress in modest Arab garb and hide her hair and much of her face with the traditional Muslim veil; she switched between the short hijab, the somewhat more elaborate shayla and – her favourite because of its name – the al-amira, a two-piece cap and tube-shaped scarf that otherwise pretty much resembled the hijab. In this modest disguise, which took up little space in her pocket when she whipped it off to quickly alter her profile, she could visit the cafés frequented by jihadi operatives all across Europe, eavesdropping on their conversations while pretending to direct her imaginary friend Leila to the café over her mobile phone. She could dress in a modern business suit and pass off as yet another stressed Western executive taking time out for a quick snack before hurrying on to her next appointment, all the while listening in and recording.

She trained for this kind of operation, she was remarkably accurate and consistent with a sidearm, and in the army she had served for a term as her Caracal unit's Krav Maga instructor. Krav Maga is an Israeli martial art that takes many different forms – there are special versions for the military, the police, for civilians, even specifically for women – but what all the variants have in common is their focus on harnessing your immediate environment to your advantage. You transform whatever is at hand into your personal weapon. And if all you have is your own body and nothing else, not even a rock, then so be it. An elbow, a knee, your forehead, can all be deadly if used properly. The basic tenet is to inflict the maximum amount of damage with the least exposure to yourself as you bring down your assailant and make good your escape. Avoid a fight by all means, but if you do strike, make sure it's so hard and so effective that your opponent is incapable of pursuit. Terminally, if need be.

But Amira Hart's capabilities were never deployed in this kind of 'hot' operational capacity. True, there were repeated refresher courses and unimaginably tough physicals with clockwork regularity. But she spent most of her time behind a desk and a bank of computers, with a row of disposable, untraceable mobile phones each neatly labelled with its intended target – a bank, an Arab businessman overseas, a European-run import-export business located in Belgium or France or Germany or England or wherever.

Much of her work was aimed at detecting shifts in patterns of bank holdings. Sudden large deposits that did not have an obvious reason, major withdrawals without a corresponding order for goods or shipments or services. Boring, humdrum work, but work that required a sharp eye and a constantly enquiring mind. And an ability to see hidden contexts.

It's not as though she had to monitor every single business in all of Europe. Her unit knew pretty much who was involved in what. What they didn't know, but always kept an eye on, was the 'when'. When things changed, when patterns altered, when the paths that money took suddenly became different – and therefore of interest. Because that almost always indicated that something that had been planned was now entering the active phase, assets were being deployed to get an operation off the planning table and onto the ground.

It was Amira Hart's job to notice when operations hit the ground – when, where, and who.

And Amira Hart thought she had just picked up on something interesting. But not where she had expected. Not anywhere near where she had expected.

Chapter 12

Sergeant Ron Amichai had done his bit. The pattern was as clear as a picture painted in the brightest colours imaginable. Only the truly blind couldn't have seen it. Which said a lot about the eyesight of both his superiors and the university-educated techies who manned the humming computers at headquarters.

But he'd submitted the information and had been asked to stand by for a visit at 2 that afternoon from some secret service spook or other. Probably some old geezer coasting his way to retirement, cruising from one air-conditioned office to another to pass the time before he got his bouquet of flowers and a thank-you card from the top floor. Or perhaps one of these jumped-up youngsters, a reedy youth with glasses the size of twin computer screens – a theoretician who'd never put a foot in the real world.

His 2 pm appointment turned up. Surname of Hart. Ron Amichai had been wrong on both counts. His visitor was admittedly a man, admittedly a youth, but he looked more like a commando who'd been forced at gunpoint into civvies and didn't feel quite at home in his clothes. He was tall, easily stretching two metres skyward and looked at first sight to be almost the same across the shoulders. Blond hair, fit physique, open smile.

He entered the police station and headed straight for the desk. "Shalom, I'm looking for Sergeant Ron Amichai," he said.

Amichai looked at him. "That would be me. You're Hart?"

Benny nodded, stretched out his hand in greeting and asked if there was somewhere quiet they could chat.

"Quiet isn't what we do here, but there's nobody in the cells at the moment and I can kick the on-duty officer upstairs for a while, if you like," replied Amichai, leading the way downstairs.

Entering the first cell and settling uncomfortably on the hard concrete bench which also doubled as a bed, Benny Hart asked Ron Amichai to go through his findings with him. "I've been through your report, everything is there like you say – all these incidents have taken place. But tell me why you reckon this is significant. I mean, what do you reckon it means? Is it just a trend, like that rash of ram-raiding incidents the police dealt with about 4 or 5 years ago – something that is fashionable among the low-lifes today but will be replaced by different methods tomorrow – or do you reckon it indicates something else? I'm not a police officer, I don't have your training, I don't see what someone with your experience can probably feel in your fingertips."

Ron Amichai looked his visitor up and down. He was young all right, what could he be – 25, 26? But he certainly was diplomatic, he knew how to soft-soap people to get the best out of them. The guy may be built like a tank but he got what he wanted out of you by coaxing you, appealing to you, making you want to please. No, that wasn't charitable – the boy was only doing his job, and it was an important job. The Shin Bet wouldn't be here if they didn't reckon this was something potentially serious.

So he drew on his years of experience as a patrol cop. He explained why these thefts were different – because they were taking place all over the country, because they were immensely specific. Opportunistic thieves took everything they could lay their hands on, and in all his years on the beat he'd never – *ever* – come across a case where a thief had left behind small, portable, high-value electronics and credit cards. There was a pattern, and it wasn't mere criminality. Because criminals involved in robberies did what it said on the box – they robbed. They robbed whatever they could lay their hands on.

"Exactly," said Benny Hart and bit his lower lip in concentration. "Your report was flagged red. Not sure if your super has given you any feedback or if he's one of these assholes who likes to take credit for the successes of his officers, but I want to tell you that it was your name on that report and we are really grateful to you for your eagle eye. In all fairness, your commander did attach a memo to your findings saying that you'd done a thorough job and that we should go directly to you with any questions we might have.

Just wanted to let you know, in case he didn't bother to let any of that filter down to you."

Ron Amichai looked pleased, but frowned as he replied that nope, he hadn't heard a word of thanks from the station commander himself and that he was grateful for Benny Hart's kind words.

With that, they stood up. Benny passed Ron a card with his contact details. "Anything else turns up, you just give me a call, day or night. And thanks once again, I think we've got something potentially big here that we have to follow up closely."

They made their way up and to the front door, shook hands and turned their separate ways.

"This kid's going to make one hell of a brilliant politician one day," muttered Ron Amichai as he smiled ruefully to himself and returned to his desk.

Chapter 13

Adan Hamati and Haydar Murad had just concluded a three-hour meeting with five women and five men in a small airless backroom at the rear of a shop in the Palestinian Arab city of Tulkarem. Five married couples, most of them parents of young children, plus Hamati.

On the table was a large drawing of a building, and on the floor beside the table was an even larger sheet of paper with a street map. All the legends on the drawing and the map were in some European language. Not English.

There were different coloured pencils strewn all around the table. No laptop, no crisp PowerPoint slide presentation, no Google Earth map on a computer screen. Just a wooden table, a dozen white plastic chairs, paper and pencils.

"Is everyone clear on what they have to do? You have just over three months to get here," Adan Hamati tapped the map. "You put in your applications with the passport authorities, applying for permission to exit to Jordan for the purpose of making the Hajj. You do it in the company of your spouses. Yes, I know that is not customary, but believe me when I tell you that a married couple travelling together, leaving their children in the care of their grandparents while they go on pilgrimage, is less likely to attract suspicion than a man travelling alone. And nobody is looking for women operatives. I have a different exit plan for myself."

He continued: "From Amman you will travel to your various way-stations throughout Africa, where you will stay out of sight and out of trouble, cutting off any connection between yourselves and Palestine. From there you will make your way first to Europe, and then on to here," he tapped the map once again, "and go to the addresses you were given. You're not travelling in a group but as separate couples. I know you feel there's safety in numbers, but this is less conspicuous and it's going to work if you just do as agreed."

"And when you get there, you'll see just what a warm welcome awaits you. Sweden is ripe for plucking. We're going to create the first Islamic Republic in Europe – and we're going to do it with the help of the Swedes themselves. Sweden is a big country in terms of physical size, but it is a tiny country in terms of population – just nine million, of whom almost half a million are Muslims. Strategically too, it is a tiny country, tucked away in a corner of northern Europe, and its Scandinavian neighbours are also tiny countries with significant Muslim populations – Norway and Denmark. Sweden itself is weak, divided, ruled by a succession of squabbling coalition partners. They have a king whose family came from France and a Brazilian queen whose family came from Germany. They can't agree on anything – there's nothing to unite them."

Adan Hamati looked at each of them in turn and smiled slowly. "We're going to unite them." He broke into a grin. "And Palestine will come out the winner."

Hamati surveyed the assembled group. “Any questions?” he asked.

Silence. “OK, this is the first and last time we will be meeting here as a group, the next time we see each other is over there,” he jerked his thumb in the direction of the map.

“May Allah be with us in our endeavour and crown our operation with success.”

And with that the meeting dissolved and each went their separate way. The next time they met, things were going to be very much colder – as the situation got very much hotter.

Chapter 14

Night in the Palestinian Arab town of Kalkilya, a sprawling community of about 50,000 people.

A combined IDF and Shin Bet operation is under way to locate and arrest a man who has admittedly been off their radar for some weeks now but who was suspected of being involved in bomb-making and who was better-known for having instigated a long-running series of rock-throwing incidents targeting Israeli car drivers.

The foreign media tended to report on Palestinian rock-throwing as though it were merely a minor disturbance, a bit like skimming pebbles along the surface of the water at the seaside while people were out bathing. Or perhaps not much more serious than aiming a pea-shooter at a student sitting in the front row of a classroom.

But rock-throwing is a major threat to civilians, and it surprisingly often has a fatal outcome. It's not only that the rocks are just that – real, big, heavy, jagged rocks, not small interestingly coloured stones that a young child might otherwise collect and keep in a box. Rocks this big and sharp hitting the soft tissue of the human body or the delicate skull that shields the human brain can cause serious injury or death. It's also that a torrent of rocks landing suddenly on a car can cause drivers to panic, lose control over their vehicles, making them crash and then leaving them an easy target for the killers closing in on them with still more rocks, iron bars and broken bottles to finish off the job up close and personal.

To Israelis, it is a barbaric act of cowardice – the multitude against one, in a reprehensible throwback to primitive means of putting people to death by stoning. Not so primitive, in fact, since stoning was still practised with impunity by many UN member states that were signatories to the Human Rights Act, some of which were in fact on the steering committees of various UN-sponsored human rights organisations.

To the Palestinian Arabs, it was David against Goliath – and it was they who now occupied the role of little David against the Zionist Goliath. They were prevented from having weapons by the Israeli army, and they felt they had no other way to defend what they saw as their land than with the weapons that their land had in such abundance – rocks. The black humour of the Palestinian street even claimed that they should thank the Zionists for this, because the situation meant that the Palestinians kept hunting further and further afield for their rocky 'ammunition', thus forcing them to clear potential arable land of rocks and freeing up more space for farming. Palestinian agriculture was expanding at the same rate as the Zionists were being driven back...

Dressed in black jeans, a black shirt and with a black balaclava pulled up onto his head as he waited for the assault team to go in, Benny Hart rolled up his shirt cuff, checked his watch, blacked out his watch again and gave the signal.

Pulling down his balaclava to cover his face, he pulled his gun from the holster at his side and followed the troops.

The capture was totally non-dramatic. Calling out in Arabic on a loud-hailer, the unit commander ordered Haydar Murad to come out of the house backwards, no shirt on and his hands raised in the air.

Haydar Murad, under strict orders from Adan Hamati not to draw unnecessary attention to himself, did exactly as he was told. It was probably just another routine roundup of Arabs to harass them. OK, this time he'd be a paragon of cooperation.

He came out of the house exactly as instructed, his hands were secured with plastic cuffs and he was led away to a waiting IDF Land Rover Defender, which pulled away.

But this wasn't going to be an ordinary arrest. Because after Murad was led away Benny Hart entered the house. The other occupants were Murad's parents, his wife and three young children. Their eyes blazed with defiance and hatred as they followed the Israeli soldiers' movements.

Through an interpreter (where was Amira when he needed her, thought Benny) he told the family that they would trouble them as little as possible and try to disturb as little as possible of their home, but that they had to conduct a thorough search for any possible concealed bomb-making equipment.

Sneering disdainfully at the Israeli soldier's Arabic accent, Haydar Murad's wife Alina responded in crisp English that they had no weapons of any description in the house, unless the soldiers were now also going to confiscate their cutlery, and that they should clear off.

Through his interpreter Benny replied that they wouldn't dream of removing anything from the Murad household that wasn't strictly illicit, and that they had no intentions of taking away cutlery or any other personal belongings.

While this exchange continued, a shout was heard from what was obviously Haydar and Alina's bedroom. Benny left Alina and the rest of her family in the company of three soldiers and headed for the bedroom. A hand-held X-ray scanner had revealed a significant amount of some kind of organic-looking substance bundled beneath the double wardrobe, behind the front cover panel that stretched from the floor of the wardrobe down to the tiled floor of the room. Suspecting they may have stumbled upon a sizable stash of explosive material or perhaps drugs, the officers went to work on the wardrobe, prising apart the 14 centimetre high front covering panel.

What they pulled out was money. Lots and lots of money. Bundles of US dollars, euros, pounds sterling, shekels. All wrapped neatly in plastic bags.

Benny let out a low whistle. "Keep searching. I want this entire house turned inside out. But nothing – and I repeat absolutely nothing – is to be destroyed. Take apart every stick of furniture and every floor tile if you have to, but I want everything to be returned to its original condition before we leave here. We're not in the business of collateral damage or collective punishment."

By the time the first slight hint of pink was visible in the dawn sky to the east over the hills of Jordan, the search party had completed its mission. Three more stockpiles of money had been discovered – inside a cooking-gas cylinder that had been opened, filled with money and then almost invisibly welded shut, under the cot of the youngest child, an infant of about 8 months, and inside what looked like a large array of solar collectors mounted on the roof of the building.

Before leaving the Murads, Benny had to call up the services of a large army truck to haul away the find.

But he was as good as his word. By the time the soldiers left, the Murad home was as near undisturbed as possible – if one excepted the absence of Haydar Murad and an as yet uncounted but undeniably massive haul of ready cash.

Chapter 15

In a police station in the nearby Israeli city of Netanya where he had commandeered an office, Benny Hart was questioning Haydar Murad.

Only problem was, Murad wasn't answering. Benny knew he was a patient person who was good at getting people to open up, even when they didn't want to, but Murad simply wasn't opening his mouth. He sat with his hands, now uncuffed, in his lap. He had refused a drink of water, declined coffee, and now refused to speak further.

Benny sat back, experiencing a creeping sensation of failure. He knew that if he couldn't persuade Haydar to open up, there were other people chafing at the bit, ready to use more robust methods to get him to reveal where the money had come from and, far more important, what it was intended to be used for.

The usual suspicions seemed somehow irrelevant: drug-running, weapons purchases, bribes. Faced with the prospect of years of incarceration in what they often called "the Zionist University" where most Palestinian security prisoners chose to gain advanced academic qualifications through multi-year studies paid for by the Jewish state, many hardened security offenders did indeed clam up in interrogations, preferring to sit out their time acquiring an academic degree at the expense of the Israeli taxpayer.

But Haydar Murad didn't fit the bill. He was a family man, he had everything to lose. If not for himself, he'd normally be speaking – volubly – just to protect his wife and children from imagined abuses at the hands of the Jews. The Israeli mind-set, Israeli public opinion, Israeli human rights watchdogs, ensured that nothing of the sort ever happened – and if it did there was swift retribution in the courts for any IDF or police officer caught abusing Palestinian Arabs. But with suspects in custody, Shin Bet officers routinely threatened all sorts of dire consequences for loved ones back home if the suspect didn't cooperate. Yet Haydar was saying nothing.

"Come on Haydar," said Benny, visibly exasperated. "Look, this isn't even a security services interrogation, we're just questioning you about money, that's all. You're not even cuffed – this simply isn't that big a deal. So some tourists were robbed and their money turns up in your home, big deal. Come now, spill the beans. You know I'm the good guy here. If I can't get anywhere with you, there are people in the next room who're going to spread the word that you cooperated fully and gave us everything. Your wife and kids will be run out of town, nobody likes a collaborator. And how about your parents? What are they going to do when it comes out that you gave it all up? If you do let us have what we want, we'll put out the word that you took it like a man, we couldn't get a word out of you so we had to rough you up and even that didn't break you. You'll be a hero. We'll carry out high-profile operations in lots of areas not even remotely linked in any way to you. Then we'll wait a good time before we act on your information, nobody will know how we got it – they just won't make the connection."

Silence.

Benny pushed his chair back. "Ok, I'm sorry you won't cooperate – that's your choice. Now it's up to people who won't play nice like me." And he got up and walked around the desk to pass Haydar on his way to the door.

Before anyone could react Haydar jumped to his feet, grabbed a plastic pen off the desk and stabbed Benny in the neck with it. Blood spurted out in a throbbing fountain before the agent-cum-interpreter who had been sitting beside Benny pushed back his chair, drew his weapon and placed three rounds at point blank into Murad's body – two in his chest and a third in his left eye.

All hell broke as the Shin Bet agent wrenched open the door and bellowed out into the station: "Get an ambulance! Now! Do it! Officer down, get an ambulance immediately!" He tore off his beige cotton safari jacket and pressed it into the wound in Benny's neck, wrapping it around the pen which was still stuck in the deep wound.

"Quick!" he screamed, "get an ambulance! Is there a medic in the station?" Police officers milled around and soon in the distance was the wail of a siren approaching at high speed.

"Back off! Back off!" shouted the station commander. "Make room for the ambulance personnel. Everyone back to your stations! Look sharp – everyone out of here!"

The ambulance crew rushed in at the double and took charge, clearing the room of everyone as they attended to Benny Hart, who was becoming visibly paler by the minute.

"How's it look?" asked the shaken station commander as the stretcher was wheeled away.

The female paramedic handling the rear of the gurney shook her head. "Can't say. Touch and go. We're taking him to Laniado Hospital, not sure where he'll go from there – if we get him to Intensive Care in time."

The scream of the siren was punctuated by sharp bursts of its ear-splitting bull-horn as it barged its way through downtown traffic to Netanya's main hospital.

The station commander surveyed the blood, the smashed furniture, the dead body of Haydar Murad.

"Where are you going?" he demanded as the Shin Bet agent slipped his phone into his pocket and headed for the door.

"I'm going to the hospital to be with Benny," he replied tersely.

"I've got news for you. You're staying exactly where you are. You may be Shin Bet and you may feel like a hero for having shot an unarmed man in my station, but that's exactly what this is: my police station. You're going nowhere until you've been questioned and a full report has been placed on my desk. And you can make as many calls as you like," he added as the agent pulled out his cell phone. "I'm going to lock down these premises and keep both the press and your mob out of here until that report is complete, so get cracking."

And with that he signalled to four officers to escort the Shin Bet agent to another room to take down a detailed and comprehensive statement, while he dealt with the mayhem that was all set to be unleashed with a dead body on the floor of his station and a seriously – perhaps even fatally – injured Shin Bet officer on his way to intensive care. Or the morgue.

Perhaps he'd been too hard on the Shin Bet officer now hurriedly giving his statement to the four policemen. They were on the same side after all; same problem, different roles.

He'd have to apologise before the man left the station. He'd better do it in public – the fewer ruffled inter-agency feathers, the better things would be.

He had a pounding headache – and he just knew that today was one day he wasn't going to get home in time for dinner with his in-laws, who were visiting from Eilat.

Ah well, small mercies.

***

The jungle telegraph in the West Bank is nothing if not efficient – and speedy. Within an hour after the last presence of the Israelis had vanished from the home of the Murads, Adan Hamati was on his way. Travelling around the West Bank by bus, he visited each and every one of the people he'd met with just days previously.

He had just a few words for each of them when they opened their doors. "Things may change, there may be a change of timetable. No change in the plan – that stays the same. Just be ready to move early if necessary."

Then he turned and made his way to the next person on his list. The list inside his head.

Nothing written down, no electronics, no phones. All communication mechanical, physical, analogue.

The last person he visited was Alina Murad. He asked her if she'd heard from her husband. No, she'd heard nothing, not from him, not from the Israelis. He gave her the same message, looked meaningfully in the direction of the children's bedroom, and left.

Chapter 16

After the first rush of adrenalin faded away, a meeting was convened at Shin Bet headquarters. The agent had read through and signed his police witness statement, the report was immediately stamped 'Eyes only' and locked in the station commander's safe until it – and he – was taken to a conference room at Shin Bet HQ.

The meeting was a short, and not particularly acrimonious, one. No fingers pointed, no blame apportioned. Just a swift, level-headed analysis of what Haydar Murad's response was all about.

There were two conflicting narratives – or more accurately, two conflicting reasons for his seemingly irrational behaviour.

Either he couldn't face the thought of long jail time and the fear of what might happen to his family on the outside, or he couldn't face the prospect of extended interrogation.

The former was understandable, a perfectly human fear.

The latter was puzzling. Was he afraid that he would be subjected to physical torture? He'd been arrested many times previously for security offences and he knew torture just never happened. Fair enough, he'd been smacked about a bit. But it was nothing serious. Neither the IDF nor the Shin

Bet was allowed to physically abuse their prisoners. An occasional smack across the head with an open palm, perhaps. A heavy boot 'accidentally' treading on a suspect's toes if he was being particularly disruptive or unhelpful. But nothing worse than that. Certainly no systematic beatings, no water-boarding, no denial of food, water, sleep – nothing that could be even remotely interpreted as torture or demeaning behaviour. The USA's Abu Ghraib debacle was something that was heavily frowned upon in the Israeli security establishment – that kind of behaviour wasn't an assertion of dominance, it was a sign of abject weakness and a total breakdown in human empathy and leadership qualities.

Haydar Murad was an old hand at this game. He wasn't afraid of having information tortured out of his lips, or that his family would be victimised by the Israelis.

Why was it then that that he couldn't face the prospect of an extended interrogation?

It had to be because of something he knew. He must have been terrified of letting something slip about the source of the money and, more to the point, its purpose.

So his attack on Benny Hart was not driven by a desperate attempt to escape custody. It was such a hopeless attack, there was no way that he had tried to kill a Shin Bet officer in order to escape – he had done so in order to die. And he didn't want to die because he had nothing to live for – he had a wife and three young children to live for. No, he didn't want to die; he *needed* to die. He needed to die so he wouldn't risk revealing whatever information he had.

It had all the hallmarks of a deliberate 'suicide by cop'.

What was the information that Haydar Murad had been so desperate to keep secret?

Chapter 17

Whenever large, unaccounted sums of money turned up in situations with a potential link to Islamist terrorism, it was red-flagged and Amira Hart's unit was automatically notified.

With the huge sum in mixed currencies counted and logged, the unit was advised that an "overseas operation" revealed the presence of a large figure in untraceable cash. The Palestinian Territories being neither officially annexed by Israel nor under direct Israeli jurisdiction pending an agreement between Jerusalem and Ramallah – if ever such an agreement got off the ground – the Murad haul was flagged as an overseas operation, and thus landed on Amira's desk.

She knew no other background details, just that this was a large sum of money with potential links to international terrorism perhaps targeting Israeli or Jewish interests at home or abroad. If an investigation revealed that the tracks led to Israel, the information would be turned over to Shin Bet and the Israel Police, as a domestic security issue. If the indications all pointed overseas, it was the Mossad's responsibility to find out when, where, how and who.

And she'd already had previous unrelated indications of activity in northern Europe. Sweden, more specifically.

She accordingly started delving deeper into possible Swedish targets with an Israeli and/or Jewish link. Working on the assumption that the money was going to be used to fund an operation in Sweden, she cast her net wide and then began narrowing her search parameters, working in concentric circles to see if the computer picked up on any interesting activity in Sweden.

What on earth could be of interest in that far-off corner of the globe? Her father was Swedish. Well, had been Swedish once upon a time, and although they had been to Sweden on vacation a number of times during her school years, to meet his family, she'd never really taken to the place.

They'd always visited in the summer, during the school vacation. Sweden was beautiful, the people were pleasant and the country was quiet. Way too quiet, for someone brought up in the constant hustle and bustle that is Israel, even in what was then a relatively small city like Ashdod.

But what was it with this never-ending daylight? It just never got dark at night in Sweden. At least, not on any of her visits there, admittedly all in the summer. Her recollections were of days and nights that appeared to blend seamlessly with one another – the sun rose at about 3.30 in the morning, and it sort of became a tiny little bit less bright at around 11.30 at night. But even those intervening four hours weren't really dark – just for fun she'd sat outside at midnight once to read a book, just to prove that she could. Who could ever have a good night's sleep in such conditions?

Not only that, her father's folks had told her that the winters were exactly the same, only not. That is, in the winter it never ever got light. Ever. They may have been exaggerating, but she doubted it. She was prepared to believe anything of a country where the elk got intoxicated every autumn on fallen fermenting apples that they ate off the ground, where winter meant you could drive a car across a lake – imagine driving a car across Yam Kinneret, the Sea of Galilee! – and where summer meant you were eaten alive by swarms of mosquitoes if you poked your nose out the door.

Who would even want to live in Sweden, let alone target it for terrorism? Did anything even happen in Sweden?

Amira Hart was about to find out.

But not before events overtook her.

Chapter 18

The unearthly monotonous 'ping' of the monitor was strangely reassuring because its measured beat was proof that Benny was stable. His face was unnaturally pale, looking even paler against the faded light blue of the hospital sheets.

His parents and sister sat by his side, occasionally holding hands and gazing at Benny as his chest rose, shallow but regular, the sound of his breathing amplified by the quiet of the room.

Sarah and Dov sat in stunned but dignified silence. No remonstrations, no hysteria, no sobbing as they saw their son at death's door. The people of Israel had been witness to countless scenes of Arab violence against Jews over the past century, in fact even from decades before the May 1948 rebirth of the Jewish state in its homeland, officially sanctioned by no less a body than the League of Nations, the forerunner of the United Nations – the collective body representing the nations of the world. There had been Muslim pogroms against the Jews of Hebron, for instance, as far back as the 1920s – was that because the Arabs were miraculously able to forecast that four decades later, in 1967, the State of Israel would 'occupy' the West Bank? That is to say, terminate the Jordanian occupation and retake areas from which Jews had been thrown out by the Jordanians in defiance of UN resolutions?

Then there was Jordan's ethnic cleansing of every last surviving Jew from East Jerusalem and the rest of the Jewish provinces of Judea and Samaria, not just Hebron, while the world stood silently and watched. Not a word of protest was uttered as Jews, who had lived for dozens of generations in communities throughout Judea and Samaria, were uprooted and resettled beyond the Armistice Line or Green Line, which the Arabs suddenly decided was to be designated the 'border'. Modern-day Jordan was what the League of Nations and its successor the United Nations had originally designated as the Arab State of Palestine, accounting for more than seventy percent of Mandate Palestine. And more than seventy percent of Jordan's population was made up of ethnic Palestinian Arabs – the Hashemite king and his family were actually immigrants imported from what is today Saudi Arabia, brought over from that desert kingdom to rule over the nascent Jordanian Arab Palestine, after a sliver of land corresponding to about 23 percent of Mandate Palestine was set aside for Jewish settlement. So it was actually a Palestinian Jordanian occupation that had ethnically cleansed the Jews from Judea and Samaria.

But nobody talked about that Jordanian occupation. It was only when Israel responded to imminent threats of yet another invasion by the joint forces of Lebanon, Syria, Jordan and Egypt in 1967, repelling the Jordanians and taking back the territory from which Jews had been illegally expelled from their homes back in 1948, that the Arab world – and the world at large – suddenly decided that 'occupation' was after all a reprehensible thing. When that charge could be laid at the door of the Jewish state.

All these thoughts and more coursed through Sarah's and Dov's minds as they caressed Benny's hand and prayed for his recovery. Their minds were numbed at the image of their huge blond giant of a son lying vanquished in a hospital bed.

Amira took it differently. The normally calm, sedate, quietly confident Amira was seething inside. This was her brother lying there. The brother who worshipped her and whom she loved, if anything, even more than she loved her parents. She had failed to protect him. Huge and well-trained as he was, he was still her kid brother, and he was her responsibility. And she had failed in that responsibility. She hadn't caused any of this, she didn't even know the details of what had happened, but nobody did this to Bunny and got away with it.

Her phone had been vibrating with incoming calls and messages for more than two hours now. She had ignored them all. But she had to take stock. She needed a situation assessment. First job was to get hold of a doctor and find out what Benny's prognosis was. Second job, depending on what the doctor said, was to check in with her unit and let them know where she was and why she'd gone AWOL. She had to follow up on the digital investigation she had initiated, to see what possible connection there was between Sweden and the recent relocation of known Islamists from places like Somalia and Syria to that Scandinavian country – or she had to delegate that responsibility to someone else. After that, there had to be a solid analysis of the uncovered intelligence, to see where all this was leading.

But before any of that she had to find a doctor. First things first.

And if it was the last thing she ever did on this earth, she was going to find out what had caused her brother's assailant to attempt to murder him in broad daylight. In an Israeli police station.

Because if there was one thing of which Amira Hart was sure, it was that Haydar Murad had not acted alone, or on a whim. Someone was pulling the strings.

What those strings were, and who was pulling them, was firmly on Amira Hart's agenda.

Someone was going to pay for Bunny.

Chapter 19

As August moved into September and the date of the October Hajj in Mecca loomed closer, hundreds of Israeli Arabs joined their fellow-Arabs from the Palestinian territories in the trek across the Jordanian border for the first leg of their pilgrimage to Islam's holiest site in Saudi Arabia.

Among the scores making the crossing every day was Adan Hamati. He knew that Alina Murad had already left two days earlier, and that the rest of his team, married couples all, would be performing the very same journey in the days ahead.

Haydar would be sorely missed. As far as he was concerned, the Zionists had killed an unarmed man while he was in their custody. They could make all the absurd allegations they wanted about him supposedly attacking an armed Shin Bet operative while in a police station, but the fact was that Haydar was dead and it was the Jews who had killed him. Simple.

He would have to think up some suitable retribution. But later, not now. First he had an important job to do.

A single man himself, he would now team up with Alina once they were both safely across the border. They would pose as a married couple. He didn't like living in close proximity with women. It wasn't a question of sexual preference – he just preferred to maintain his freedom of movement and action. He preferred not having responsibility for anyone else when a mission was going down – man or woman. And a woman, especially one who had recently lost her husband under such tragic circumstances, had the potential for being a particular burden. He'd have to draw up some strict ground rules when they met up.

From Jordan he would travel west to Turkey. The other members of his team would be spending their time in places like Albania, Greece, Bulgaria and Romania after their initial sojourn in Muslim Africa. Countries where a small bribe went a long way and where a big bribe bought a new life.

Because they were all going to be reborn before continuing their journey north. They were all going to become refugees fleeing the constantly escalating horrors of a vicious civil war 'back home in their beloved Syria'.

Europe had a fairly generous policy of accommodating Syrian refugees, but the Swedes had gone one step further: with national elections looming in another 11 months and mindful of the changing electoral demographics in Sweden with a Muslim population of no less than half a million souls, most of them fairly recent immigrants from war-torn communities throughout the Muslim world, the current government, a weak and failing coalition, was on a fishing expedition. It was fishing for votes, and the bait was its generous asylum policy.

The Swedish government had only recently announced that any Syrian refugee who made it to the Swedish border would be granted fast-tracked asylum status and permanent residency and citizenship since the human rights situation in Syria was deteriorating by the day. What a gift! And free besides, no strings attached. Such generosity! It was like Eid al-Fitr – the festival at the end of Ramadan when gifts were given to one and all. Except that this generous gift of Swedish asylum didn't just last a few days like the Muslim festival did; it was as though it were Eid and the Crusader gift-giving festival of Christmas and that thing the Jews did at about the same time of year, when they lit candles and gave presents to their children for seven or eight or nine days, some rubbish to commemorate some idiotic miracle hundreds of years ago before the Prophet Mohammed, peace be upon him, brought the one true religion to light up the hearts of people the world over.

Who cared anyway? Arrive at the Swedish border, present Syrian papers, and warm welcome to the land of the cold.

Adan Hamati cleared all thoughts from his mind as he presented his travel documents to the Jordanian border guard who gave the papers a cursory glance, stamped them with three separate stamps and handed them back, waving impatiently for the next traveller to step forward.

Chapter 20

Gothenburg on Sweden's west coast is a beautiful city. It was given its town charter in 1621 and had from the time of its founding always been a major hub for trade and commerce, industry and shipping.

Historically one of Sweden's most cosmopolitan cities, it was heavily influenced by the Dutch who were brought in to design the city's graceful canals and avenues. Built right on the water with the Göta River slicing the city in half and with Dutch-built canals criss-crossing the southern part of the downtown area, Gothenburg is graced with public parks, beautifully laid out green jewels dotting every neighbourhood, with huge forests, large lakes and rolling tracts of fertile farming land surrounding the city to the north, east and south. The North Sea limits the city to the west, and across that huge tract of choppy sea lie the British Isles.

Swedes pride themselves on their hospitality, their open-mindedness and their general lack of racism. Mindful of Sweden's rather dubious distinction of having successfully stayed out of World War Two, which ravaged the rest of Europe and saw millions of civilians killed for no other reason than their Jewish religion and ethnicity, Swedes generally feel both a sense of pride at having rescued and given a safe home to so many Jewish refugees, and a sense of guilt and shame that the price of their country's neutrality during the war was free passage for Hitler's troops to Nazi-occupied Norway and a plentiful supply of high-grade steel to the Nazi war machine. Hints of war profiteering have periodically raised their ugly head over the years and as is so often the case with relatively recent events of historical significance, it is difficult to separate the truth from the suspicion that such damaging allegations are routinely made simply for political point-scoring.

What was above all suspicion, however, was that modern Gothenburg was a powerhouse of heavy industry, cutting-edge medical research, advanced digital technology and a remarkable number of nondescript companies with not always clear links to various Swedish military industries.

The biggest name in town, of course, was iconic Swedish automotive manufacturer Volvo. The car division had been sold off to the Chinese a few years ago but still produced a highly successful range of automobiles, and Volvo's heavy-vehicle division produced trucks, buses, construction machines, marine engines, aero engines and industrial power generators. In a fusion characteristic of the pragmatic Swedish mind-set, the Swedish air force's Saab fighter aircraft were powered by Volvo aero engines, while Volvo's very first attempt at building an experimental electric-fossil fuel hybrid bus used a Saab turbocharged car engine to generate electricity on board, because at that time nobody else had succeeded in producing so much power from such a small and lightweight internal combustion engine.

Pragmatism. That defining characteristic of the Swedish approach to everything. In the event of a difference of opinion, the natural Swedish inclination was always to first look for the middle ground, check the scope for possible compromise. Compromise where both parties would lose a bit, but not as much as they would if they lost it all.

A safe bet for Swedes doing business, but a godsend for predators – businesspeople or others with a far darker agenda – looking to establish a presence in this wonderful country. A country that had not fought a war for over two hundred years and that regarded itself as the conscience of the world.

Hence Sweden's generous policy on asylum for refugees from the increasing volatile Arab world, and its open-door policy on anyone claiming asylum from Syria in particular.

With such a massive influx of immigrants in so short a time, even with the best intentions in the world integration was always going to be a problem. Add to this the tolerant but traditionally aloof attitude of Swedes in general, and a natural drift towards segregation was unavoidable. Swedes lived on their own, and Muslim immigrants tended to live among their own kind.

The politicians deplored this trend, social workers warned that it was creating a tinderbox, a pent-up store of immigrant resentment against the majority society, and the police had the hapless task of serving two increasingly distinct communities with ever fewer bridges between the two.

The new Sweden. The Sweden to which Adan Hamati made his way in mid-October, together with the rest of his team. All claiming asylum from Syria.

It was laughably easy. The Swedish Migration Board officials were totally out of their depth. They always had been. The Migration Board was more a political tool than a measured response to a carefully assessed – and fast-growing – problem. Always understaffed, the Board seemed to be governed by the attitude that asylum-seekers from the Arab world spoke Arabic and that all Arabic was the same. There was no appreciation of the need to gauge nuances, accents, dialects in order to determine the authenticity of claims of origin. There had been cases in which native-language interpreters had been bribed to assist asylum-seekers with the 'right' answers, so the Migration Board solved the problem by using increasing numbers of native Swedes with an academic degree in the Arabic language. For the sake of security. Which simply compounded the problem because Swedish Arabic speakers had even less understanding of regional dialectal nuances.

The result was laughably easy entry to Sweden. Infiltrators with one agenda or another making their way into this beautiful Scandinavian haven among the thousands upon thousands of truly deserving asylum-seekers fleeing the horrors of human-rights atrocities in countries spanning the entire Arab and wider Muslim worlds, from Libya and Tunisia to Egypt and the Palestinian Territories, from Syria and Iraq to Afghanistan and Pakistan.

Strangely enough, the one country with a sizable Muslim population from which there had never been any Arab asylum-seekers, despite the constant barrage of accusations of 'institutional apartheid', 'racism' and 'ethnic cleansing', was Israel. More than 20 percent of Israel's population was Arab, both Muslim and Christian, yet never since the founding of Sweden's Migration Board had there been a single case of an Arab seeking asylum from the Jewish state that everyone claimed treated its Arabs so badly.

And nobody put about that claim more stridently than the Swedish mainstream media. Backed up by a range of opportunistic politicians. All looking to acquire either more readership or more votes. They all understood it was a game, they didn't really believe their own lies, but over the past couple of decades institutional Israel-bashing had just become so much par for the course that nobody really reflected on it.

Nobody, that is, apart from the Swedish security service, SÄPO.

Like their colleagues in uniform, Sweden's SÄPO dealt with an entirely different reality than the image reflected in the media and presented by the country's politicians. Officers in uniform had to deal on a daily basis with integration-related issues in sprawling ethnically segregated suburbs such as Rosengård in the southern Swedish city of Malmö, Husby just north of Stockholm, and Bergsjön in eastern Gothenburg. Pressure-cookers of resentment where on many an occasion even ambulances and fire-engines had been stoned for daring to enter what some local firebrands declared was 'Muslim territory'.

While uniform dealt with these issues day to day, the plain-clothes 'squirrels' at SÄPO monitored the stream of potential troublemakers entering the country and kept track of them once they were inside.

Ignoring the often rather puzzling posturing of Swedish politicians and media, the Swedish security service had an excellent symbiotic working relationship with its Israeli counterpart. It was a relationship that rose above the petty politicking of the civilian ranks and was based on mutual respect bordering on admiration for the way each service did its difficult job under immense domestic constraints.

So it came as no surprise when the phone rang at the Israel desk at SÄPO headquarters and some rather troubling news was delivered by a female Mossad officer at the other end. Several Palestinian Arabs who had left the West Bank to attend the Hajj had failed to return after the end of the pilgrimage. There was a pattern: most of them were young couples, they had left behind families – some including young children. The Jordanians, with whom the Israelis had an excellent security relationship despite the negative public hype in the press, had confirmed their entry into the country, but there was no record of them moving on to Saudi Arabia. In fact, all had travelled elsewhere, on return tickets paid for in cash. Problem was, they had not returned to Jordan. There was no pattern to their destinations, which seemed to cover various parts of Muslim Africa. And years of intelligence had shown that if anything nefarious was being planned overseas, northern Africa was usually an ideal departure point for destinations in the West, usually via a number of EU states along the Mediterranean.

This lack of a definable pattern was also a pattern, said the Israeli intelligence officer. And there was one other matter. Recently a large amount of stolen money had been discovered by chance during a raid on a house in a West Bank town, but the money in no way corresponded to the huge sums stolen in a massive robbery spree in Israel that had lasted a long time and that had abruptly ceased following the discovery of that cache of stolen funds. The suspicion was that the rest of the money had been hidden away elsewhere, either for use in domestic criminal activities or terrorism. Or had gone abroad to fund an operation overseas.

The Mossad was making routine enquiries with all friendly agencies: to keep a lookout for unexpected cash sums suddenly surfacing, and also for anyone with a possible Palestinian origin. Sweden was outside the euro zone, so it was unlikely that any large sums of foreign currency would suddenly appear – the Swedes exercised rigid control over all foreign currency transactions at home. Rather, the thing to watch for was large amounts of money being traded overseas for Swedish kronor.

The Mossad officer assured her Swedish counterpart that she was asking the same of all her other EU counterparts and those further afield, but that the focus was on a European country that was either not in the EU, or a European country that was not part of the euro zone. For the simple reason that terrorists – if indeed there was a terrorist operation afoot – preferred at least one degree of separation to minimise the risk of traceability. Shekels, US dollars, euros and pounds sterling had been stolen, so it was reasonable to assume that the action was not going to be in any country that used these currencies. If for the moment one ignored countries further afield for logistical and/or political reasons, a process of profiling and elimination left a handful of potential target countries such as Norway, Denmark, Liechtenstein, Switzerland. And Sweden.

Amira Hart put down the phone and looked thoughtfully at the map of Europe on her screen.

In the shadowy world of mind-games that was the intelligence community, the lack of a pattern was surprisingly often also a clear pattern in itself. But it was all too fuzzy in this case. Something was missing. She needed a break, she needed something or someone to turn up where they shouldn't, where she could put her finger on an identifier, a marker.

She looked at the time on the bottom right of her computer screen. Time to go visit Bunny.

Chapter 21

As far as Amira Hart was concerned, Benny Hart the blond fair-skinned giant was still her baby brother Bunny. He was recovering well, had had more blood transfusions pumped into his massive frame than anyone at ER had dreamed possible – and his sister Amira, no blood relation and with a totally incompatible blood group, had felt powerless to help her brother.

All that was in the past now. Benny was regaining his strength. He was back home with his parents, on indefinite sick leave from work and raring to get back in the saddle, but his commander wouldn't hear of it. Nor would his doctor, or his parents. And nor would Amira, which is what clinched the deal. Benny was on sick leave, like it or not. He sometimes wondered wistfully if there were any other battle-hardened warriors who were as daunted as he was by a dark, wiry, pint-sized little bundle of muscle that could flash a heart-warming smile – or burst into a rapid-fire tongue-lashing designed to strike the fear of, well, of an irascible older sister, really, into the toughest of souls.

Benny Hart decided to enjoy his enforced leave of absence. He would use the time to think. Because he reckoned he knew what had put him in hospital, why Haydar Murad had acted as he did after that massive amount of money was discovered in his possession. The money was the key. No other valuables had been stolen, and no other valuables had been found. Just cash. He needed to think about this.

Amira Hart decided to make sure that he got away from it all. She suggested he take a holiday and go stay with family in Sweden. Get away from it all, breathe some of the cold, clean, bracing air of which the Scandinavians were so inordinately proud. Their relatives lived in a western suburb of Gothenburg, in a newly constructed complex of apartment buildings and semi-detached houses built on the site of what until recently had been a large school. There were farms and woodland backing onto the new houses. It was quiet, relaxing, away from the bustle of the city yet no more than 20 minutes by tram or bus to the centre of Gothenburg and its theatres, restaurants, pubs. Life, should the quiet of the suburbs become too quiet for him.

Much to Amira's surprise, and initial suspicion, Benny readily agreed. She thought about it, reckoned he was really just pleased to get away from it all for a while and would return rejuvenated and ready to throw himself into his work.

Said and done. Less than a fortnight later Benny was on an early-morning Lufthansa flight from Ben-Gurion Airport outside Tel Aviv, heading for Frankfurt in Germany and a quick switch to a Lufthansa-SAS partnership flight to Landvetter Airport just outside Gothenburg. His aunt and uncle, Lola and David, were on a month-long visit to their eldest daughter in Los Angeles, so the apartment was vacant and they were only too pleased to have someone give the place a lived-in look to ward off any potential burglars or tipsy Friday night chancers looking for somewhere to doss down and sleep off the effects of a wet weekend celebration.

He took the airport bus in to Nils Ericssonsplatsen, the main terminus located beside the railway station, and the number 7 tram heading west to Frölunda. His aunt and uncle lived on Magnetgatan, in one of the area's attractive new apartment blocks, surrounded by an open park on one side, another apartment building in front, and some woods fanning away up a rocky hill across the remaining two sides.

These pragmatic Swedes, thought Benny to himself as he took the elevator to the apartment. All the streets in this entire area had an electronic theme going – Magnetgatan, Radiogatan, Antenngatan, Transistorgatan. *Gatan* was Swedish for Street. Other areas of Gothenburg were similarly themed – there was one suburb where all the streets were named after various musical instruments, another where the theme was flowers, yet another where all the streets had mouth-watering exotic spice names and so on.

Benny knocked on the door of apartment 1406 and introduced himself, explaining that he was there to pick up the keys for next door, Lola and David. His Swedish was a wee bit rusty, he only spoke it at home with his father, but a couple of weeks would put that right. Nothing like the TV and radio for polishing up a latent linguistic skill.

He entered the apartment, switched on the lights and started putting things in order for his impromptu vacation. First things first, though: turn up the thermostats on the wall-mounted radiators – this may seem like a perfectly normal temperature for his aunt and uncle and other hardy souls with Viking blood coursing through their veins, but he was a child of the desert and he liked things warm.

After a shower and change of clothes he locked the apartment door and went out to the local supermarket for provisions. Dinner was his first priority.

Chapter 22

This was only October, and they were set to stay here for another two months. What a miserable, cold, wet, depressing place this was, thought Adan Hamati. It was grey, you could almost physically measure the days getting shorter one at a time, and long before the day was over in any civilised part of the world, here it had already turned black. And they said this was a mere precursor to what would come in the interminably long months of December, January, February, when the colour 'black' took on a whole new meaning.

Any wonder the Swedes were by and large such a shy, one might say aloof race – most of the year it was so dark they probably couldn't see each other to say hello...

Adan Hamati had settled quickly into his new routine. A room provided by a Somali sympathiser in the somewhat seedy suburb of Grumstad, no phones in the apartment, neither landline nor cell phone. His Somali host had moved out as agreed, leaving him in sole charge of the apartment. Just one bedroom, but the living-room had a pull-out sofa and that was where he would sleep.

The woman whom the Swedish immigration authorities knew as his wife, Alina Murad, lived in the bedroom. The routine was fairly straightforward. Alina cooked, went shopping for provisions in the local market, where most of the stalls seemed to be owned either by Somalis or Iraqis, with a sprinkling of Lebanese and Turks. Adan did his regular tour of the other apartments, where the rest of his team were in place. He varied his route, but always took in all four apartments once a day.

One couple to each apartment, nobody else staying there, not even the tenants whose names were on the rental agreements. No phones, no TV, no radios. Not even a credit card.

Their duties were not exactly onerous. Sleep, cook, eat, pray, do the laundry when necessary. And work out in the apartment, with the blinds securely shut and just a dim light on in the corner above the bedside table.

A shuttered life. Except in the evenings, when they exchanged the confines of their apartments for the open air, wrapping up warm and stepping out for a brisk walk, long and hard, breathing in the fresh air with its occasional chemical tang – the oil refineries on Hisingen Island were just over that ridge of trees and if the wind was right – or wrong, really – the heavy musk of processed oil would waft across the housing estate.

In the second week, Adan Hamati went shopping.

Chapter 23

The Swedish banking system is a peculiar one – and one of the most tightly controlled in the world. Most high-street banks no longer deal with cash. You can make a purchase of just a few kronor using your credit card, for which there is no charge, and you can withdraw funds from your savings account from any of the hundreds of automatic telling machines or cash-points found in every city, town, village, petrol station and corner store.

But putting cash into an account – that's virtually impossible. Because Sweden is a largely cashless society.

It's a measure driven relentlessly by SÄPO, the Swedish security service, in line with EU-wide guidelines aimed at strangling the funding of terrorism. Credit card transactions can be traced, cash cannot. Solution: strangle the use of cash. You receive your salary every month, which is electronically deposited into your bank account. Every purchase you subsequently make using a credit card is logged, making traceability and accountability an easy game for the authorities. And if you instead withdraw cash and spend folding money – well, that's fine, it's accepted everywhere. But if you withdraw a large or otherwise out of character sum of money – well, that too is logged. And automatically red-flagged.

It all makes things easier for the financial crimes squad, the people in uniform. The officers who are keen to stamp out illegal gambling, the underground world of what is euphemistically termed 'grey employment' – that is to say illegal employees who never pay income tax, and other financial frauds.

The biggest benefit, however, one that is never really talked about openly, is that it is an absolute boon for the security spooks who work in a similar world of financial irregularity but who aren't interested in tax evaders. They are the intelligence officers on a constant lookout for the funders of terrorism.

Terrorism requires money. It really is that simple. True, terrorists can create mayhem with a mere fraction of the funding and other resources needed to keep a regular army or security service in operation – the 9/11 terror attacks that had and still were having such a global impact were carried out on an embarrassingly tiny shoestring budget – but it all still required funding.

And funding meant money.

Cash is the invisible king. Credit cards spell certain discovery.

Adan Hamati knew that, hence the looting spree in Israel. It was a risk, an unnecessary affectation that might have jeopardised the entire mission. But it was important for symbolic reasons. Because the fact was that although it would have been more difficult to find cash-carrying targets in a cash-strapped mainland Europe long in the grip of a threatening economic meltdown, it was the symbolism of acquiring the money in the Jewish state that so appealed to the Palestinian.

He wanted Jewish money, or at least money intended to be spent in what the Jews thought was their land, to fund the operation that would stop their foolish dreams. It was nothing more than poetic justice, really. They should finance their own destruction. It had been working very successfully for years in the Gaza Strip: as soon as the Zionists barred the transfer of cement to the Hamas brothers who controlled Gaza, the Palestinians and their many friends overseas went into overdrive, condemning Israel for its racist refusal to allow the Gaza Arabs to build homes. And when world opinion forced the Jews to relent, reopening the supply of cement to Gaza, all the building materials – in their entirety – were promptly siphoned underground for the construction of tunnels burrowing deep into Israeli territory. Tunnels designed to permit the kidnapping of Zionist soldiers and civilians, and for packing with explosives under Israeli factories, kibbutzim, homes, schools and shopping malls.

There was a particular satisfaction among the Palestinian leadership in knowing that it was Israeli cement that made these spectacular missions possible – the Zionists were financing the undermining of their society. Literally.

It was that thought that had prompted Adan Hamati to launch his cash acquisition spree in the Jewish state. It was quite simply very fitting, he thought. They had admittedly lost a lot of funds when that Shin Bet operation had accidentally stumbled upon part of their cache, but it was only a small portion. And he was by now absolutely certain that Haydar Murad had not revealed anything about his part in the mission – otherwise the Israelis would have rolled up his operation by now.

No doubt about it, the Zionists were still in the dark.

Adan looked at his watch and then at the gathering gloom around him. Three fifteen pm, and dark grey would soon turn to jet black.

He was in the dark too. But his was a dark of his own choosing.

And so he continued shopping, paying for everything in cash.

Always cash.

Chapter 24

In Tel Aviv, Amira received a priority email from Sweden. Marita Ohlsson, a financial transactions analyst at SÄPO in Sweden, was seeing some unusual activity, but she wasn't sure what it meant or, to be perfectly honest, if it was even remotely significant. It was, well, just different, that's all. And Amira Hart had asked for any signs that were out of the ordinary. So here it was.

Amira called Marita Ohlsson on the phone and thanked her for her email. She had read the raw information, but she wanted a more personal feel, a gut reaction to what it may mean.

Marita thought before answering. Stores supplying hiking goods and equipment for outdoorsmen suddenly seemed to be doing an unusually brisk trade. That wasn't particularly odd – Swedes were after all inordinately infatuated with living as primitively as they could in their free time. They enjoyed living in summer shacks far from any habitation, no electricity or other amenities, not even a proper toilet. They loved rambling, they loved hunting, they went both downhill skiing and cross-country skiing, and when the lakes froze over they took to their ice-skates on ponds and lakes that were sometimes hundreds of feet deep. And they cheerfully did all this accompanied by nothing more civilised than a spare set of warm, dry clothes, sturdy footwear and plenty of sandwiches and coffee, with hot blueberry drink for the kids.

So nothing really strange. Except…

"They were all cash payments," said Marita. "No plastic. Why would that happen, suddenly?"

Amira pondered this new information. The traditionally docile, rather lemming-like Swedes generally tended to follow rules and guidelines, rarely bucked the trend – whatever trend – and now suddenly their purchasing pattern was not following – well, it wasn't following the pattern. And Swedes loved patterns, patterns brought a degree of comfort that comes from the familiar.

This was the autumn, so it wasn't odd that outdoors hiking equipment was being bought in unusual quantities as the stark autumn chill gradually morphed into harsh winter cold. But that change in type of payment was definitely odd.

"And another thing," continued Marita Ohlsson. "It's not just hiking goods. I may be imagining things, I may be crunching the data wrong, but it's also weird things like electric bikes – lots of them."

"Electric bikes?" asked Amira Hart. "What, you mean the things pensioners and people with physical disabilities use to get around?" She wasn't sure where this was heading.

"No, I mean like regular cycles, but with an electric motor as well as pedals. You don't have them in Israel?"

"Aha, OK I see what you mean," replied Amira. "Sure, we have them – and then some! You can't walk on a pavement anywhere in Tel Aviv without risking being knocked down by some idiot whizzing by at a hundred kilometres an hour. Wouldn't be so bad if they could build up their speed through hard work, but they just sit there with an idiotic smile on their faces while they play ten-pin bowling with pedestrians, pensioners, young kids in strollers who scatter in every direction as they come speeding at them."

When had she turned into such a grumpy old biddy, wondered a startled Amira. Where did all this complaining come from? Shaking her head she turned her attention back to the conversation.

"Does any of this mean anything to you, is it what you were looking for?" asked Marita Ohlsson.

"I really don't know at the moment. But I'll tell you what would be really useful, although I'd understand if you felt reluctant about this: can we have some kind of demographic over these sales? That is, the kinds of people doing the purchasing?"

She waited with baited breath. Asking for information that might be perceived as offending a foreign power's personal integrity laws was risky business. It could quite rightly be regarded as privileged information and, quite frankly, as rather an offensive enquiry.

"What exactly are you looking for?" came the guarded response from the somewhat startled Swede.

"Well, you know," began Amira as disarmingly as she could. "Age, gender, that kind of thing, if the purchases were registered to businesses, even though they were paid for in cash." She did not dare ask for an ethnic marker, anything that identified whether the purchasers were native Swedes or people of foreign extraction. The Swedes were famously touchy about anything that smacked of even the slightest hint of xenophobia, segregation, racial profiling. Amira held her breath.

There was a pause at the other end of the phone line. Then a little laugh. "Oh yeah, age, gender and so on, no worries. Look, let's stop beating about the bush. You want to know if there's any common denominator linking all these people. *ANY* common denominator. Political correctness is for the politicians. We're not politicians, thank God. The day we're told to pray to the altar of political correctness I'll be out of here like a scalded cat. And so too, I suspect, would most of my colleagues. I'll get back if and when I put anything together."

And with that she rang off.

Amira Hart found she was perspiring profusely. Not just because she was feeling that indefinable sensation that she was on to something, a possible entry point into a very puzzling case, but also because she knew she had walked a very fine line between asking a sister service for assistance, on the one hand, and risking alienating some very good friends by asking a question that simply could not be asked without offending a whole lot of people.

She mentally saluted Marita Ohlsson, who was obviously not someone who paid too much attention to the quagmire of social niceties. “A woman after my own heart,” thought Amira Hart and thanked her lucky stars that the call had ended without her becoming mired in a minefield of political correctness.

Chapter 25

The rented lockup was filling up nicely. The equipment arrayed in neat stacks. Eleven of everything. Even though Haydar Murad was no longer with the team – was no longer on this Earth thanks to the accursed Zionists – an eleventh set was nonetheless there, ready for use. Always good to have a backup, a spare.

It had all taken so much time. Not being able to rent a car because of the need to furnish a driver's licence meant everything had to be done by public transport. And public transport in Gothenburg meant purchasing an electronic card which was swiped across the scanner every time one boarded a bus or tram. A card costing 100 kronor would last for about 5 trips, but Adan Hamati did not want any degree of traceability. So he purchased a 100 kronor card in a corner shop, used it just the once to get to a bicycle store and then buried it deep in a trashcan outside the mall where the bike shop was located.

He knew what he wanted, and the order in which he wanted it all.

He had to avoid the buses and trams because of the need to use electronic swipe-cards. There was an alternative: the municipality of Gothenburg catered for first-time travellers without the requisite electronic card by allowing would-be passengers to board a bus or tram and then send a text message by mobile phone to a number, which deducted the cost of the journey from the subscriber's cell phone account. But Adan wanted nothing to do with cell phones – or any other phones for that matter.

So it had to be a bicycle. Which was no great problem since he needed one anyway. In fact, he needed eleven of them.

But a specific type of bicycle. Electric. And a specific type of electric bike, too.

He walked past row upon row of bikes arranged in neat order. Traditional sit-up-and-beg city bikes with three gears or five. Lighter hybrid and sports bikes, a kind of cross-over between off-road and street cycles. Serious mountain-bikes, with everything from 15 to 24 gears. Slim, ultra-fast racing bikes.

And finally electric bikes. He had a list of priorities. Lightest possible, ladies model without a crossbar. Seven or eight gears. Dampers at the front. Black, dark blue or dark grey frames. Built-in LED lights front and rear. Rigid rear without dampers. Knobbly tyres for good grip. And power: 500 watt brushless motors, integrated in the rear wheel hub. Disc brakes a must, at least at the rear, mechanical or hydraulic – whichever was cheaper. Battery capacity minimum ten amp-hours, preferably sixteen if available.

And eleven bike trailers. As many different kinds as possible for visible variation. Aluminium frames, lightweight, the shopping-trolley kind with all-enclosing sturdy canvas bag for holding the shopping, not the large rectangular open-top cart types.

One by one, Adan did the rounds of all the big cycle stores and major department stores, careful not to buy more than one bike and trailer in each place. Paid cash. And then went straight on to outdoor equipment and hiking outfitters, buying everything else he needed and loading it in the trailer. Lightweight but waterproof and windproof jackets and trousers, two sets of warm thermal underwear for each person, featuring long sleeves and ankle-length leggings. Cheap plastic wraparound clear-glass sports glasses from a hardware store, thin black polyester/cotton balaclavas and brown, black or navy-blue woollen hats to go on top. Thin windproof joggers' gloves and thicker fleece gloves to fit over them.

Day after day, Adan Hamati returned to the lockup with a fresh new full set of equipment in his bike trailer. Anyone not paying too much attention would have assumed it was the same person returning each day with the same bike. By the time he returned at the end of each day it was already dark and the differences weren't very noticeable.

When everything was finally assembled, he went to a hardware store and returned with lengths of sturdy aluminium tubing, each pre-cut to an exact length and with a predetermined chamfer at either end. Each tube slotted into space between the cycle handlebar and the saddle post; a cursory glance from afar would register a gent's bike, not a ladies' model. He then went shopping for self-adhesive contact paper, the kind schoolchildren used to cover their schoolbooks to protect them from wear and tear. He chose bright colours – eye-catching metallic red, blue, green, yellow, silver.

Then he went to work, carefully applying the contact paper and the similarly coloured crossbar to what would hopefully be the spare bike, the one nobody would ever have to use.

The transformation was total – it looked nothing like the original. He glanced at his watch, noted the time and set about totally stripping the bike of its disguise, returning it to its original ladies model in unremarkable black. His fingers working quickly, he removed the crossbar and stuffed it into the trailer, peeled back the contact paper from the frame and stuffed that too into the bike trailer. A few slivers of self-adhesive paper remained here and there, clinging tenaciously to the metal frame, but it would require a close examination to see that the bike had ever been a different colour. Time: 58 seconds.

Perfect.

Adan Hamati locked up the garage and returned to his flat.

Chapter 26

The phone rang on Amira Hart's desk and she picked it up, looking automatically for the caller ID. Nothing, which meant it was probably overseas or a switchboard.

"Hi, this is Marita Ohlsson, we spoke a few days ago, remember?"

Yes, Amira certainly remembered. Marita the Unfazed, who wasn't afraid to call things by their right names. "Hi Marita, do you have anything for me?"

"I think I might, not exactly sure though. Remember I told you there was a whole lot of purchasing for cash suddenly going on, electric bikes and hiking stuff and things like that. All in Gothenburg, and now it turns out all by the same man. Or at least, perhaps by a bunch of different men but they all look and sound pretty much the same. And they all speak English, not Swedish. And another thing: the bikes, at least, are pretty expensive pieces of kit with fairly complex gear systems, electrics and electronics and so on, but he hasn't submitted any of the warranty forms. Which is really plain stupid because without a registered warranty form, neither the shop nor the manufacturer will honour the standard one-year warranty – they insist on proof the bike was purchased and paid for, not stolen. So that's really pretty odd."

There was a pause while this strange information sank in. "And something else: he's probably from your neck of the woods."

"You mean he's Israeli?" asked a surprised Amira.

"No, I'm not saying that exactly, just that he's kind of Middle Eastern in appearance, nobody can say for sure, but perhaps Turkish, Greek, Lebanese, Israeli, Palestinian – something like that."

Amira Hart nodded to herself. Perhaps this was the break she was hoping for.

The Hajj was over, just about everybody who had gone on pilgrimage from Israel and the West Bank had returned home, with the exception of a number of couples and a few businessmen travelling alone – all from the Palestinian Territories.

Large sums of cash had been stolen from all over Israel over a long period of time.

Large sums of cash had been recovered by accident in a totally unrelated arrest in the West Bank. By no means all the money had been recovered, not even a small percent, but the type of money taken and the country in which large sums of money were suddenly turning up indicated a connection, however circumstantial.

The one suspect who may have been induced to provide information had to all intents and purposes committed suicide by attacking armed officers inside a police station – and his wife was one of the non-returnees from the Hajj.

And most interesting of all: one Hajj pilgrim was notably prominent by his absence from the register of returning residents to the West Bank – Adan Hamati. Now *that* was really interesting. As Amira was fond of reminding herself, patterns emerged not only from what was there, but remarkably often from what was missing.

And Adan Hamati, notorious troublemaker, had still not returned home, according to the Border Police register.

As if all this were not enough, there was Sweden and its remarkably forgiving policy of admitting refugees who claimed asylum from all over the fast-imploding Arab world, in particular from Syria.

"You know what?" said Amira. "I'd like to meet you and compare notes, I think we might have something for you to go on. It's a long shot, but I think it's worthwhile. If nothing comes of it, I'll have wasted a few hours in an airplane. But if my suspicions are justified – and I repeat, it's a long shot – then we may be on to something here. What do you reckon, can you clear it with your people?"

They agreed that Amira should let Marita Ohlsson know the date and time of her arrival and that they'd book a conference room to jointly pool their resources and go over their findings.

"Swedes and their conferences – they just love them," muttered Amira under her breath as she picked up her phone and started making arrangements.

Chapter 27

Benny checked his email message again. Amira was coming to Gothenburg. On business, her message had said rather cryptically. No details. She asked if the flat had space for her too.

He dashed off a reply in the affirmative. It would be great to see his little big sister, but what was bringing her here? Benny wondered if it was in any way related to the attempt on his life but he was too sensible to ask Amira over the Internet. He'd wait until her arrival. If there was something he could do to help her in whatever she was working with, it would give his enforced holiday some much-needed structure. Two minds were better than one. Of course, he was Shin Bet, and Shin Bet was strictly prohibited from operating outside Israel. But he was here recuperating, wasn't he? And he was staying at his aunt and uncle's flat in Gothenburg because they were away on holiday. He was officially on sick leave, and if he was officially sick then he was officially not working. Not working meant he was free to do as he liked.

Amira, on the other hand, was Mossad, and Mossad operated overseas. Irrespective of what many people believed, most Mossad work was not covert, under the radar of purportedly friendly nations. Most of their work was perfectly open, consisting of a lively exchange of information and tips via regular channels of contact with sister agencies.

The content of the information passed back and forth may be secret, but most of the mechanicals of the exchange process were not. It was for the most part conducted in an atmosphere of mutual – if occasionally rather wary – respect. Open, swift and constant exchange of information was the name of the game in a world of ever-developing threats such as terrorism, financial crimes, human trafficking, drug-running and money-laundering on a global scale that would make the gross domestic product of a small nation pale into insignificance.

And now Amira was coming to Gothenburg, officially.

Benny considered his situation. This holiday might actually turn out to be fun, after all.

Chapter 28

On one of these occasional sparkling and sunny afternoons that sometimes brighten up the month of October as the autumn trees shed their leaves in cascades of gold and red, Amira Hart landed at Landvetter Airport and was met in Arrivals by a young woman, perhaps late twenties or early thirties, wearing a strict blue business suit and crisp white collared shirt open at the neck, with a short blue coat over the top of it all. Marita Ohlsson introduced herself and the two women made their way to the short-term parking lot across the slip road leading past the terminal building.

“Let me fill you in on the latest developments,” said Marita as she guided an official-looking white Volvo S60 out of the parking lot and down past the cargo terminal, heading for the motorway into town.

“Once again circumstantial and it may mean nothing, but you know we’ve been admitting a lot of refugees, from Syria in particular, over the past few months?”

Amira Hart nodded as she watched the tree-covered granite hills flash by on either side of the motorway, giving an occasional glimpse of a frigid-looking lake burnished deep gold by the rays of the fast-sinking sun as it slipped down towards the horizon.

"Well, no prizes for guessing then that some of them have absconded. They're supposed to report at scheduled intervals to the Migration Board, not least to receive their regular maintenance grants while the immigration authorities process their status. Nothing really odd about that, it happens once every couple of years, but this time there are ten people missing – a suspiciously symmetrical five couples. And they're all from Syria. Or so they say. Again, nothing odd about an influx of asylum-seekers from Syria, but for ten of them to go walkies at one and the same time, well now, that really *is* odd."

"OK, so it looks like there's work for us here then," said Amira. "From your point of view, you're looking for people who have gone suspiciously off the radar, and from my point of view, I want to see if there is any link with the money stolen in Israel and the money being spent here. And if the two cases coincide, as I'm beginning to think might be the case, then it's all systems go. This isn't something I can decide on my own, I'll have to get in touch with my superiors to see how we handle this.

"Still, no point getting ahead of ourselves," she continued. "We have absolutely no idea yet if there's a connection. So, are we going to your office now?"

Marita Ohlsson slowed down to 70 kilometres an hour as she approached the steep descent of the motorway exit ramp and guided her car through the underpass and up onto the flyover that would take them past Gothenburg's new Ullevi football stadium and opposite it, the massive structure that was the city's central police station. It was here that Marita Ohlsson's Stockholm brass had commandeered an office for her use.

They left the official car in the underground car park and made their way to the office set aside for their use. Marita Ohlsson paused on the way at a small blue car to pick up an overnight bag. "I drove down from Stockholm," she explained. "Not sure how long I'm going to be here so I'd prefer to have my own transport rather than have to rely on there always being a pool car available."

They made their way to the elevator and up into the building.

Of course – there it was, the ubiquitous conference table. These Swedes and their penchant for conferences, for consensus around a table. Amira saw with gratitude that they were alone in the room – there wasn't going to be a conference, not now at any rate. The two women headed for the far end of the room where Marita pulled her slim laptop out of her bag and opened it up. After keying in her password and clicking on the files she needed, she pointed to the screen.

"That's them. Ten people – five couples – who all arrived within a few days of each other, who all failed to register after their arrival, who are all Syrians, and who are all now missing."

“Can you send these to me?” asked Amira. “I’d like to study them this evening. It’s a long shot, but we can run them through our face recognition software and look for matches in our own databases.” She peered closely at the small laptop screen. “I suggest you contact our friends in Greece and Turkey…”

She looked up as Marita Ohlsson looked quizzically at her. “Yes, despite the hype and the idiocy of the politicians, on the tactical intelligence level we continue to work very well indeed with our Turkish colleagues. In the intelligence fraternity we know what matters – only the politicians don’t. They don’t know – and they don’t matter,” finished Amira with a smile.

“Too right,” nodded Marita in agreement. “OK, you’ve got the file now. What else. Oh yeah, tomorrow perhaps, after you’ve had a good night’s sleep, we’ll set you up with what you need here in this room and we’ll pool our information, see where this gets us. Incidentally, are you fixed for accommodation? Where are you staying?”

“Sounds like a plan. I’m good, thanks, I’m staying with my brother here in Gothenburg,” replied Amira.

Marita Ohlsson looked up in total surprise. “You have a brother living here? In Sweden? Gothenburg? Why didn’t we know this?”

"No, it's nothing like that. We have relatives here, and they're in America somewhere spoiling their grandchildren rotten and Benny – that's my brother – asked if he could use their apartment while they're away. He just wanted a short holiday." She checked her smartphone. "It's in Västra Frölunda." Noticing the SÄPO agent looking up in surprise at her excellent pronunciation, she added with a smile: "Our father is Swedish. Was Swedish, I should say. We speak Swedish at home whenever our Dad can force us."

"So I've been wasting my time speaking English to you all this while? Right, Swedish it is. Where is the apartment?" asked Marita, switching languages.

Amira showed Marita Ohlsson her phone. "Oh, that's Magnetgatan in Västra Frölunda. A pretty new area, I believe. Never been there, but I know roughly where it is. I'll drive you there."

As they rode back down to the underground car park Amira pulled out her phone and called Benny's number. "Benny shalom, it's me," she spoke in Hebrew. "How're you doing? Look, feel like company? I'm getting a lift out to you with a Swedish colleague, perhaps you can get off your bum and play host or something? Coffee, baklava, cookies, dates, whatever? Play nice, I need her as much as she needs me and I don't want any hiccups. OK *motek*, see you soon."

Chapter 29

Amira Hart pressed the button beside the door to the apartment building and the two women were buzzed in.

Greeting them at the door of the apartment was a fit-looking Benny, not half as pale as he had been the last time Amira had seen him. The Swedish autumn certainly seemed to agree with him.

Marita Ohlsson stopped dead in her tracks, the smile wiped off her face at the sight of tall, blond, blue-eyed and fair-skinned Benny Hart.

“Who’s this,” she asked hesitantly, yet trying to project power. “This is supposed to be your brother?”

Both Amira and Benny burst out laughing. He stretched out his huge hand and grasped hers in a firm yet not overpowering shake.

“We tend not to think about this back home, where everybody knows us, but yes, I guess it can be a bit of a shock if you’re not prepared for it. *Amiraleh*, what a prize nutcase you are – you could have at least mentioned something to your colleague. Come in, come in, no point in standing on the cold landing when we have a perfectly good borrowed – and warm – apartment at our disposal.”

Marita Ohlsson had never been in a situation like this before. She instinctively liked Benny Hart, and she had no reason to distrust a fellow officer from an overseas agency, but it certainly was odd to conduct a conversation in Swedish with two such disparate-looking Israeli siblings who both claimed the same Swedish parentage. Decidedly unusual.

One thing was for sure: Benny Hart wasn't going to win any prizes on Masterchef – there was no baklava, no cookies, no dates. Just coffee. Without either milk or sugar. "I'm returning to my Viking roots," said Benny with an apologetic shrug of his shoulder as his sister looked daggers at him for his abject failure to be a good host. Was the boy ever going to grow up, she wondered.

The evening flashed by quickly, and after their guest left Amira had a shower and settled down for a chat with her brother.

"*Nuuu*, spill the beans! What's this about?" asked Benny. "And don't give me any of that official secrets crap or I'll pull your hair till your grey roots show."

"To be perfectly honest, I'm not really sure. It's just a bunch of loosely connected threads. In fact, I don't even know if I'd say they're loosely connected, or even connected at all."

And with that she gave him a brief sketch of what she'd come up with so far, the possible links with the money and why they may, just may, lead to Sweden.

As she was scrolling past files on her desktop Benny caught sight of a file with the SÄPO logo.

"What's that?" he asked his sister.

"Probably nothing particularly relevant to our case, just some people who've gone missing and Marita was wondering over a possible connection. We're both casting our nets wide, as you can see, hoping to catch something, anything."

But Benny's interest was piqued. He read the Swedish text, and without asking for permission clicked on the icon to expand the photos of the missing people.

And stopped dead. Stared hard. Looked across at his sister. And looked again at the photos. At one particular photo.

"That one!" he said, his forefinger almost trembling with barely suppressed excitement. "The name is all wrong. That's not her name. And she's not Syrian. And she's not married. At least not to him." He pointed again, at another picture.

Amira looked up at him quizzically.

"That's the wife of the man we arrested, who stabbed me. Something Murad. Alia, Alisa, something like that. No, wait," he snapped his fingers. "Alina! That's her. Alina Murad. And she has three young children. Where are they? Why are they not listed as entering with the mother? Why are they not listed as missing?"

Amira looked in triumph at her kid brother. He may choose to disembark aircraft in an unorthodox way with a glorified umbrella fanning above his head, he was so tall the weather was probably different at his ankles and around his head – but that head was working and it had saved the day.

They finally had their longed-for break.

Chapter 30

16-year-old Samira Hersi lived with her father on Länsgatan, in a third-floor two-bedroom apartment in the northern suburb of Grumstad in Gothenburg, facing an access road lined on the other side by a long row of lockup garages.

Samira and her father were the only survivors of a massacre that had killed her mother and her two younger brothers in Somalia. That was nine years ago. Sweden had taken in the decimated family, and for that her father Abdurrahman was eternally grateful.

He had worked hard at a variety of menial jobs after arriving in Sweden, accepting the Swedish language course that the state provided free to all asylum-seekers, as well as all financial and other assistance for his young daughter Samira, but refusing the proffered unemployment handouts.

That didn't go down well with the Swedish bureaucrats. A registered asylum-seeker was entitled to various benefits, and it was unheard-of for these benefits not to be accepted. In any case, there was no administrative mechanism for returning selected parts of the state's centrally stipulated financial package.

So Abdurrahman Hersi was forced to accept the full amount, but he promptly donated the excess to the local mosque. In its entirety. And went looking for work. After four long, hard years he finally secured a job as a hospital porter in

Gothenburg's universally acclaimed Sahlgrenska University Hospital, where his ethos of hard work and his quick mastery of the Swedish language soon made him a highly respected and well-liked member of the hospital's huge payroll.

And that ethos of hard work, of doing what is right, had rubbed off on his daughter Samira. At sixteen, she was tall for her age, attractive to look at but always modestly dressed, never going out without a hijab to cover her hair and the sides of her face. She spoke Swedish without the slightest trace of a foreign accent, and did very well at school.

Abdurrahman and Samira were among the relatively few recent arrivals to Sweden's shores who seemed to have understood that integration in a new society did not have to mean assimilation or the wiping out of the culture from which they had come. They were both devout Muslims, gave generously to charity, attended mosque services whenever they could, observed all the festivals, kept to all the strict Muslim dietary laws – yet lived as Swedes. They spoke good Swedish, although always used their mother-tongue at home. They chatted with their non-Muslim neighbours and always seemed to find the time to exchange a word or two of greeting with young and old alike on their way to or from their apartment.

In short, they were the best of what the new Sweden was supposed to be: people from a different culture who proudly maintained their own ethnicity and religion, but who also adapted smoothly to the ways of their new home.

And one of the things that Abdurrahman had taught his daughter was that criminality was not to be tolerated. Because if you make allowances in one case, you'll likely be tempted to do so again. And again, and again.

So when Samira Hersi saw a suspicious-looking man going in and out of a lockup garage across the road every evening, always with an expensive-looking bicycle but almost certainly not the same bicycle every time unless her young eyes were deceiving her, she became interested.

She'd never seen him before, and didn't particularly relish the idea of finding out where he lived. That was nothing to do with her. But if he was stealing bikes – and what *was* it with all those different-looking trailers every day? – then this certainly was something that someone needed to attend to.

That someone would have to be her father. She'd tell him this evening when he returned from his late shift at the hospital. Meantime, she had to prepare dinner and then get on with some homework, and if there was time after that she'd give her girlfriend Hanan a call, see how she was getting on with that project they would have to finish writing up and hand in on the following Monday: the historical origins of the modern-day city of Gothenburg, which in the dawn of time had first been built about 45 kilometres up the coast in today's picturesque little village of Lödöse. She was of course going to see Hanan the following day. Not at school, though, because tomorrow was the day her entire class was leaving town for a field trip to Lödöse to see the place first-hand. Stig, their history teacher (known behind his back as "Stigma" because he was very self-conscious of his prematurely balding head) was assembling them all at some unheard-of time outside the local library, where the coach would pick them up.

Six-thirty in the morning! Who'd ever heard of such a time? And that's when they were departing – which meant getting up way before some of the rougher element in her class – some of the hard drinkers and party-goers – even got to their beds. Their problem, not hers. But she'd have to get up early. Really early, like five-thirty or something.

Putting together her backpack of supplies for the following day's field trip, Samira completely forgot to tell her father about the strange guy in the lockup across the road.

Chapter 31

Nobody had been looking for them, nobody had shown the slightest interest in the fact that there were new faces in apartments previously home to other people. The refugee scene was very transient at the best of times – people came and went, they took under-the-table jobs to eke out their government allowances, they often lived away from their designated homes to be closer to family and friends from the old country.

So nobody had paid even the least bit of attention to the five pairs of newcomers in their various apartments spread all over Grumstad.

Good. Time now for a dry run, time to emerge into the open and train along the routes they would actually be using.

Adan Hamati pedalled off to his team members, one after the other, to tell them to get ready for the following morning. They would meet at his lockup at six-fifteen in the morning, prompt. They glanced at each other. That hour of the morning in the raw early November chill was going to be a barrel of laughs. But nobody protested, this was what they had come here to do. Things were moving up a notch. Finally.

The following morning they assembled near the garage in ones and twos, arriving early to make sure they didn't keep Adan Hamati waiting. They didn't huddle together while waiting for Adan to arrive, instead walking past the garage door as though they were on their way elsewhere. And they didn't acknowledge each other. Nothing very odd, then.

Yet it was odd. In fact, it was very odd. The ceiling light was switched off and the curtain swished open in Samira Hersi's bedroom as she readied herself to leave for the day's school field trip. Sure, there were people living here who got off to an early start in the mornings – there was the early shift at the Volvo car plant, not least – but never in all the time she and her father had lived here had she seen so many people at one and the same time walking up and down past that row of lockups across the road.

It wasn't as though they were loitering, they didn't give the impression they were casing the building for a break-in – they just didn't seem to be heading anywhere else in particular.

And then a lone figure appeared, walking briskly but without running. He walked purposefully to a particular door – the one that seemed to be home to a different cycle every day – unlocked it and pulled the sliding door up and over, and entered. And all the dark-clad figures – why hadn't she noticed earlier that they were all wearing dark clothes? thought Samira to herself – all quickly converged on the same door and entered. The door was pulled down – but not before Samira caught a fleeting glimpse of what looked like a whole warehouse of bikes as well as neat stacks of what looked like sports bags on wheels. And cardboard boxes! Lots and lots of cardboard boxes.

She really would have to speak to her father this evening. Her father may know the chap with the garage. Or he'd know if she should mind her own business. She would definitely speak to her dad when he got back from work.

She surveyed her room. Everything neat and tidy as usual, bed made, all her school stuff neatly stacked on her desk and on the white IKEA bookshelf above the desk. Samira left quietly, easing the front door latch into the locked position behind her so as to not disturb her father after his late shift the night before.

Chapter 32

The women got into their training clothes behind a hastily rigged blanket at the far end of the lockup, while the men got dressed at the front of the remaining space. Surveying the bikes, Adan quickly allocated one to each member of the team. Alina Murad looked at the remaining cycle, the unclaimed bike intended for her dead husband Haydar. Everyone else averted their eyes.

"Time to go," said Adan. They wheeled out their bikes one by one and set off.

The early shift at the Volvo Cars factory starts at 6.32 every weekday morning, and a surprising number of workers cycle to and from work every day. It's not solely a financial issue – despite the recent introduction of wallet-stinging road tolls in Gothenburg, the top management of Volvo had negotiated an agreement with the notoriously stingy Swedish tax authorities whereby the company would pay the toll for any of its employees who drove in to work, thus absorbing the financial burden of the privilege of driving to work to earn a living, as one left-leaning local politician had put it.

No, the reason why so many cycled to work was because they wanted to. Swedes enjoy fresh air, they appreciate exercise. And to top it all, now Volvo Cars – which as its name suggested built cars, very good ones at that – had implemented an incentive scheme to get people to leave their cars at home and either use public transport or cycle to work. The benefit was a healthier workforce, said the company's top management. True – but the financial inducement to each employee who cycled to work corresponded to less than half the daily road toll charge the company would otherwise have to pay on their behalf, so there was no little measure of self-interest mixed somewhere in there with all the hype of a healthier workforce and easing the burden on the company's health-care clinic.

The fact is, everyone really was a winner.

So lots of people cycled to work along the beautifully smooth separate cycle road, marked with special cycle road signs and regulated with its own set of cycle traffic lights. The cycle road ran for the most part parallel to the main road but behind a sturdy steel barrier that kept motorised traffic at a safe distance.

It was along this cycle motorway – there was no better term for this amazing bit of engineering – that Adan and his compatriots pedalled. Swiftly, steadily, electric motors off on the flat or when the road dipped down, and switched on to carry them equally swiftly up the steepest gradients or when a head wind buffeted against them.

That was the beauty of the electric bike – nothing slowed you down. You could maintain a steady speed no matter what. Well, until the lithium-ion battery pack signalled that it needed a top-up. But that still gave a range of about 35 to 45 kilometres, used judiciously. Less, of course, if the rider was heavy – or the bike was towing a trailer.

But today there were no trailers. The Palestinians on their bikes blended in seamlessly with other riders making their way to work, some at the assembly plant, others to early meetings in offices, still others heading for the various peripheral services that all made up the self-contained city that was Volvo – canteen staff, cleaners, building maintenance workers. There was even a bank, a day-care centre and a travel agent on site in Volvo City, so there was always a steady stream of people converging on the site, pretty much at all times of the day.

Reaching the turn-off to the car assembly plant, Adan pulled over to the right, on the gravel verge and got off his bike. The others followed suit. Seventeen minutes. Not bad, not bad at all. Now came the important bit: how long would it take to reverse direction and get away from the factory?

He signalled the group and they all pedalled off back down the way they had come.

Chapter 33

It hadn't been easy.

Amira Hart was in Sweden on official business. She was Mossad, and was working with her Swedish colleagues in an investigation that seemed to have ever clearer links between their two countries.

But Benny Hart was nobody. He wasn't in Sweden on official business. And if he had been, he'd have been breaking the law because Shin Bet is not empowered to operate outside Israel. It would only make matters worse if he had been working in Sweden without even the courtesy of a heads-up call to the relevant authorities here.

So Amira Hart had her work cut out to explain – out in a somewhat draughty reception hall – that her brother really was here on holiday, in fact he was on sick leave and hadn't even known about her impending visit. His only link with the case – and it was a vital link – was that he could positively identify a person who had entered Sweden under false pretences, using a false name and travelling on false documents. That had to count for something.

Very grudgingly the still exceedingly miffed SÄPO top brass gave him a plastic ID tag to hang around his neck and said he could enter the building and offer whatever assistance he could. But he was not to speak unless spoken to, and he was never, ever, to be left on his own, not even to go to the toilet. Benny shrugged and agreed. He just wanted to get to the bottom of this, he wasn't interested in turf wars and if truth be told, he had to admit that he too would have been more than a little suspicious if the roles had been reversed.

In the conference room they all pooled their information. Benny Hart related everything he knew about Alina Murad, which wasn't a whole lot because his attention had been on her now deceased husband. But he had definitely recognised her face, there was no mistake about the identity of the woman in the photograph.

Amira Hart meantime had received confirmation from her outfit back home – the other nine people had all been positively identified as Palestinians living in the West Bank. There was nothing unusual about Palestinians being in Sweden, but when a group left home at the same time, arrived in Sweden at the same time, all on false papers, and then disappeared off the grid all at the same time, that had to indicate something was in the works.

But what?

Local undercover surveillance units were contacted and ordered to keep a special lookout for any unusual activity, especially anything related to, but not limited to, Palestinians, Arabs or Islamists. This brought the room to an uncomfortable silence – no-one in Sweden is happy about singling out people on the basis of their ethnicity or religion, their skin colour or gender. It is so deeply ingrained in the public psyche that there had in fact been countless cases of some pretty nasty criminals slipping through the net because the authorities were unwilling to sanction profiling that might be deemed discriminatory in any way.

But the world was changing, and changing fast. As though by unbidden consent they all nodded to indicate that nothing was leaving the room – this had the potential of becoming political dynamite and they needed to keep everything as close to their chests as possible. The surveillance officers had to know what to look for, that went without saying, or nothing would be attempted or achieved. But otherwise, total silence.

They went through the list of possible targets. High-profile individuals, major infrastructure, anyone or anything that had recently caused offence in the highly volatile Middle East.

But there were no particular indicators, nothing of any great importance that had happened recently with any links to the Middle East. On the contrary, Sweden had acquired a whole lot of goodwill in large parts of the Arab world thanks to its generous asylum policy for refugees fleeing the brutal dictatorship of Syria's Iran-supported Alawite dictator Bashar al-Assad and his equally murderous Sunni political opponents as the country descended ever deeper into total anarchy. So why now? And who? And where?

A call was put to Marita Ohlsson, asking her to collate the financial aspect. The surveillance units were out on the streets looking for any relevant signs. Amira Hart was asked to dig deeper with her people back in Israel – what possible links there might be, was the Israeli ambassador in Sweden due to make any high-profile visits, was there any date of religious or historical significance coming up in the Jewish calendar? That kind of thing.

The task force agreed to reconvene at nine the following morning, same place.

Chapter 34

The field trip had been a lot of fun, surprisingly. For such a tiny little hamlet, Lödöse had a rich history stretching back a number of centuries, and it was picture-postcard pretty.

Of course, it meant a whole lot of homework that evening after Samira returned to the apartment. As she drew shut her bedroom curtain, she glanced across the road and remembered. The lockup – yes, she was definitely going to take this up with her dad this evening, he'd know what to do.

Abdurrahman Hersi returned from work, went straight into the shower as was his regular custom and then sat down to dinner with his daughter, who was chattering away about her eventful day on the field trip.

He listened with undiluted pleasure. This girl, this absolute treasure, was everything a father could wish for. Bright, almost always cheerful, hard-working, respectful – and she didn't go chasing after boys like so many of the others he saw around him. At age sixteen, she was still a child as far as he was concerned – time enough to grow up when the time came. No need to think about adult responsibilities just yet.

But Samira had a particularly adult question to ask him. It was to do with responsibility. If she had seen something that was suspicious, was it better to stay out of it or report it to the police? She didn't want to be seen as an interfering busybody, and she certainly wasn't a tattle-tale, but how did one draw the line between not seeing and pretending not to see?

She explained her dilemma to her father. He had always brought up his daughter to do what her conscience dictated – right was right – but was there really much point in bothering the police with a lot of unsubstantiated suspicions? It wasn't as though someone had been beaten up or killed; at worst, someone was possibly stealing cycles. There were worse things in the world.

On the other hand, as the police themselves so often said in their own defence: they don't interpret what they see, they do their duty and leave the legal intricacies to the legal system. Surely the same applied here? Perhaps they should go to the police station – he'd never let his young daughter go alone – and explain what she had seen, and let the police decide if it was significant? That way her conscience would be salved, and no harm would be done if it turned out that an investigation revealed the lockup was just an overflow warehouse for a particularly large batch of imported bikes. Let them decide, she wasn't jury or judge, she was just a chance witness of … well … perhaps nothing, really.

Accordingly they took the number 5 tram to the police station in Backaplan and registered their observations with the constable on desk duty there.

Job done, conscience clean, father and daughter returned home.

Chapter 35

Marita Ohlsson knew her limitations. She was good with following up financial trails, she knew how to read a balance sheet buried under eight or ten layers of dummy corporations, even if half of them were offshore companies with incestuous ownership relationships with one another designed to throw the most battle-hardened fraud-squad officer off the scent.

But she wasn't much good at initiating active searches for hidden parameters, concealed patterns of purchasing and divestment superimposed on recent activity, to see if a pattern emerged.

She accordingly contacted her colleague Martin Lindell over at Data Analysis. She explained her dilemma. She had a pattern. Sort of. There was a sudden spike in cash purchases, purchases of a specific sort. From a variety of stores. It looked like the same materials were being bought from several different shops. Why?

Could Martin please take some time off from watching endless episodes of The Simpsons on his office computer and actually do some real work instead? What she wanted was for him to write an algorithm that monitored recent patterns of purchasing, patterns of crime, patterns of police reports, patterns of arrests – anything that caused his super-expensive taxpayer-funded computer to actually come up with something useful for once?

The general image of a computer nerd is someone who looks like one of the stars on “The Big Bang Theory” – a weedy, bespectacled, nervous geek with buck-teeth and an inability to be in the same room as anyone of the opposite gender.

Not so Martin Lindell, who was built like Arnold Schwarzenegger before the actor turned to flab, with Hollywood looks and an always-ready smile showing a dazzling array of even white teeth. On the downside, he was married – unfortunately happily so – had two young kids and he spent what little spare time he had away from the pressures of the job and family life working out in the gym, training judo, and jogging. He didn’t even have a home computer, and his young children spent their time playing board games, climbing trees, reading books. So much for the stereotypical image of a computer nerd.

But Martin Lindell knew his stuff, all right. At work his computer was his world and his mind raced as he keyed in parameters and wrote long lines of complicated code to get an approximation of what he had been asked to do.

Called up the program, let it run, frowned, closed it down, adjusted various columns of code and tried it again. On and on through the morning and the whole afternoon until he reckoned he had a structure that would automatically check key data, cross-reference it with other relevant data in parallel directories, weight each data set with a figure and a colour denoting its significance in a table of priorities, and then collate the whole lot in a series of overlaid diagrams to provide an easily digestible graphic readout. Anything that overlapped would – statistically at least – be potentially significant.

Martin leaned back in his chair, rotating his neck from side to side to ease the strain of sitting for so many hours. Glancing at his watch he realised with a start that he'd completely missed lunch and if he didn't get his skates on, he'd be late picking up his daughter from pre-school.

He quickly checked his screen, nodded in satisfaction and clicked Enter on his keyboard. Tomorrow morning would reveal if his programming had turned up anything of interest. Home now.

He got up, put on his coat and left his office, switching off the light as he went out.

Chapter 36

Adan Hamati continued on his shopping spree. Powerful battery-operated industrial staple-guns were top of his list of priorities. These were designed to fire sharp C-shaped metal spikes into plywood, MDF, chipboard and other wooden materials and were popular in the house-construction industry. He bought two spare fast-load cassettes of staples for each staple-gun, spreading his purchases across different stores around town. Adan's electric bike and trailer were truly proving their worth.

On other trips he purchased several litre bottles of kerosene and denatured alcohol from various supermarkets, never more than one bottle from each store. This was the fuel people used to light barbeques in the summer and fondues in the autumn and winter. At a charity shop he bought several cheap second-hand cotton garments – shirts, T-shirts, aprons and smocks. His bicycle trailer was being put to very good use indeed.

He also bought one DIY worktable and a small vice, as well as thick leather work-gloves with a padded surface on the palms. At a local Järnia hardware store he purchased several coils of sturdy four-millimetre steel wire, the type usually used as the top and bottom guide for chicken-wire fences, holding the mesh in place.

At the same store he bought a substantial pair of wire cutters and a mains-operated grinder with plenty of spare diamond-tipped grinding pads. And he rounded it all off with two pairs of plastic safety goggles – no point in taking risks with one's eyes, God's most precious gift to man after life itself.

Letting the electric motor take the strain, Adan Hamati cycled back to the lockup with his heavy load and got to work. Experimenting with the wire, he cut a few sample pieces into varying lengths – eight, nine and ten centimetres long. Three of each length. He twisted the matched lengths together to create jagged six-pointed barbs. Donning his goggles and thick work-gloves, he attached the vice to the work-table, plugged in the grinder, placed the barbs in the vice one at a time and sharpened all six points of each.

What he finally ended up with were three finished barbs, each tapering to six vicious points, each of a different length.

He took them in his gloved hand, looked at them as they nestled there against the padded leather, then dropped them onto the floor, examining how they landed. Using his toe to separate them one from the other, he fetched a small but stout block of wood about the length of his shoe and about three centimetres thick, placed it on the first barb, and trod heavily on it.

He repeated the process with the other two. It was the shortest one that was best, that deformed the least. And it punctured the wood at two separate points, whichever way up it landed – the sharpened points were that close because of the short overall length of the wire.

Picking up his three experimental pieces he threw them into a metal bin and got down to it.

Working rhythmically, he used the cutters to snip off the stout steel wire into lengths of eight centimetres and dropped them into a cardboard box on the floor below the worktable.

With assembly-line efficiency, and pausing only for frequent sips of water and the occasional bite of a banana or apple, he sharpened the tips to a razor-sharp point and, when that was done, proceeded to bind them together in threes.

By the end of the day, the bones of his fingers stiff with the repetitive strain and the muscles of his neck aching from poring over the work-table all day long, he had completed a huge armoury of vicious, impenetrable barbs.

He disconnected the grinder from the mains socket, put everything neatly away and swept the floor clean, ready for a new day's work.

Chapter 37

Martin Lindell's hard work had paid off.

Well, sort of – if you knew what you were looking for. He didn't – that wasn't his job. His job was to produce the raw data, now it was up to Marita Ohlsson to make of it what she could.

"You owe me lunch," he said on the phone. "Didn't have time for any yesterday because someone, not saying who, insisted the world come to a standstill because she wanted special treatment. And I want dessert too – it's my gym day today so I need to stoke up on extra energy. Sending you the data ... now," he said as he clicked the Send icon. "Let me know if it's any use to you. You may want to look extra closely at yesterday's police report on a possible incident in Grimmered or Grumstad, can't quite remember where."

And with that he put the phone down and decided that he had definitely earned himself a fresh cup of coffee for a job well done.

***

Marita Ohlsson felt a rising tide of excitement as she scrolled through the data. She needed a thorough overview. Her 27-inch Samsung screen wasn't big enough to display all the information. She needed a printout, high-resolution, and fast.

While the files were printing Marita cleared the conference table of all the accumulated clutter of half-used legal pads, pens, plastic coffee-cups and crumpled paper napkins, dumping it all in a corner on the floor or in the bin as appropriate.

Retrieving the printouts from the laser printer, she spread the papers all across the table, following the patterns that emerged with growing interest and saucer-shaped eyes.

It was there. No doubt about it. The epicentre had to be Volvo – or did it? Svenska Mässan, the Swedish Exhibition & Congress Centre, was currently closed for refurbishment. There were no conferences or other events planned there until April when it threw open its doors once again, which was what? ... almost six months hence. So did the purchase of construction tools – always for cash – tie in with something planned for there, while construction work was ongoing? That was definitely a possibility.

Gothenburg's famous autumn book fair always drew high-profile authors to what was northern Europe's largest event of its kind. Perhaps next autumn's programme included a featured writer with whom the Palestinians had a bone to pick? An Israeli or perhaps an American author? That too was definitely possible. But why now, almost an entire year in advance of the late September book fair?

And every summer Gothenburg played host to soccer teams from all over the world, youngsters – boys and girls alike – who came to the city for the fortnight-long Gothia Cup soccer fest featuring hopefuls from Europe, Africa, Asia, North and South America. And including both Palestinian teams and Israeli teams. Was that where the bikes came in – some kind of tenuous sports connection? That too was definitely possible.

The problem was there were too many things that were definitely possible. She needed to get someone else in on this, a second pair of eyes. Why not that Israeli woman? Or, more to the point, her extremely attractive brother? Yes, that would be even better – three pairs of eyes, three brains scanning the material to identify what was definitely there, but oh so elusive.

It was at this point that her phone rang.

"It appears your Israeli friend is playing some kind of game with us," said her superintendent. "Just how much have you revealed about our ongoing investigation?"

Marita Ohlsson was nonplussed. Was he referring to Amira Hart or her brother Benny? And what kind of game could this be? After all, SÄPO had been approached by the Israelis with information about a possible unfriendly operation by a third party, on Swedish soil. They had volunteered the information without being asked. And the Swedes were finally beginning to see a pattern emerge. Why on earth would the Israelis be pulling a stunt on them? And what stunt, exactly?

"I'm not quite sure I understand you," she said. "Benny Hart was admittedly not really entitled to be part of this investigation but he did have significant information for us, he identified a possible, in fact a likely, subversive who has submitted false information and is closely and unequivocally involved with nine other people who have similarly lied their way into this country. I'm not sure what sort of game he could be playing," she continued.

"It's not him – it's her, the sister. Samira. She walked into a police station yesterday together with a male colleague – no, not the guy posing as her brother – and reported seeing suspicious activity in a lockup in Grumstad. If she had information pertinent to our enquiry, why didn't she give it straight to us, why sneak behind our backs and get uniform involved?

"No more contact with her or her brother," he continued, "until we arrest her and find out what she's holding back from us. No, no buts," he added as Marita Ohlsson started to protest. "We're not going to have cowboys – or cowgirls – running around behind our backs on our own turf. She is to be brought in, and she tells us everything, after which she and her 'brother' (Marita could almost see him over the phone, framing the word in quotation marks with his fingers) will be expelled from the country."

She wanted to protest that to the best of her knowledge both brother and sister were actually Swedish citizens and therefore could not be expelled, but she diplomatically held her tongue. Let the desk jockeys rant and rave, it made them feel important.

But none of it made sense. She had to get to the bottom of this, or else she wasn't going to get any help from Amira or her brother to interpret Martin Lindell's data.

Chapter 38

What was conceived as a simple arrest of a potentially hostile alien agent working undercover in Sweden went down in the annals of SÄPO history as one of its deepest – and most public – embarrassments.

As Samira Hersi made her way home to her apartment after school, she noticed but did not pay attention to a dark grey Opel Insignia parked facing the wrong way on the other side of the road, its engine idling. When she thought back on the incident, if there was anything that struck her as odd at all that afternoon before her world was turned upside down, it was the fact that the engine was idling.

With Gothenburg's strict environmental laws in force for so many years now, there was a whole generation of drivers who had been brought up indoctrinated with the belief that leaving a car engine idling was the work of the devil incarnate, that only the spawn of the Horned One would ever pollute the city's beautiful environment by leaving an engine on without actually driving anywhere. It simply pumped out carbon dioxide and all sorts of other nasties that the world would be so much better without. So for more than ten years now, the people of Gothenburg – and indeed people in most of the rest of Sweden – had gotten into the habit of switching off their engines if they weren't actually driving.

But at the time, none of this registered consciously with Samira. All she knew was that as she drew level with the front passenger door, two burly, dark-clad men opened their doors and started walking purposefully towards her. She quickened her pace and, glancing back over her shoulder, saw that they too were speeding up. With panic rising to screaming level and adrenalin pumping through her veins, Samira threw her backpack in the direction of her pursuers and started running as fast as her legs would carry her, in the vain hope that they were muggers looking for easy pickings.

But they didn't pounce on her satchel and make off with their easy spoils. They didn't even break stride as they closed in on her, fanning out one on each side as they approached her in a lateral pincer movement. By now Samira was screaming at the top of her voice and windows and balcony doors were opening. People were staring horrified at the sight of a young black girl being overpowered by what looked like two racist thugs – blond, close-cropped hair, square jaws, dressed head to toe in dark clothes all the way down to their heavy, polished boots. What was it they called them? Shaved-heads? Hard-heads? Skinheads? Something like that?

People started yelling from their windows and others raced downstairs to come to the aid of the girl. Many had recognised her – it was Samira. Samira, of all people, being attacked and abducted by two thugs in what passed for broad daylight on a late autumn afternoon.

They were wrong, of course. There weren't two thugs – there was a third behind the wheel of the grey car that pulled up diagonally across the road as the first two men bundled the hapless, screaming girl into the rear seat. With a squeal of its front tyres as they scrambled to find purchase on the wet leaf-strewn road surface, the car sprinted away down the street as ever-larger crowds gathered at the spot.

Except the road was a dead-end – the end of the housing estate. The Opel turned and started making its way back. With a gathering roar the crowd – virtually all immigrants from various African and Middle Eastern countries, teenagers, middle-aged men, a few women – first stood their ground in the middle of the road and then started running towards the car as it approached them, nowhere else for it to go.

The driver gunned the engine and the car lurched ahead but the crowd moved relentlessly on. At the very last crucial second, the driver hesitated – and all was lost. He couldn't bring himself to drive deliberately into a crowd of people.

They pummelled the car body and its windows, but couldn't smash them. Inside the car Samira was screaming hysterically while her two abductors pulled out pistols and waved them menacingly at the crowd. The driver pulled out a cell phone and was speaking urgently into it.

The crowd weren't backing down, but the gun-toting thugs weren't shooting either. Perhaps they understood that if they shot through the windows at the mob trying to rescue the girl, then the smashed windows would also mean the rioters could reach into the car and drag them out. Stalemate.

In the distance the scream of sirens was approaching at breakneck speed. There was no knowing what was happening, or who was on the way, because in Sweden police, ambulance and fire service sirens all sound the same.

It was the police. Report a burglary or an attack in Gothenburg and you could wait hours for an overworked police officer to arrive to take your statement. And that was only if they deemed it serious from the tone of your phone call – most police precincts were seriously understaffed and although the officers do an excellent job there are only so many hours in a day. Now, within just a matter of minutes, no less than three police cars arrived, two marked and one unmarked with a blue flashing light stuck on its roof with a powerful magnet.

They parked across the street and two officers got out of each car. The four officers in uniform needed no introduction, they were all local patrolmen and were well-known, if not always well-liked. The two plain-clothes officers looked like drug dealers gone to seed. But the uniform officers seemed to know them, and they did flash genuine police warrant cards.

"We want no trouble, you can all go home," said the lead officer, the one with a beard that looked like a rat that had forgotten to lick its fur clean that morning. "This is a simple matter, no-one's in trouble here. We're here to question a suspect who is able to help us with our enquiries, that's all. Amira Hart, that's her in the car there. These are undercover police officers (he smirked slightly in the direction of the three hapless abductors) and we're taking her in to answer a few questions. Go on, disperse now, there's nothing to see here."

In the car, Samira felt both a sense of relief and a burning sense of outrage. It was somebody's idiotic mix-up, yet she was still stuck in the back of a car between two gun-wielding hoodlums – one of whom smelled like he wasn't too well acquainted with the luxury of soap and water.

The crowd were having none of this. Everyone was now shouting one louder than the other, drowning out the voices of the police officers as they tried in vain to maintain the peace.

Finally an elderly man with a traditional knitted Muslim skullcap on his head raised his hand to shush everyone else. "You have the wrong person," he said quietly and with dignity. "We all know that girl there. Her name is Samira Hersi, she is a schoolgirl who has never done anyone any harm. She lives there in that apartment. Her father, Abdurrahman, works at the big hospital in the city centre, he'll be home in about 3 hours. We saw what you did," he glared at the male occupants of the Opel, whose doors and windows were still firmly shut, "and we won't let you take her away. She stays with us. Here!"

It took a further fifteen minutes of argument, remonstration and abject apologies before the crowd thinned out and returned home. Not before Samira got out of the car and said she understood there had been a mix-up and that she would accompany the police as they wanted to clear up the matter – but that she would only ride with the uniformed officers in their marked police car.

Flushed red with embarrassment, the three SÄPO agents in the grey Opel had to endure the taunts of their uniform colleagues for what one termed "an almighty cock-up – and you're supposed to be picked from the cream of the force. I guess the cream's off then," which elicited raucous peals of laughter from his colleagues in uniform. Any opportunity to stick it to the spooks was always welcome – and the uniformed police had not liked lying to the crowd by pretending that the three idiots were their own undercover officers. They couldn't reveal their identity as SÄPO agents, but neither did they have to like carrying the can for them.

What a debacle. Things just couldn't get any worse.

But they could.

Much worse. And there were only a few days left in November.

Chapter 39

Back at the police station, to which Abdurrahman had been brought in the back of an unmarked police car so as not to arouse suspicions at his place of work, the three SÄPO officers once again offered their abject apologies to daughter and father alike and explained that it had been a case of mistaken identity – the person they were looking for had a similar-sounding first name and the surname started with the same letter, and all these foreign names sounded pretty much alike.

Any tiny measure of goodwill they had snatched back with their heartfelt apologies turned to dust before the eyes and ears of their stunned colleagues. Seriously, these guys were in dire need of a refresher course in social sensitivity. One thing was for certain – they needed to be removed from the premises before they put their size nineteens right into it.

On their way out Samira and Abdurrahman Hersi passed two burly uniformed officers escorting a stunningly beautiful young black woman into the building. A third officer was trailing behind, walking gingerly as though he were balancing a particularly delicate – but invisible – glass vase between his legs. He was sweating profusely and looked slightly cross-eyed. Without concentrating on where he was going he blundered into the back of the woman under escort. She spun round and took a step back, left arm stretched out in front and right arm drawn back, ball of the hand facing out and up, ready to strike.

"What, you haven't had enough?" she blazed at him in English. "You want more of the same?" The other two police officers, one on either side of her, stepped back and out offset in front of her, standing clearly in her field of vision.

"Look, he just stumbled, OK? Enough now. We've apologised for the mistake. We were asked to bring you in because our colleagues arrested the wrong person. You're here to help them with their enquiries, and he," the officer gestured at the third policeman, searching for the right word in English, "wasn't trying anything on – he thought you were resisting arrest."

"And I told you that as a serving officer of a friendly nation invited here by your own intelligence service to help them with an ongoing operation, you had no right to try and arrest me. All you had to do was ask me to accompany you. You don't come bumbling into my home trying to muscle in on my private space," retorted Amira Hart. "Bring it on and you'll feel the result."

The lead policeman rolled his eyes in an exaggerated show of curbing his impatience, and said: "OK, everyone understands everything. Now let's get a move on. I for one am already supposed to be off duty – let's get you in there, off our hands so we can go home." Bloody Israelis, he muttered audibly under his breath in Swedish. They treat the Palestinians like dirt, reckon they call the shots here too.

Quick as a flash Amira replied – in Swedish – that Israel didn't treat anyone like dirt. Least of all based on their ethnicity, religion or nationality. If he wanted a lesson in contemporary history and didn't have anything against learning the truth, he was welcome to visit her country and she'd show him just what it was like, warts and all. Then he could make up his own mind.

There was an awkward silence in the foyer. Nobody had reckoned that their Israeli charge could understand a word of their language. And they hadn't been particularly kind or diplomatic during the drive from Magnetgatan to the police station on Skånegatan in the heart of the city. She hadn't said a word on the entire drive. But apparently she'd heard plenty.

He shook his head disconsolately. Just give me riot control or traffic duty any day – way less complicated, he thought to himself.

Chapter 40

Adan Hamati addressed the group after they were kitted out and ready for their regular reconnaissance ride out along the Hisingsleden dual carriageway that leads to the sprawling Volvo production facility bedded in among the granite outcrops, undulating parkland and thick forest so typical of this part of western Sweden. From the road it was actually hard to imagine that set amidst all this beauty was Sweden's biggest industrial concern, the car production facility now fully owned by a parent company in China. And within a stone's throw were Volvo Group plants that manufactured trucks, marine engines, bus chassis and more.

But Adan's attention was not on the beautiful landscape. He was focusing on the job at hand. And on the need to maintain his team's level of motivation. There were still a few weeks to go before the operation went down and his group still had to conduct reconnaissance rides to two other targets, all the while being constantly reminded of their goal, the justification for their action, the means they would use.

"I know you're wondering why we are here when the real action ought to be in Stockholm. It's a legitimate question. The entire world will be watching on December 10. The media will be present in abundance. The Western media. And that's good. But not good enough. We need something that will also capture the attention of the Arab and wider Muslim media.

"The Nobel prize ceremony is a media attention-grabber," he went on. "But the Arab and Muslim media rarely – if ever – pay it any attention. And why should they? Arabs and Muslims are almost never picked to win Nobel prizes.

"The fact is, at just 0.2 percent of the world's population, Jews have nonetheless received twenty percent of the Nobel Prizes ever awarded. That is racism, pure and simple. We're being discriminated against as Muslims. And as Palestinians we are being denied the chance of a good enough education to nurture a generation of scientists and academics who can rise to these heights. This has to change."

"But that's what I've been saying all along," interjected Alina Murad, in a somewhat surly tone. "That's why we should be targeting the Jews in Stockholm, not messing about anywhere else. I mean, that's the whole point, isn't it?"

"Not true, Alina, and you know we have already reached consensus on this issue. For one thing, the Nobel Prize is an institution not just of national pride to the Swedes, it is of international renown in the rest of the world. We don't want to alienate the Swedes or other Westerners who are already sympathetic to our cause.

"No, we're not going to target the Nobel awards, we're going to exploit the fact that world's media are already here in Sweden, we're just going to realign their attention on us instead. It'll be our greatest PR coup since the Munich

Olympics operation, when we took out eleven Zionists. Nobody'll be talking about anything else – and that's what we want. For the world to stop focusing on Afghanistan, Iraq, Syria, Somalia, Yemen – our cause is fading into the background. We can't have that. Without constant world attention on us, we're nothing. It's good that the world finances us, but we need media attention too. Constant media attention, so the world doesn't ever have the opportunity to forget that we are the only cause worth supporting. Our brothers in Afghanistan and elsewhere can sort out their own problems – our cause is paramount. Because a cause that isn't seen doesn't exist. And our cause exists, our people exist.

"Before we wheel our bikes out and set off on today's reconnaissance run, just hold that thought steady in your minds: we have to succeed because our people need us to succeed. Nothing else matters."

They all nodded assent. Adan opened the garage door, looked left and right, gave the signal and ten bikers exited and set off.

Nobody looked up and across the road, where a curtain twitched in an unlit window.

Noting the exact time on her mobile phone, Samira wondered when, if ever, the police were going to act on the information she had given them.

Chapter 41

Marita Ohlsson's cell phone vibrated in her pocket as she sat in yet another one of these interminable conferences.

She cast a surreptitious look at the screen and scrolled down to the incoming email. Martin Lindell was wondering if she'd had time to extrapolate anything from the information he'd given her. Meantime he'd fed some more parameters into his program, letting it crunch the raw data looking for anomalies, departures from recent trends, changes in familiar patterns.

What his program had come up with was interesting. There was nothing out of the ordinary.

And *that* was really interesting.

Because in the normal run of things there are always events that peak in environments where such things are the norm: acts of violence, arson, car thefts, sometimes even murders. It was politically *very* incorrect to monitor ethnic groups on the basis of religion or political affiliation, for instance, and of course there were no written directives authorising such operations either by uniformed police or SÄPO.

But unofficially everyone understood that you stopped trouble most effectively by dealing with it at source, not after it broke out. If you wanted to get a handle on the drug trade, for instance, you initiated a proactive undercover operation to insert agents somewhere along the route, you tracked the supply of money that made the drug trade possible, you monitored locations where dealers and their clients were known to conduct their trade.

The same thing applied to prostitution, to illegal gambling, to the burgeoning trade in stolen luxury cars which all somehow seemed to end up in countries like Ukraine, Azerbaijan, Albania.

And the very same thing applied to extremist Islamist groups. It was excruciatingly difficult for the Swedish authorities to curb radicalisation in the country's expanding, segregated Muslim communities – many people used the term 'ghettos' – but that didn't mean the police didn't do their utmost to get to grips with it. Not always with much success, but it wasn't for lack of trying.

Swedish law enforcement had learned the hard way that their most effective weapon was not the sidearm that police officers carried in their holsters, or the police cars that were increasingly beginning to resemble armoured combat vehicles.

Their best weapon was bandwidth. Computer power. Data.

And the programmers and analysts who were smart enough to unravel the billions of bytes of information being constantly generated, able to extract some kind of sense from all the raw information.

Computer nerds like Martin Lindell.

His computer wizardry had come up with the interesting result that nothing of interest was happening.

Which in itself was interesting. Very interesting.

Had the country's often surprisingly overt al-Qaeda extremists suddenly been hit by the law-abiding bug? Had the nation's al-Shabab supporters suddenly turned over a new leaf? Were the normally so active Hezbollah activists giving up on their cause? Were the pro-Hamas agitators finally tiring of their lost cause as not only Israel but now also Egypt battled the fanatical Islamist regime in the Gaza Strip?

Was there no end to the peace and quiet that was suddenly breaking out all over the country?

Marita took in the gist of Martin Lindell's email, excused herself with an apologetic shrug, muttering something about a "computer meltdown" and left the stuffy room and its stuffy conference participants.

"Great," she thought to herself. "Now perhaps I can get some real work done."

She pulled out her cell phone as she walked and called Martin Lindell.

"Don't bother coming to my office without something to eat and drink – you still owe me," he said. "But get here quick – we might have something to work on. And there's more all the time. You can almost see a picture. Well, sort of."

November was drawing to a close.

Chapter 42

"That's her," said Benny Hart as the thrill of the chase set the hairs on the back of his neck tingling with anticipation. "It's definitely Alina Murad. I've been staring at this photo ever since those guys took you away. This is undoubtedly the wife of the man who tried to kill me, Haydar Murad. But what's she doing here, and what is she doing here with these people?" He pointed at the other nine file photos. "If Adan Hamati is involved, you can bet they're not here to train the Palestinian team for the world skiing championships."

Amira and Benny Hart pored over the printouts.

"That girl, Marita Ohlsson. You need to get her back here, we need to put our heads together," Benny said as he sat back in the sofa.

"Yeah, right, you'd like to get your head really close to hers, I can clearly see that," said his sister with a smile. "But I reckon you're right – up to a point. '*We*' (she emphasised the word) don't need to put our heads together, she and I do. You're out of it, remember? Here you're just a civilian, you're not working and these people are going to get very, very upset not only with you but with me too if it looks like you're interfering. I'll give her a call, try and get her to come over, but your interaction can only be here, in this apartment. Beyond the front door, you know nothing and say even less. Got it?"

"Yes ma'am!" he barked crisply as he jumped to his feet and snapped off a smart salute. Bossy-boots as ever. But his sister was right, of course. He'd have to use all the diplomatic skills at his disposal to provide the greatest assistance he could while appearing to remain totally out of the action.

***

Marita Ohlsson walked into Martin Lindell's office carrying a bag of fresh sugar-dusted cinnamon buns, two bananas and two apples.

"Here," she thrust the carrier bag at him. "I wasn't sure if today was one of your healthy or sinful days, so I've covered all bases. You have to provide the coffee, though. You still got that machine that dispenses hot floor-cleaner disguised as coffee? Make mine white, no sugar."

She pulled out her laptop and the copies of the printouts she had been provided with earlier, waited for Martin's return so they could get down to some serious work.

"Here's what's bothering me," said Martin Lindell as he placed a cup before her and took the other one round to the seat beside her.

"You know how it is that we're used to a certain level of background chatter in the course of our work – things that happen, criminal incidents, police reports and so on. Well, when the volume of that background noise suddenly drops … well, not suddenly, exactly, but distinctly. Yes, that's the word I'm looking for – when there's a distinct drop in the level of activity that the police and SÄPO are accustomed to dealing with, well, that's got to mean something, right?"

He searched Marita's face, fearing he'd see a look of disappointment or worse still derision, but hoping to see at least a hint of understanding. After all, an analyst's job was to search for patterns, it wasn't necessarily to look for explanations. And Marita's job was in the financial trail of anything that might interest SÄPO, she wasn't concerned with day-to-day operational problems. It's just that he sensed a kindred spirit in her, that she was keen to embrace a more proactive approach to their task rather than following in the well-worn rut dictated in stuffy conference-rooms.

What he saw in Marita Ohlsson's face, to his relief, was a slow smile of understanding. Appreciation, even. Yup, they were on the same wavelength.

"You set this against what you know – these people who've turned up in Sweden with false identities, this spike in odd cash purchases, possibly all by the same person, that report of suspicious activity in Grumstad…"

Marita's hand flew to her mouth in alarm. The Amira/Samira debacle! In all the fallout after failing to properly bring in not just one but both the young women, Marita had forgotten to pursue the information. What had uniform uncovered from that lockup in Grumstad? Did the information from there have any bearings on what tantalisingly always seemed to escape developing into a real case, or was it all just the lively imagination of a teenage schoolgirl?

She pulled out her phone and made a call. Screwed up her eyes in frustration when she heard the answer and shook her head in despair.

“Look: first thing tomorrow morning,” she said into the phone. “Stake it out from before dawn. No, definitely *not* uniform. Plain-clothes officers, nothing to alarm any passers-by or neighbours. No entry, just observe and report. And no repeat of the mess with Samira Hersi. Softly if you please! Right. Get back to me as soon as you have anything to report tomorrow.”

She put down her phone and looked guiltily at Martin Lindell. “Should have had this rolling today. But it doesn’t matter, that schoolgirl Samira says the only action takes place early in the morning, so that’s when we’ll be there to watch. Let’s stake this out and see what possible link there is to what we have here.

“Meantime,” she continued, “I have a feeling you’re onto something here: not having a pattern is also a pattern; not having action where there is usually action is also a pattern. I’m going to have a word with that Israeli officer to see what she has – she says she has information about some, possibly several, of those people who came in on Syrian papers and then disappeared into thin air."

"OK," replied Martin. "Don't thank me or anything, it's all part of the service down here. But I don't mind being the only person with manners in this room, I'd like to say 'thanks' for the buns and fruit. We're well brought-up here in the Data Analysis department..."

Marita kicked him lightly on the shin before pushing her chair back from the table, gathered together her papers and laptop and left, waving a cheery 'thanks' over her shoulder. Paused at the door, hand on the doorknob. "You people really ought to get Health & Safety onto that so-called coffee machine of yours – it smelled like melted candle-wax and tasted even worse."

And with that she was gone.

The following day, just after nine in the morning, she received her long-anticipated call from the police surveillance crew.

There were ten people. Not sure from the distance from which they were forced to watch but they reckoned not all of them were men – it was difficult to see clearly in the dark of the early morning. They all converged on a lockup and entered, and thirteen minutes later ten people departed, on bicycles. Yes, they thought they might be the same ten people, but couldn't be sure. No, they hadn't followed them

– their job was to stay and watch the premises. The bikers returned exactly seventy-two minutes later. Yes, they returned from the same direction in which they had departed. No, they had no idea where they had been for those seventy-two minutes.

Bingo! Of sorts.

Marita Ohlsson pulled out her phone and called her opposite number from Mossad, the young Israeli woman who had been arrested the day before, during which arrest she had taught at least one Swedish policeman the value of protecting the part of his anatomy that he prized most.

They would meet that evening after work. Yes, she'd be happy to come to the apartment where Amira Hart was staying with her brother.

The final day of November was drawing to a close, December the 1st was just around the corner.

Chapter 43

Was it Amira Hart's imagination or did Benny volunteer a little too eagerly to go do some shopping before that female SÄPO analyst was due to drop by for an informal early-evening chat and to compare notes?

No matter, she needed him out of the way for some time while she considered just what the scanty information at their disposal might mean. It all seemed to be there, yet irritatingly just out of focus. There was no doubt there were large areas of the picture that were blank or at best blurred – but what was the picture supposed to depict?

She felt like she was trying to put together a jigsaw from a box that contained pieces from three of four different puzzles. Like she had a few of the key corner sections worked out, but wasn't sure if the random sections she had pieced together for the middle actually belonged to the same puzzle.

Money stolen in Israel. A West Bank Palestinian who committed suicide by cop rather than risk revealing information – almost killing the arresting officer, her brother – in the bargain. The wife of the suicide victim apparently abandoning her children at home, no doubt in the care of loving family members, but still. And turning up here, in Sweden! Not only that, turning up here apparently in the company of a number of Palestinian Arabs who had all arrived on false Syrian papers. And who had then gone off the radar somewhere in Sweden. And one of those Palestinians was Adan Hamati. Where there was smoke...

But *where* was the smoke? She was simply going to have to lay all her cards on the table when Marita Ohlsson turned up and hope that the Swede would do likewise. This wasn't the time for jealously guarding turf, it was imperative that some sense be made of these disparate clues and hints before her brain boiled over and they had to send her back home a blubbering, incoherent mess.

***

Who would have thought that Benny Hart actually knew how to put together something worth eating? OK, he didn't actually cook anything, but he had gone to the Prince of Bengal Indian takeaway in Frölunda Torg, a ten minute walk from the apartment, and had apparently ordered every item on the menu.

"Well," he said as nonchalantly as he could to no-one in particular, "I wasn't sure if anyone had nut allergies, preferred fish, was a vegetarian or whatever, so I bought a bit of everything. There's naan and paratha too – they're different types of Indian bread. Eat while it's hot. Anyone want orange juice, or do you prefer water?"

Once the dishes were cleared away (amazing how domesticated Benny had suddenly become in one fell swoop, thought Amira, biting her lip hard to stop herself from smiling) they sat down with coffee to discuss what they had met to thrash out.

A thread, a pattern, a link.

And there it was – a positive ID of a woman whose husband had died in police custody in Israel and who was here in Sweden on false papers. She was part of a group of ten people, half of them women. The man who was making the odd purchases – always for cash – was apparently part of that group. Whatever it was the group was up to, it had to be local. Why else would they be riding bicycles – you couldn't get far on a bicycle – and why else would they be stocking up on outdoors clothing and machine tools? OK, the clothing was understandable – the weather had certainly shifted to autumn, and winter was definitely in the air. But machine tools? And bicycles?

What was with the bicycles?

***

That evening a nondescript green Volkswagen Golf parked in the visitors' parking lot on Ministergatan in Grumstad. Two police officers got out. They were both women, and they were both in plain clothes – sensible after the fracas of the previous police visit to the area.

They walked down the long road from the parking lot, checking off the numbers of the apartment buildings as they passed. They verified a particular building's number, pressed a button beside the door and after exchanging a few words, were buzzed in.

Abdurrahman Hersi was standing in his open doorway as the two officers approached. The two women were somewhat hesitant – what was the protocol for greeting an elderly gentleman dressed in the garb of an observant Muslim? Did one shake hands? Wasn't there something about strictly religious Muslim men not having contact with women who were not their wives?

Seeing their hesitation Abdurrahman smiled, stood aside and gestured for them to enter. "Please," he said, "do come in. My daughter Samira is here, she's just finishing her homework in her bedroom, she'll be out in a moment. Would you like something to drink? Something hot, perhaps, or cold if you prefer?"

Samira entered just as the two women politely declined, saying it was too late for coffee – they'd be up all night if they drank coffee this late – but accepting a cup of mint tea each. Polite chit-chat over, they got down to business. They wanted to once again apologise on behalf of the police for the terrible mess the other day, and wondered if Samira would care to go over what it was she had seen, when, what caused her to notice it. Anything of interest, really, because of course the police were always grateful every time the public took an interest in proactive crime prevention. No, Samira didn't need to worry if it led nowhere, her name would be kept out of it anyway. The police were determined to show that they really did mean it when they said they were serious about tackling any suspicious activity.

Samira relaxed as she related her observations, pausing only once to ask again if the two women really wouldn't care for something to eat along with their tea. No, really, they were fine. Please continue.

The officer taking the notes looked at her colleague who had taken the lead in the questioning, and asked the question that had brought them to the Hersi apartment in the first place: would Mr Abdurrahman and his daughter mind if the police used their apartment for a surveillance operation? It would require access to Samira's bedroom.

Samira looked shocked and not a little embarrassed.

"Oh dear, I can see I'm not expressing myself very well at all," said the policewoman. "Don't worry, we won't have anyone entering your room or anything like that. Well, just the once, to set up some equipment – if you and your father agree, of course," she added hastily.

"You see," she continued, "we had officers watching the lockup this morning but it is really difficult to do this again without arousing suspicion. You don't often see cars or vans parked on the street below because this entire residential road is a drop-off zone only, so if we have a vehicle loitering here again we're going to stick out like a sore thumb.

"So," she went on, "if you give us permission, we'll get one of our technical officers to come here with his equipment – while you are at home, of course – and calibrate it to record any activity in and around the garage. Once he's set it up, he won't bother you until it's time to remove the equipment. The only request we would have is that you leave your curtain and blinds in the exact position he sets them – just don't touch them. That's all. Our equipment will transmit images and audio directly to our control centre. And no, before you can ask, it is not capable of picking up either images or sound from your room – the microphone is unidirectional and will be pointed only – I repeat *only* – at the garage, while the camera lens also only faces the lockup. In fact, he'll drape a thick black cloth around the back of it so all you'll see is a shrouded tripod with some electronic gadgetry attached to it. What do you say?"

She leaned back and mentally crossed her fingers. After the way the girl had been treated the other day, it wouldn't exactly come as a surprise if she and her father promptly declined. She couldn't really blame them.

Father and daughter exchanged a few sentences in a language the officers could not understand, then Samira turned to the policewomen and smiled. "It's OK. I started this, it's important to my father and me that we do the right thing. If you feel this is the right thing, go ahead."

The lead officer could feel a wave of relief flooding over her as she spontaneously reached over and grasped Samira's right hand in both of her own. "Thank you very, very much. I promise you, once our man has finished you won't even know he's been here – if you don't mind looking at a black-clothed thingy standing in front of your window, that is!" She smiled.

"And now I have another request. "We didn't want to presume anything so we haven't brought our techie along with us, but we can call him now and he can be here, in and out of your apartment within an hour. Would that be OK with you? It is a school night after all, we wouldn't dream of disrupting your homework or anything."

Samira smiled and said that was fine, she could watch TV with her dad in the living room until the police technician was finished in her room, she'd wait to have a shower until after he left their apartment.

And with warm thanks for their hospitality and for agreeing to the use of their home for surveillance, and showers of gratitude heaped on whatever gods had smiled down on them for navigating what could have been such a tricky diplomatic mission, the two police officers left the apartment and walked back to their car.

By the time Samira and her father got into their respective beds that night, the motion- and sound-activated surveillance equipment had been installed, calibrated and expertly concealed by the police technician. Who very surprisingly turned out to be a twenty-something woman, not a man.

Samira smiled to herself as she snuggled under her duvet. OK, so some police officers had behaved rather unprofessionally the other day, but that didn't mean they were all thoughtless. She just knew that the two officers who had visited them earlier that evening had gone out of their way to find a female technician to do the job in the teenage Muslim girl's bedroom. Now that was genuine consideration.

Samira yawned, wondered what she would look like in a police uniform. She could easily see herself as Sweden's first female uniformed officer wearing the traditional Muslim head covering.

Chapter 44

The audio didn't pick up much that was intelligible – something to do with the closeness of so many bodies packed in the small enclosed space of the garage absorbing too much sound to produce anything discernible; Marita and Amira didn't quite understand the technical jargon.

But the stills and moving images were crystal-clear. What wasn't crystal-clear was why ten Palestinians would suddenly develop a penchant for going on cycling trips in the cold damp of the Swedish autumn, early in the morning, every morning, after taking the trouble to enter the country on false papers.

They had to be followed, there was no alternative if the police and SÄPO were going to get anything out of them.

And better audio pickup had to be obtained from the lockup, while the cyclists were out. That gave the police about fifty minutes, less actually since the road to and from the garage was long and straight and afforded a rearward view of the lockup long after the cyclists left, should they glance back, and long before they arrived as they headed towards the garage.

So 40, maybe 45 minutes tops, just to be on the safe side.

Shouldn't be a problem. Just insert a tiny microphone somewhere unobtrusive. Preferably also a button camera to provide pictures inside the premises.

Piece of cake for the inordinately well-equipped and extremely well-funded SÄPO, whose responsibility this part of the surveillance had become.

Chapter 45

The problem with modern, virtually undetectable electronic devices is not the devices themselves, but the often visible traces left by the human beings who fit them.

There is no doubting the technical excellence of SÄPO's electronic surveillance capabilities. As so often, the devil is in the detail.

And when there are small details where there shouldn't be any – tell-tale signs suggesting that someone has been where they have no right to be – then no amount of technical excellence is good enough.

Adan Hamati and his team returned to the lockup and paused while he stopped to fish the key out of his zip-up side pocket. That was when he noticed a patch of dry asphalt outside the garage door. Everywhere else was wet from the slow drizzle that had accompanied them throughout this, their last reconnaissance ride before the mission.

A dry rectangle of asphalt could only mean that a vehicle had been parked there. It did not necessarily mean anything – someone could have left their car there for a few minutes while they hurried across the road to the apartments on the other side to fetch or deliver something.

But still: their particular lockup of all the others? Judging by the size of the dry area of tarmac, this was no small hatchback or medium-sized family car, more like a pickup truck or some other commercial vehicle – the track was wide. And the rain from the surrounding area was only just beginning to trickle into the dry patch, so it must have left only recently. Why would a commercial vehicle be out here in the suburbs at this early hour of the morning?

Had they noticed a large pickup truck or van leaving as they approached? Not really ... except, yes, there was a large chocolate-brown Mercedes-Benz high-top panel van that had pulled up at the T-junction heading away from their lockup as the cyclists turned into their road. What was strange, when one thought about it, was that it had no signage – nothing proclaiming that it belonged to a company, or a rental firm, nothing. Which was odd – no company small or large ever failed to exploit every single opportunity to advertise its products wherever possible, especially for free on the sides of its own vehicles. And of course virtually every van rental company in Gothenburg, indeed in all of Sweden, operated white vans – they were the cheapest fleet colour and they were bought in bulk with identical specifications.

What was perhaps more striking, thought Adan as he let the team into the lockup and closed the garage door on them, was the dark blue or black Volvo XC90 4x4 that was driving right behind the brown van. He wasn't the sort of person to have predisposed notions of people's social and financial status, but Grumstad wasn't exactly a well-to-do area. Most people around here drove boringly dependable Japanese and South Korean imports – usually into their second or third owners. Not clunkers, but certainly not expensive SUVs easily costing more than half a million kronor.

Without saying anything of his concerns to the others, Adan bustled them out as soon as he could without arousing their suspicions and after they left set about working silently and methodically. He was searching for signs of entry, interference, anything.

He found it after twenty-five minutes. Ridiculous really. Almost undetectable because it was so obviously in plain sight that it wouldn't really merit a second glance. On the left rear wall halfway between floor and ceiling, there was an unused plug point. Only problem was, it hadn't been there when Adan Hamati had first taken the lockup, and bearing in mind that it was disused it wasn't anything like as dusty or grimy as it ought to be. Two screws holding the electrical socket's white plastic casing to the wall, but the two screws weren't identical. Closer examination revealed one genuine screw head visible to the naked eye, and one tiny fish-eye lens inserted into the aperture intended for the second screw.

Adan meandered around the garage, pulling away cardboard boxes from one pile and stacking them up in the middle of the little free space available, and then, looking around as though searching for a better place for them, piled them up one on top of the other in front of the camera he had just detected. Finishing that job, he looked at his watch and then surveyed the rest of the lockup, as though deciding whether to continue tidying up or call it a day. He appeared to have made up his mind to pack up for now and leave the premises.

After he shut and locked the garage door behind him, Adan squatted down to slowly retie his shoelaces. If someone had placed a camera in the lockup, that meant their location was blown. If so, why hadn't they been arrested, or at least pulled in for questioning? There had to be a reason. Perhaps the police weren't sure they'd identified everyone involved. And more to the point, how had anyone latched onto them?

As he straightened up and then knelt down again to tie his other shoelace, Adan's eyes swept the apartment building opposite him. This was a weekday morning, by now everyone had gone off to work, to school, to whatever it is that people in the suburbs do on a cold late-autumn morning in Gothenburg. All the blinds were open in all the windows, all the curtains were drawn open to let in what meagre daylight there was at this time of the year.

Except one. That was interesting. A late sleeper? An unemployed youngster? A stay-at-home parent? Possibly entirely innocent. But definitely worth following up.

Which Adan Hamati did that afternoon, all by himself. Dressed in dark clothes and with a black woollen hat pulled low down over his ears to fend off the damp cold, he huddled among the trees at the end of the row of lockups and waited. He waited and watched for anyone entering the door of that particular apartment block. Four apartments on each floor, two at the front and two at the rear. Three storeys, which meant twelve apartments per entrance. No elevator, because Swedish construction codes for these older buildings only required elevators in apartment blocks of four or more storeys.

He waited and he watched. Several people entered the building, starting with school-age children arriving from about three in the afternoon onwards. Typical latchkey kids, thought Adan with a sad shake of the head; returning home alone to an empty home, nobody home to welcome them, nobody to walk them home after school in a society where both parents had to work to make ends meet. A sad indictment on the purported blessings of modern western society, where parents didn't have time for their kids, where there was no family stability, the warm feeling that came from knowing that there was always someone there to welcome you home from school, give you something to eat and drink, ask you about your day. All that had to wait until exhausted parents returned from work, asked cursory questions while busying themselves in a flurry of activity in their second jobs, as homemakers in the hours they weren't at their jobs as income-makers.

Finally, at about a quarter to five, a tall, slender girl in a long brown coat and a modest hijab entered the door. A minute or so later, lights were turned on in the front left apartment, in the room on the left of the blacked-out window. The girl appeared in the other windows and lowered the blinds one by one, but nothing moved in the blacked-out room.

Adan Hamati never left his post all that evening except to relieve himself in the woods behind the chain of lockups, always returning to his watch as soon as he could. He almost missed a tall, thin dark man, certainly African judging by his skin colour, entering the building. Against the backlighting of the lit-up rooms he could see what must be the girl and the man moving around, then nothing for about half an hour, then the tell-tale blue flickering of what must be a TV set in the room on the left.

Still nothing in the darkened room.

Just after eleven that night the light came on for about ten minutes in the room on the right and was then switched off, replaced by a dimmer glow lower down – no doubt a bedside lamp.

By eleven-thirty that night, all the lights were out. Nothing had changed in the darkened room throughout the evening.

So that was it then, thought Adan. That was probably the prime surveillance site, giving a wide-angle view of the scene opposite the road, while the bug inside the lockup provided additional coverage. Well, they wouldn't be getting any more images from inside thanks to the strategically stacked cardboard boxes, but for all he knew that device may also have included audio, or there might have other devices that he had failed to locate. Audio was the danger – depending on configuration a microphone could pick up sound from anywhere in a closed space like a room.

They may have to reschedule. Tomorrow was only the third of December and things weren't really set to kick off until the 8th, but if needs must... A mission without the capacity for flexibility was a mission that had little chance of success.

Adan Hamati was flexible. Very flexible. It's what had kept him alive all these years.

Tomorrow would reveal just how flexible he was.

But first, cold, wet and hungry as he was, he had some business to attend to in the apartment building across the road.

He left his concealed position among the trees and walked around the side of the garages, crossing the road until he came to the front door of the apartment block. Craning his neck and shading his eyes from the light glaring out at him from the entrance lobby beyond the securely locked front door, Adan Hamati read the board just inside the door displaying the names of the building's tenants. Most, but not all, were Muslim-sounding names. So much for Sweden's famed integration, but good for Adan Hamati this late evening.

He pressed all the buttons in the panel by the door and waited for someone to either buzz him in or ask him who it was calling at this late hour. Nine times out of ten someone would just hit the key on the intercom and remotely unlock the downstairs entrance door; it was amazing that people weren't more security-conscious in this day and age.

No such luck today though. An angry voice asked in a language he didn't recognise but which he assumed was Swedish what he wanted. He muttered in Arabic that he had come to pick up his friend who wasn't answering his phone, he was probably fast asleep and wouldn't make his night shift if he wasn't roused.

Amazing. The door buzzed open. Adan Hamati entered and waited until the door shut securely behind him. He had four choices – the third-storey apartments. They wouldn't be the two apartments at the rear of the building, which narrowed down his choices to two. Memorising the names he walked up the winding stairs.

Mentally ticking off the two names that belonged to the families at the rear of the building, Hamati was left with two surnames: Hersi and Kekkonen. He had no idea what kind of name Kekkonen was, but it wasn't Muslim. His earlier observations and the timeline of arrivals in the building meant he was looking not just for a Muslim name, but a Muslim African name, perhaps Sudanese, perhaps Somali, judging by the appearance of the young girl and the elderly man. He knew that in that part of the world it was customary for older men to take young wives, but this one really did look like a schoolgirl. Still, stranger things had happened before.

He made a mental note of the Hersi surname, turned and walked silently down the stairs, exiting the building and making his way home.

Chapter 46

The following afternoon Amira called Marita Ohlsson and said she had a question. Perhaps a bit of a tricky question – she didn't want to trample on anyone's toes since she was a guest agent on foreign soil.

"What's the problem?" asked Marita.

"Here's a thing. I want to get a feel of where all this is happening, the lockup where the activity is going on and the family that is allowing their home to be used for surveillance. But I don't want to risk doing anything that might upset SÄPO.

"And before you can say anything," she continued hurriedly, "I don't want to talk to anyone, or even really stop on the road or anything; just pass by, get a feel of the place, the atmosphere, see the location for myself, and then return home. If this had been our operation we would insist on all operatives knowing the ground first-hand, but of course this is not my scene, it's SÄPO's. So what do you think, will it ruffle any feathers if I do a discreet sweep through the area?"

There was a short silence as Marita Ohlsson considered this unorthodox request. She could see it from the Israeli's perspective, but she was a desk jockey, she wasn't trained for this kind of hands-on work and, quite frankly, it didn't really appeal to her, the skulduggery of covert operations. She liked the big picture, not the nitty-gritty. On the other hand, if Amira Hart was bringing her brother Benny along, that might make it all quite worthwhile.

"Tell you what," she said. "I'll pick you up about six-thirty this evening and we'll take a ride out there together. Take a look, turn around and head home. We can have a drink at my place afterwards, if you're not busy later."

"Sounds good," said Amira. The last part of the suggestion didn't actually sound all that good. Amira had never ever acquired a taste for wine or any strong alcohol, and her brother was notorious for never drinking anything other than orange juice or water. Whereas Amira enjoyed Coke and Sprite and all the other fizzy sodas available in Israel and elsewhere, Benny had an instinctive dislike of anything with bubbles in it and could probably count on the fingers of one hand the number of beers he had opened in the course of his life – opened and sipped but not actually drunk. Still, even Swedes had to have things like orange juice and mint tea at home, right?

At twenty-five to seven Marita's car drew up. A tiny metallic blue Toyota Aygo hatchback, about three or four years old, it would fit in anywhere without ever eliciting a second glance. Amira sat in the front passenger seat, placing her small backpack on the floor in front of her, and Benny climbed in the back. No child seat, he noted – promising. In fact, not much of a rear seat either, for that matter. This wasn't a car, it was a toy. But it did the job around town for a single young woman, and it was the 'single young woman' bit that appealed to Benny.

Chatting about what kind of a pattern the electronic eavesdropping might reveal when it was all collated in a few days' time, Marita guided the car out past the huge revamped Frölunda Torg shopping mall and out to the wide dual carriageway that led via Gnistäng Tunnel and onto the Älvsborg suspension bridge, heading for the island of Hisingen that was home to Volvo – and the Hersi family of Grumstad.

***

Adan Hamati knocked twice on the door, waited and then knocked twice again, as was the agreed signal. The door opened and Omar Obaidi let him in.

Adan greeted him and nodded respectfully at Obaidi's wife Suhila. They were probably the best-trained, most highly motivated members of his team. Married with two young children currently in the care of doting grandparents back home, they were committed to the cause and would get the job done without unnecessary questions.

Politely accepting Suhila's offer of a glass of mint tea, Adan and Omar chatted about nothing in particular until the three of them were sitting at the small table in the sparsely furnished kitchen, each with an untouched glass of aromatic tea gently steaming in front of them.

“I have reason to believe someone is onto us,” he launched straight in. Suhila and Omar were not given to hysterics, they would not waste time looking for someone at whom to point the finger of blame. Take stock, assess and adapt.

Adan explained what he wanted. He knew they would both want to do it. He knew who he would prefer for the job but he didn’t want to interfere in their decision-making process. Suhila Obaidi made the choice easy for him. “It’s best if I do it,” she said. “I’ll arouse less suspicion, it’ll be easier for a woman to gain access than a man. Are we doing this tonight?”

They agreed that Omar would stay at home, well away from the action. This would be a ladies’ night. Adan would meet Suhila at the top of Länsgatan at six-fifteen that evening and they would make their way together to the apartment from there.

They spent the next twenty or so minutes discussing various options, likely scenarios, sipping their tea as they talked.

As Adan thanked Omar and Suhila for their hospitality he wondered if this was going to work out. It would have been so much better if they could have stuck to the original plan, but since that was no longer an option, the Obaidis were his best way out. And Suhila Obaidi was the best of the best for the task at hand.

***

As Marita Ohlsson's Toyota Aygo turned in at the top of Länsgatan she said: "It's further up this road, near but not quite at the end of the road. I'll slow down as we approach the apartment building."

Amira was busy pulling something out of her small backpack, something that looked like a length of black fabric. "Just pull in here for a moment," she said. As the car slowed to a halt she arranged the black fabric over her head and draped it over the top of her shoulders. A hijab. In a second she had been transformed into a modest Muslim woman – blending in perfectly in this area with its high concentration of immigrants.

"You know what?" she said. "Let me out here, I'll walk slowly down the road, like I'm looking for a particular address. That will give me the opportunity I need to get the flavour of the place. I'll walk all the way to the end – this is a dead-end road, right? And on my way back I'll check out the lockup on the other side of the road. Job done. You can turn around and drive off, wait a few minutes around the bend near the T-junction and then come back and pick me up."

Amira Hart got out of the car and walked slowly down the road, pretending to have an animated chat in Arabic on her mobile phone. A young woman on her way home, or visiting a friend perhaps. Nothing to merit a second glance.

Up ahead of her on the left, from behind what looked like the end of the row of garages which must also contain the lockup she was interested in, she noticed a woman exit from the cover of some trees. The woman was wearing a hijab. And modern clothes – just like Amira was in fact. Slim-fitting jeans, a warm dark green jacket, woollen gloves. It struck Amira as odd that she had emerged from the trees – there was nothing there. Amira slowed down and looked from one building to another as though she were searching for the right address, giving the other woman the opportunity to cross the road at a diagonal and approach her side of the road. As she crossed under the yellow sodium street light, Amira's heart gave a little leap of surprise. She recognised the face! It belonged to one of the ten Palestinians whose location was currently unaccounted for, the ten who had arrived on false Syrian papers. She couldn't for the life of her remember the name, but there was no mistake about it – she was definitely one of the ten missing Palestinians.

Keeping behind her she walked along the pavement in the footsteps of the Palestinian woman, both heading in the same direction.

No doubt about it – the woman was heading for the apartment block where the Hersis lived. Amira quickened her pace very slightly. She didn't want to get too close to the suspect, but because she had no way of getting into the building herself she didn't want to be so far away that she wouldn't be able to enter with her.

Still carrying on her imaginary conversation in loud Arabic, Amira walked in the direction of the Hersis' door while keeping a watch on the actions of the woman up front. It appeared she was pressing all the buttons and hoping for an answer.

Suhila had in fact pressed all the buttons except that of the Hersis. No point alerting them unnecessarily. Someone buzzed open the door.

As she heard the audible buzz ringing out across the quiet street Amira quickened her pace into a run, shouting gaily into the phone "But I told you that dress is perfect, Bilal! We'll meet tomorrow at the store so you can try it on again, OK? 4 o'clock? Fine, see you then sweetie!" Amira snapped her phone shut and caught up with the front door of the building just as it was shutting.

Made it in the nick of time. Up ahead Suhila glanced over her shoulder and saw a dark Muslim woman, a Somali perhaps, who was putting her phone away and adjusting her hijab in the reflection of the glassed-in board with the tenants' names. She smiled at her and continued on her way. Just so long as the newcomer wasn't coming up to the third floor. Alina continued climbing the stairs. Nobody was following. Good, perhaps the newcomer was visiting someone on the ground floor.

Knowing that the Hersi family lived on the top floor, Amira kept up the charade and rang the first doorbell on the ground floor. If anyone answered, she'd say she was looking for the Hersis and apologise for ringing the wrong doorbell. If nobody answered, so much the better – no-one would know she had been there.

Nobody answered. Good.

She started walking slowly and quietly up the stairs.

On the third floor, Suhila Obaidi breathed in and out deeply, once, twice, three times. Fixing her most open, most friendly smile on her face she rang the doorbell.

It took a while before she heard some slight noise from behind the door. The security eye in the door darkened and Suhila knew she was being scrutinised. She had taken a step back away from the door and stood under the overhead ceiling light on the landing so she could be clearly seen. She wanted to seem as non-threatening as possible. Everything depended on the next few moments.

A man's voice behind the door said something that sounded like a question, in a language Suhila did not understand but that she recognised as most likely Swedish – it had that lilt to it, Swedes sounded as though they were chronically out of breath. An odd language indeed.

But Suhila didn't have time to reflect on the linguistic properties of strange languages. Adan had said that at this hour of the evening, the young girl would be home alone, now instead the man of the household was already there. Perhaps a shift worker.

No matter, assess and adapt. Speaking clearly and slowly in Arabic she introduced herself with her real name, said she was a new arrival in Gothenburg and that the imam at the newly built mosque in eastern Grumstad had told her that the Hersis were always generous to fellow-Muslims in need of help. Speaking to the closed door, she said she didn't need money or even a bed for the night, just access to a phone so she could call her friend who was supposed to pick her up from the Länsmansgården tram stop at six o'clock that evening but had failed to turn up. Suhila had nowhere to go and no way to contact her friend unless she could get to a phone and call her. She would be most grateful if she could just make that phone call. And yes, she knew how strange a request this was and apologised most profusely for disturbing a hardworking family man out of the blue like this. She didn't even need to come into the apartment to make her call, she'd understand any reluctance to admit a stranger like this, even one who came upon the recommendation of the local imam. Perhaps Mr Hersi could just lend her a mobile phone for a minute? She'd be perfectly happy to make her call from out there on the landing, she wouldn't dream of disturbing his family any more than necessary.

Suhila Obaidi almost felt sorry for giving Abdurrahman Hersi such a moral dilemma. But she was on a mission, and there was no scope for feeling sorry for anyone or anything that might compromise that mission.

The door opened and Suhila smiled at the man who opened it. Taking a swift step forward she punched him straight in the solar plexus, twisting her body to put her entire weight behind the punch.

Abdurrahman Hersi never had the chance to warn his daughter – he couldn't catch his breath, let alone shout out a warning to the teenager in her bedroom doing her homework. What he did do to warn his daughter, however, not so much by design as by sheer accident, was to stumble awkwardly back and to the side against the hall mirror, knocking it off its hook and sending it crashing noisily first onto the small chest of drawers beneath it and then onto the floor where it smashed to smithereens.

Inside the flat Samira heard first what sounded like a scuffle and then the loud splintering crash of glass breaking and she leapt out of her desk chair to go see what had happened.

On the first-floor landing making her way quietly upstairs, Amira heard the commotion and bounded up the stairs two at a time, reaching the top landing just as the Palestinian woman stepped over a mass of broken glass in through the doorway and a beautiful dark girl appeared at the end of the hallway from inside the apartment.

An elderly man was writhing in agony on the floor of the hall just inside the door, the woman was bending down over him and about to punch him once again. It looked like she was aiming for his face. The young girl's face was contorted into a soundless scream.

Her training snapping her automatically into action, Amira took a big step forward and aimed a roundhouse kick with her right foot into the right side of the crouching woman.

Suhila Obaidi gasped as a dagger of pain shot into her ribs. She fell onto her left side but quickly scrambled around to regain her feet. Amira took another step forward, both hands held in front of her face in a boxing guard. As she moved in close her right forearm snapped out and up from the right, swinging the point of her elbow into an arc that struck Suhila on the point of the chin in a vicious uppercut. She immediately followed it up with a left hook to the liver and as Suhila Obaidi grunted in pain and bent involuntarily to her left, Amira drew back her right hand, now balled tightly into a compact fist, sinking a massive right hook into Suhila's left kidney.

Staggering back in pain but quickly recovering her feet, Suhila snapped an upward front kick towards Amira's groin, but Amira saw it coming and twisted slightly out of the way. It struck her straight on her left thigh and almost crippled her, sending sheets of blinding white pain rocketing through her eyeballs and almost lifting the top of her skull. She hobbled back a step and waited for the pain to subside. The two hijab-clad women eyed each other, with the hijab-clad Samira still standing in shock at the end of the hallway. She had neither moved nor uttered a sound throughout.

Testing her weight on her left leg, Amira decided to continue on the offensive before her opponent had time to mentally regroup and take stock of the situation. She feinted down and to the left with her left hand and when Suhila ducked to her right to ward off the oncoming attack Amira leapt into the air and smashed the full force of her right knee into the point of Suhila's chin. The Palestinian woman went down like a sack of potatoes, hitting her right shoulder painfully against the protruding corner of the small chest of drawers that stood below where the mirror had hung. She fell onto the floor amid a loud tinkling of glass. As Amira followed up her advantage she saw an ominous red stain spreading rapidly beneath Suhila's body.

Suhila was staring up wide-eyed. She didn't seem to be in pain, more surprised really. But she wasn't moving, other than an involuntary recurring spasm in her right leg, which twitched continuously. Speaking to her in Arabic Amira told her not to move, stay calm and breathe while she checked her. Going against everything her compulsory medical training had taught her, she gently and very slowly rolled Suhila Obaidi onto her left side, looking behind her for signs of injury.

The back of her jacket seemed to have been shredded to bits by sharp slivers of glass, and from the back of her neck a large jagged piece of glass jutted out at an acute angle. Working quickly but smoothly, Amira snatched off her hijab and, looking around for something else to cushion the wounded woman's head and neck, caught sight of Samira in the hallway, the girl's eyes large with horror.

"Quick!" she commanded in Arabic. "Give me a jacket or towels or something. Anything soft." No reaction.

"Move!" she shouted, this time in Swedish, "Get me some towels, now!" Her tone seemed to galvanise the young girl into action. Samira darted away and reappeared a few moments later with an armful of towels. Amira gently placed a soft cushion of towels under Suhila's head and neck and carefully lowered her back to the floor. She knew better than to move her again.

Turning once again to Samira she said: "Two things: first call for an ambulance, tell them someone slipped on broken glass and has puncture wounds, it's bad. Then take care of this man. He's your father?" she asked.

Samira nodded mutely. "Go now – phone first then help your father." The girl disappeared, presumably to get her cell phone from her bedroom and make the emergency call. She reappeared a few moments later and rushed to Abdurrahman, who was gasping for breath but slowly regaining some colour in his face. He took one look at Suhila as Samira helped him to his feet and he knew what had to be done. He'd worked as an orderly at the hospital long enough to pick up more than a rudimentary knowledge of what to do in this kind of situation.

"Get me the duvet from my bed," he told his daughter. "We have to keep her warm until the ambulance arrives."

Amira meantime kicked the sharp shards of glass out of the way and knelt down beside the injured woman, who was rapidly turning very pale indeed. She put her mouth close to her ear and whispered in Arabic: "What is your name? Who should we notify?" Amira said nothing about who she was, how she happened to be there at the time of the attack.

Suhila's lips moved but no sound came out. Amira pushed back the woman's hijab and stroked her hair. "The ambulance is on its way, but I'm not sure it will get here in time. Is there someone you want me to notify? Anyone at home?"

Again Suhila's lips moved, this time forming the words: "Omar Obaidi. My children's father. My children are in Palestine, with my parents. I have to go back to them. Promise!" She grasped Amira's jacket with surprising strength, but it soon faded away as the pool of blood beneath her spread wider, seeping out from under the duvet that Abdurrahman had placed on her body.

Suhila Obaidi's eyes started flickering as they searched out Amira's. She still doesn't know who or what I am, thought Amira to herself, she just thinks I happened to prevent what looked like an attempted break-in. Better that she slips away without that knowledge, no point in distressing her last few moments in this life.

"Bury me at home!" Suhila's words could barely be heard. In the distance the wail of a siren could be heard. Amira bent her head down, her ear to Suhila's mouth. "My children..."

Amira whispered in Suhila's ear: "I give you my word you will go back home. Your husband is Omar and I will notify him. I promise. Go in peace." She uttered the traditional Muslim blessing and held both Suhila's hands in hers as her life slipped away at the same rate as the ambulance approached.

As the diesel clatter of the ambulance engine shut down and she heard the heavy tread of boots on the stairs through the still-open front door of the apartment, Amira gently closed Suhila's eyes.

Suhila Obaidi had not completed her mission – and Amira Hart still had no idea what that mission was.

What she did have was a shocked young girl, her father, two ambulance paramedics, and a blue Toyota Aygo that had trailed the ambulance all the way to the door of the apartment block.

Marita Ohlsson could not afford to be seen here. She sent Benny up the stairs behind the ambulance paramedics with strict instructions to extract Amira as quickly and unobtrusively as possible.

Too late. Amira was deep in conversation with Samira and Abdurrahman. Without going into any details, she explained in Arabic, addressing the father out of respect but frequently glancing at the daughter, that she was working with the intelligence services and that they had reason to believe that the woman who had just died was a Palestinian terrorist who had gotten wind of the surveillance equipment in their apartment. Amira would ensure that the family received thorough protection and that nothing further would happen to them. Without disabusing them of any impression they might have gained that she was working for SÄPO as opposed to working *with* SÄPO, Amira said she would take the necessary steps and have the situation in hand.

The ambulance personnel meanwhile called in the status of the victim and prepared to move the body after uniformed police arrived to take witness statements.

There was nothing for it, Amira would have to stay and give a witness statement – she couldn't risk upsetting her host country by removing herself from the scene of a crime – a crime moreover that she had admittedly helped prevent but in which she had nonetheless played a key role and about which she was able to give a full account.

This had the potential of turning into a bureaucratic nightmare.

She needn't have worried. When Benny returned to Marita Ohlsson and explained that uniform officers were on the way, Marita shrugged and made a call.

Far from tearing her off a strip, it turned out SÄPO was immensely relieved that the Hersis had come to no harm, despite SÄPO's assurances to father and daughter that even Samira would scarcely notice the presence of the surveillance equipment in her own room. Some promise...

So no, there would be no fallout and the issue was cleared up through the combined efforts of uniform and security police in a matter of half an hour after their separate arrival.

Before leaving, Amira took both Samira's hands in hers and told her she was a very brave and a very upright citizen for her principled stance. Samira, still convinced that the black female agent who had quite possibly saved their lives was a SÄPO officer, smiled and her thoughts drifted once again to her dream of the previous night. OK, so she wouldn't be the first hijab-wearing Muslim officer in the Swedish police, because here was a woman who'd obviously made it ahead of her. But it just went to show – nothing was impossible in the new Sweden. Her mind was made up. She knew what college programme she would be applying for after she finished high school.

And with that everyone left the apartment, with the exception of Samira and Abdurrahman inside and a uniformed officer sitting on a chair outside their door. He was going to be there for three hours before his relief arrived. He settled in his chair, eyes and ears ready to detect anything unusual.

Chapter 47

From his concealed position in the scrub of trees beside the row of garage lockups, Adan Hamati viewed with increasing consternation the swelling tide of activity at the Hersi residence. None of this was going according to plan. Suhila was supposed to gain access to the Hersi apartment using a modest amount of non-lethal violence if necessary against the elderly man if he was home and the teenage schoolgirl, ascertain if there was any surveillance equipment in the blacked-out room, and either destroy the equipment or bring it away with her for analysis. It wasn't a difficult mission for any one of the team's members, least of all for Suhila Obaidi.

What could possibly have gone wrong? He had seen no police or other security activity either before or during Suhila's mission. In fact, the only other person who had entered the building before the ambulance arrived, sirens and lights blazing, was a modestly clad Muslim woman about Suhila's age, possibly a bit younger, who had arrived at almost the same time.

But trailing the ambulance was a small four-door hatchback. The driver was a woman Adan had never seen before, the passenger a big man. He could have been light-haired, it was difficult to say under the woollen bobble-hat he was wearing but there seemed to be a ring of blond hair peeping out from underneath. There was something vaguely familiar about him, although not the woman. Perhaps Adan had seen him passing by before on one of his many visits to the lockup.

Hamati stayed hidden among the trees. His feet were freezing. It wasn't only the cold, it was the damp – that really multiplied the effects of the cold. What a country to live in – and yet so many Muslims lived here. Not just his own countrymen but also people from other parts of the Arab and wider Muslim worlds. They must be mad.

When a marked police car arrived, strobe lights clearing a path down the long approach to the apartment building, followed by two discreet black Volvo S80 sedans, Adan was on the verge of melting away into the darkness behind the lockups, ready to make his way through the woods and into the safety of anonymity elsewhere. But he realised nobody could really see him and unless he saw signs that the authorities were setting up for a search of the area, he saw no reason to leave – he might as well stay and learn as much as he could from his invisible vantage point.

His reward came about forty minutes later, when first the ambulance paramedics appeared, carrying a stretcher which they loaded into the ambulance and drove off. No lights flashing. Not an emergency then. The body on the stretcher had its face covered. Someone had died, that was obvious. But who?

Adan felt he had received his answer when, in short order, first one then a second man came out of the building carrying bulky black bags which they stowed in the luggage compartment of one of the Volvo S80s. At about the same time, the blinds in the previously blacked-out room were adjusted slightly and light appeared between the slats of the blinds. So that was the end of the surveillance operation, reckoned Adan – and there had indeed been one. He saw two blurred outlines moving against the closed blinds. It was reasonable to assume that both Hersis were intact, since as yet he had not seen any sign of police officers escorting Suhila away from the premises.

Question was, how much had the surveillance revealed, and why hadn't the police moved against them? There was little doubt in his mind that the two black cars belonged not to the regular police but to Sweden's secret service, which had some unpronounceable name.

Just as he was about to leave, two more people appeared in the doorway of the building: the tall blond man who looked vaguely familiar, in the company of a much shorter but stunningly beautiful black woman. But *this* one he definitely recognised – this was the woman who had entered the building immediately after Suhila, in fact before the door had even shut, Adan now recalled.

The two of them went first to the first of the two black SÄPO cars, exchanged some words with the driver or possibly the front seat passenger. Adan was too far away to hear what was being said. The two walked back in the direction of the nondescript blue Toyota hatchback, where the female driver had spent most of her time talking animatedly into her cell phone. Or, more accurately, listening to her cell phone. As the young woman and the blond giant passed beneath a street light Adan caught a clear view of their faces.

And that's when it struck him in a flash of recognition that buckled his knees. Not the female – the blond man. Of course he knew him – but not from here, not from Sweden. He looked typically Swedish but he wasn't, he was Israeli. He worked for Shin Bet, Adan just couldn't place his name. But if so, he was way, way out of his own territory. And who was the Muslim woman working hand in glove with the Zionist? To make matters worse she even took him by the arm and momentarily leaned her head against his shoulder – which she barely reached. Despite the hijab she had worn on her way into the building, then, she probably wasn't Muslim. At least not as observant a Muslim as she would like people to believe – observant Muslim girls didn't do this sort of thing in the street. The man and woman exchanged a few words he couldn't clearly hear, but the lilt was all wrong – it was not Swedish, nor did it have the cadence of English or Arabic and by now he was prepared to swear it was Hebrew. They then made their way past the marked police cruiser and on to the blue Toyota hatchback.

Once in the car, the three of them drove on, turned around at the roundabout at the end of the dead-end and made their way back past the lockups on their way up to the T-junction and away. Followed soon after by both black Volvos driving swiftly in close formation.

All that was left was a marked police car, with the driver speaking into his radio before finally starting the engine and driving off.

Alone.

Which meant that one officer, his partner, had remained behind.

Enough for one night. Adan turned and melted quietly into the wooded shadows behind the lockups, heading for home.

But first a visit. One he dreaded making.

***

Omar Obaidi did not remonstrate, he did not curse or smash up the furniture. He sat quietly, his thoughts on his two children – and their grandparents, Suhila's mother and father. The struggle for a free Palestine had claimed another martyr in the holy war to end the Zionist occupation and deliver liberty.

Now there were nine of them left to make their mark, to see if they couldn't once again refocus the world's attention on what must always remain the world's most pressing problem, no matter what it cost in human lives.

At its own peril would the world ignore the plight of Palestine.

Adan grasped Omar's hands and together they recited the prayer over the recently departed.

Adan Hamati left Omar Obaidi. He had one more port of call before he could lay his weary head on his pillow.

And luckily it was just a few minutes away on foot.

Pressing a push-button marked "Amir" he was buzzed into a typically 1960s high-rise green-painted rental apartment block in a nearby part of Grumstad. The ground-floor apartment door was already ajar by the time he got to it. He entered, shut the door behind him, and spoke for less than two minutes to the man who met him in the hallway.

"It will be done, brother, exactly on time and exactly at the right locations, you can rest assured," said Amir.

They shook hands, and parted. Adan left the building and made his way home. Sleep at last.

Chapter 48

On the night of December 4th unmanned petrol stations all over Gothenburg started burning.

The police had little doubt it was a case of deliberate, aggravated arson, but initially went off at a tangent because only Shell stations were being set alight. Obviously someone with a grudge against the Dutch-owned company. The police deployed all their meagre patrol resources to the city's remaining Shell petrol stations, manned and unmanned alike.

As fire crews from the city's three biggest fire stations battled the blazes, the police started receiving reports of fires in unmanned Q8 petrol stations.

This wasn't some nutter with a grudge, imagined or otherwise, against a particular chain; someone was targeting unmanned filling stations everywhere.

Statoil petrol stations followed soon after, and crews were called in from all the fire stations in the city and the neighbouring counties to assist in putting out the conflagrations.

The MO was always the same: a car turned up, a credit card was inserted, the fuel pumps started, fuel spilling onto and under the car, the nozzle put on autolock and then a lit matchstick dropped into the liquid. Which spread and engulfed the car and raced back up the fuel filler hose to the dispenser. Which continued spewing out fuel by the litre until the automatic volume mechanism reached its limit, usually 80 litres, and switched off. But by then the forecourt and its equipment were firmly ablaze.

By morning the police and fire crews were nearing the point of absolute exhaustion but no new fires had been started since about four in the morning, so it looked as though daylight had put a stop to the spate of arson attacks.

Forensics and computer records would doubtless reveal the identities of the credit card holders, but equally doubtless was the certainty that they would all be revealed to be either stolen or cloned.

As late evening turned to night on the 5th of December, all police leave was cancelled and every officer who had worked less than one and a half consecutive shifts was pressed into service, union regulations be damned. Fire crews were on standby for a repeat performance of the previous night's events.

They need not have bothered. Gothenburg was as calm as a duck-pond on a lazy summer afternoon.

Instead, the spate of arson spread east to Jönköping, Borås, Karlstad and Växjö. With resources stretched thin to breaking-point and Gothenburg still perfectly calm, officers and fire crews from the city were despatched east to aid their colleagues.

Gothenburg was left severely undermanned.

But nothing untoward happened in Gothenburg that night, and by morning the exhausted police and fire-fighting personnel returned to their bases on the west coast.

By the time the 6th of December rolled around, there was a sense of tense expectancy all across the middle of Sweden. Would the violence continue spreading east, heading for Stockholm? The Nobel Prize Award Ceremony was due to be held in just a few days' time, on the 10th, and that was a world-renowned event that captured the attention of the global media. In fact the media were already in place in the Swedish capital and some pretty unfavourable background reports about the breakdown in Swedish law and order were making headlines in various European, North American and Middle East papers.

Stockholm breathed a sigh of relief as the night of the 6th passed by in peace and quiet. Instead, the cities of Malmö and Lund in the very south of the country exploded in an orgy of arson. Petrol stations, schools, public libraries, even day-care centres, were torched and Malmö's desperate appeals for assistance were answered by fire-fighters from neighbouring Copenhagen, the capital of Denmark, forty-five km away via the Öresund Bridge, which is actually a combined tunnel and bridge link between southern Sweden and eastern Denmark. Danish fire crews battled blazes in Malmö and now also in Trelleborg and Helsingborg a few kilometres away, before returning across the water to Copenhagen in the early hours of the following morning.

As Gothenburg cleaned up the mess and slowly started breathing a collective sigh of relief, the city's 170 year old synagogue on Alströmergatan was attacked with Molotov cocktails on the night of the 7th, swastikas daubed on the walls of the building and rocks hurled through its beautiful Moorish stained-glass windows.

The police threw a security cordon around the listed building, their job made easier by the fact that the synagogue backed onto a canal and all three streets on the other three sides were one-way thoroughfares.

As all this was playing out, Amira and Benny were deep in dialogue with SÄPO on their particular problem and the possible links with the rash of violence spreading across the country.

From their particular perspective, of course, Amira and Benny Hart were focusing firmly on the Palestinian Arab angle. A pod of West Bank Palestinians were definitely involved in something, and it was obvious that they were determined to stay beneath the radar – hence the cash-only transactions, the use of bicycles and no motorised vehicles which would require licences, registration, insurance, credit cards.

Was there any significance in the fact that most of the action seemed to be in Grumstad on the large island of Hisingen? That, after all, was where Swedish automotive manufacturer Volvo had several facilities – building cars, trucks, buses and more besides.

Was there any significance in the fact that arson and related violence had spread from the west coast first east to the Midlands and then south, but not east to Stockholm? That, after all, was where the world-famous Nobel awards ceremony would be taking place in a couple of days' time. Was this a silence before the storm, or was the Swedish capital being avoided because the rioters assumed it would be far too well defended by police owing to the Nobel ceremony? The King and Queen of Sweden would be presiding at that event, so law enforcement, both uniform and covert, would be taking no chances.

Was there any significance in the fact that in previous arson epidemics, and there had been plenty of such rioting in previous years throughout Sweden, it was usually the work of gangs of what the media and politicians euphemistically termed 'disaffected youths', politically-correct-speak for predominantly Muslim immigrant gangs terrorising native Swedes and fighting turf wars over drug-peddling rights?

This latter was the angle that the Swedish police were focusing on, and coming up with surprising results. Whereas previously the media carried sob-stories about young 'unfortunates' from mostly-immigrant suburbs protesting their lack of integration into mainstream Swedish society, this time there were no youths coming forward to protest that this was their way of making their voices heard. On the contrary, they all steered clear of the media, they had no comment, or if they did it was to say that they had nothing to do with it and it was all a terrible shame that so much was being destroyed.

So no disaffected-immigrant angle, then, apparently. In fact, from the more notoriously raucous extremist mosques and strident Islamist organisations there was not a peep – not a word in Stockholm, Gothenburg, Malmö. Nothing. And they were traditionally the first to jump on the bandwagon to protest how badly Sweden's Muslim minority was being treated, ignored and shoved into segregated suburbs where they were denied equal job opportunities or even the chance to mix with native-born Swedes. That was their way of seeing it, and there were many Swedes who saw it that way too.

But right now, not a word from them. That angle seemed to be a non-starter. In fact, in a city where terrorist organisation Hezbollah held rallies outside Town Hall every Saturday a stone's throw (literally) from Gothenburg's main synagogue, Hezbollah's presence on the streets had also suddenly evaporated. It was like the most extreme Islamists had somehow come to their senses and decided to keep a low profile. The police were nonplussed.

And they didn't know where to turn for information. The suspect who had attacked Abdurrahman Hersi in his home – and would probably have gone on to attack his daughter Samira – had obviously been after the police surveillance equipment. And she had died. A human tragedy of course – and very unfortunate because the police were going to get nothing from her. So the police surveillance equipment was now their only lead.

Whether deliberately or by chance, the camera embedded inside the lockup had been blocked by a pile of boxes, but the audio feed was still operational. For SÄPO and the Swedish police, however, the problem was that nothing much was ever said inside the lockup. And repeated viewing of the digital footage captured using the equipment in the Hersi apartment revealed nothing useful. All it showed was ten adults, all of Middle Eastern appearance, about half of them women. According to the Israeli liaison officer Amira Hart they were all West Bank Palestinians, Fatah stalwarts from the Palestinian Authority President's own political party. Her brother Benny Hart, who by coincidence or otherwise happened to be in Gothenburg while all this was going down, said there was no doubt there was a link but he wasn't prepared to offer details, for reasons that had to do with ongoing Shin Bet operations. He was not here on Shin Bet or any other official business, and in any case he was not authorised to talk about Shin Bet operations.

With Stockholm and nearby Uppsala on Sweden's east coast still ominously silent and peaceful, all the attention was focused there. That had to be where the action was going to be. The rest was either a trial run or a softening-up mission. Perhaps just a preliminary exercise to gauge police response. The ultimate target had to be the Nobel Awards on the evening of the 10th of December. That was just two days hence.

The Nobel Awards Ceremony would be the obvious high-profile target. The Swedish royal family would be there. But they were scarcely likely to be a target for potential Palestinian terrorists. Sweden was probably the most outspoken – if embarrassingly naïve – supporter of the Palestinian cause in the UN and EU. Sweden was the biggest per capita donor in the world to the Palestinians, funding a wide variety of Palestinian aid organisations and Palestinian groups, a few of which were overt terrorist groups, while the best one could say about most of the others was that they were virulently anti-democratic, misogynistic and racist in their dealings both as regards Palestinians who didn't toe the line, on the one hand, and as regards Israeli civilians – men, women and children – on the other.

It just would not make sense to jeopardise the sympathy many Swedes felt for the Palestinian cause. Of course, every year there seemed to be a preponderance of Jews and Israelis who won various Nobel awards – perhaps they were the target?

Jews and Israelis had been targets countless times in what the Arab press and many European media outlets referred to as 'overseas operations' carried out by 'Palestinian militants'. There was a lot of sympathy, latent and sometimes remarkably open, for such missions, even on foreign soil. Had not the Germans, the British, the French, all voluntarily released convicted felons, what Israel termed Palestinian terrorists and mass-murderers with blood on their hands, following assassinations of Jews and Israelis on European soil? As was the custom, Israel's ambassador to Sweden would be invited to the Nobel Awards Ceremony, as would all other ambassadors to the Swedish capital. He was always a target, he always travelled in an armour-plated Volvo and usually in a convoy of two, sometimes three cars packed with highly trained SÄPO bodyguards bristling with light arms and some pretty heavy-duty firepower too, should push come to shove.

The car was interesting. Shunning protocol, the Israeli Foreign Office had specifically requested that their top representative in Sweden use a domestic Swedish make. The long-troubled SAAB brand had recently collapsed, which left that other Swedish automotive icon, Volvo. SÄPO preferred heavier and more powerful German BMWs and Mercedes-Benz V12 and V8 models, but for Israel this was a point of principle – they wanted to demonstrate their goodwill and commissioned a heavily armoured Volvo S80L powered by Volvo's now decommissioned but massively powerful and lightweight Yamaha-developed V8 engine mated to four-wheel drive transmission taken from the company's XC90 soft-roader. A special build from start to finish. The SÄPO minders didn't like the car, but Israel insisted – it was a matter of courtesy to their host country and various Volvo models were also the transport of choice for government ministers back in Jerusalem.

But alongside the US ambassador to Sweden, the Israeli ambassador was probably the best-guarded foreign dignitary in the country, and his protective shield was 24/7. Nobody was ever going to be able to get through to him, end of story. And in any case, none of this made any sense. What possible connection could there be between a group of suspects in Gothenburg on the west coast and Sweden's capital Stockholm, 550 kilometres to the east? Not least because the suspects – whatever they were suspected of – were on bicycles. They weren't going to make it to Stockholm in less than a week of hard riding on cold, wet and slippery roads that would soon turn icy with frost and the first snows. This just had to be the least plausible connection ever in the history of crime detection.

But the sheer absence of any action in Stockholm was worrying. The Nobel Awards were going to be held there on December the 10th. And that was just two days hence.

As is so often the case, it was the back-room boys, not the first-responders or the undercover police pounding the streets, who came up with what looked like a possible break.

Martin Lindell, to be specific. Yet another of those interminable morning conferences had revealed just how dry the trail was, so Martin Lindell set himself the task of feeding all sorts of parameters, from the likely through the less obvious to the ridiculously tenuous, into his box of tricks to see what sort of links, what sorts of patterns, it came up with.

And it turned out the link had been there all the time. So minor that nobody had registered its significance.

Chapter 49

There was a reason for the Gothenburg presence, after all. And it was an Israeli link too. Just not the one anyone expected.

With the focus firmly on protecting petrol stations, Sweden's royal family and the Nobel Awards, all the while piling additional police reserves into Stockholm as unobtrusively as possible since this was the only major city in Sweden not to be hit by the recent arson epidemic, what had escaped everyone's attention was the impending visit by the importer of what was probably one of Volvo's smallest dealerships anywhere in the world: AutoSwed of Tel Aviv, Israel. AutoSwed CEO Daniel Nimrodi was arriving for a ceremony to symbolically accept the keys to the latest batch of ninety-eight new Volvos ready for shipment to Israel to serve with various Israeli government ministries.

Most of the cars were regular assembly-line products, but twelve of them were lightly armoured and three, intended for the holders of the top cabinet positions, were heavily armoured special models.

All sensitive Volvo models are withdrawn from the regular assembly line and their build completed in a separate high-security division of the car factory. This applies to cars such as police specials for domestic and overseas markets, SÄPO cars requiring special equipment, taxis with their nonstandard heavy-duty specification, all cars destined for diplomatic missions overseas, and of course special-bodied models such as hearses and ambulances.

In Sweden it is illegal to vet people for jobs on account of their ethnicity, religion, gender or sexual preference, and most Swedish employers are so keen to demonstrate their absolute even-handedness that what actually happens is a pronounced inclination to hire staff from groups often perceived as under-represented in the workforce. A kind of unspoken positive discrimination to which no Swedish employer would ever own up.

So too at Volvo Cars' Special Build Facility or SBF. Yousep Yonan, whom everyone at work called Josef or Joe, was a skilled car electrician who had earned his degree in automotive electronics at Gothenburg's world-renowned Chalmers University of Technology. Born and bred in Gothenburg, Yousep's Assyrian parents had arrived in a labour-hungry Sweden in the early 1960s intending, like so many others, to work for a few years, make a lot of money in the high-income Scandinavian country and then retire back home in low-cost eastern Turkey – if the domestic political situation ever improved enough for them to return to Turkey. And just as with so many other labour immigrants, it didn't quite work out that way. The children of that generation were more Swedish than Assyrian, annual visits to the old country notwithstanding. While the children of many subsequent groups of immigrants to Sweden developed a kind of semi-lingual status, with insufficient skills in either their mother-tongue or Swedish, children of first-generation Assyrian families were generally thoroughly acclimatised, one foot firmly in each camp and usually truly bilingual. They had mastered that otherwise so uniquely Jewish-immigrant art of becoming totally integrated in their new home country, yet without becoming assimilated and losing their own identity. They succeeded, for the most part, in maintaining their own culture, traditions and religion, while becoming part and parcel of the country in which they lived.

Like so many other so-called 'second-generation immigrants' of Assyrian descent, education was everything for Yousep Yonan and his family. And like so many other children of immigrants from that generation and background, he was careful to cultivate smooth relations with people of other religions and ethnicities – Yousep had no interest whatsoever in importing the religious and political tensions of the old country of his parents to the country of his birth.

But not everyone had such a generous attitude. The shape and name of the battlefield may change, but for many the war still had to be fought – and won.

And the war that occupied the hearts and minds of so many recent immigrants from the Arab and Muslim worlds to Sweden was what they termed the colonialist, imperialist war that the Zionists were continually waging in Palestine with the aid of their allies, the Americans.

Every weapon was a legitimate asset in this war, every tactic permissible, since this was a holy war. Al Quds had to be liberated from the Jews, its blasphemous Jewish and Crusader name of 'Jerusalem' for Islam's third-holiest city had to be expunged from the world's consciousness. Cost what it may.

And right now, Yousep Yonan was being asked to pay the price. True, he wasn't a Muslim. And true, he wasn't a believer in the cause – or indeed had ever expressed any opinion on the matter. But he did have a wife and two young children, so it would be in everyone's interest if he fell into line. The threat was not elaborated upon, but it was perfectly clear.

It wasn't as though he had to do anything. Nothing at all, in fact. No act of sabotage, no stealing – in fact, he didn't even have to lie.

All he had to do was give the signal. That was it. Simply notify them when what they wanted was ready – nothing else. That was his part over, for ever. Just give them a date and a time, and an exact location. Nothing else.

Yousep Yonan was nothing if not a pragmatist. He was a proud Assyrian, and he was a proud Swede. But he was also a very happily married man and an inordinately proud father. Nothing – absolutely nothing – was going to jeopardise the lives of his wife and kids. Nothing. It was one thing taking the moral high ground when it came to his own wellbeing, he knew how to look after himself. But here it was his wife and two young children whose lives were being threatened, so morality and conscience be damned. He'd give them what they wanted now, and maybe speak to the police afterwards. But first he had to get them off his back.

So on the afternoon of the 8th of December he went to the public library in Grumstad, logged onto the free Internet service provided by the library, and sent a one-line email message to an address he had memorised following a particularly unpleasant visit by a group of large, very threatening, men. Men who had knocked on his door at home – while he and his wife were putting their young children to bed. That had no doubt been their intention – a none-too-subtle yet wholly understated invasion of the most vulnerable private space a family man could imagine.

So there was never any doubt that Yousep Yonan was going to send that message when the time came.

***

Israeli Volvo importer AutoSwed's CEO, Daniel Nimrodi, was scheduled to visit Gothenburg on the morning of Thursday the 10th of December. The same day as the Nobel Awards Ceremony.

And the Israeli embassy's commercial attaché in Stockholm, Amikam Taub, would be travelling down to Gothenburg for the official signing ceremony.

That had to be it. Martin Lindell passed on his findings to his operations commander and washed his hands off the whole affair. He'd come up trumps, and his part in this was now over. Let the muscle-heads take over.

An interdepartmental conference was hastily called. It was agreed that this being the 8th afternoon, nothing was going to happen until the 10th morning at the earliest, when both the Israeli importer and the Israeli commercial attaché would be at Volvo HQ. There would be no overt surveillance of the lockup until the 9th night – they didn't want to spook the suspects. They still had audio inside the lockup, so if there were any indications of heightened activity before that they would move in.

Every unit was assigned its role for dawn of the 10th of December. Vehicles, equipment, tactics. A strong security cordon would be placed around Volvo HQ where the handover ceremony was scheduled to be held. Both uniform officers and Volvo's own unarmed security personnel would be there in force. Nothing too visible or rigid, they had no idea what to expect so they didn't want to commit all their resources to any given locations, although the handover ceremony surely had to be the ultimate goal.

So three concentric rings were laid out.

The first, closest to the target, at Volvo Cars HQ. Armed police, plus unarmed but uniformed Volvo security personnel.

The second, placed some way off on Assar Gabrielssons Väg, the slip road that veered left off the public highway and led into the Volvo complex. Unarmed Volvo security personnel.

And the third, the outermost, at a quickly created road-works site near the T-junction leading to the row of lockup garages and the building that housed Abdurrahman and Samira Hersi's apartment. Low-level plainclothes police officers. Armed, as all police officers always are while on duty in Sweden, but whose sole job was observation and communication – and a show of digging a ditch on the grass verge that local council workmen would have to fill in later after completion of the observation mission.

The front-line interceptors, both uniform and SÄPO, would be deployed in their cars and unmarked vans at the district police station on Hjalmar Brantingsplatsen, a fast four minute drive from Grumstad with flashing lights and screaming sirens, or seven minutes in silent stealth mode obeying all the traffic regulations so as not to draw attention to their approach.

Winter having officially descended on Gothenburg, the city's police motorcycles and police bicycles had already been taken off the road.

Mistake number one.

Chapter 50

Asymmetrical warfare is just that – asymmetrical. You break the rules. In fact you don't even recognise the rules. You cannot match the sheer manpower and firepower of a numerically superior force so you use their size and strength against them. You go where they cannot, and you disappear where they cannot follow you. In conventional warfare, strength often means weight, and weight means slow speed, it means a traditional mind-set, an inability to think along parallel tracks.

And it was precisely parallel tracks that were going to be Adan Hamati's advantage – literally.

Everything indicated that the action was going to get moving early in the morning on the 10th of December.

Which as far as Adan Hamati and his team were concerned meant that any date and any time other than early morning on the 10th of December was perfect.

Wrong-footing the enemy, always keeping them off-balance, always doing the unexpected. By holding to a rigorous pattern of early-morning cycle rides in three different directions, Adan had ensured that this was exactly what the police expected. Which is what they were not going to get when the operation went live.

Late at night on the 9th of December, the nine remaining members of Adan Hamati's team arrived singly and in pairs at the lockup. The WiFi-linked motion-activated camera in the cab of the excavator parked beside the hastily staged road-works recorded the movements of human being and vehicle alike – as well as the occasional deer and hare making their way from one stretch of woods to the other when all was quiet.

But there was nothing odd about seeing the occasional person walking towards the block of apartment buildings – there were late shoppers, people returning from a late shift at work, people visiting friends and family. The SÄPO officer manning the screen at police HQ saw individual people walking past the road-works in both directions, he saw the occasional car drive in and out. Nothing untoward at all.

It was only when he saw a convoy of nine men's bicycles – brightly coloured in various shades of red, blue, green, yellow, silver – approaching from the direction of the row of garages, each towing a trailer, that he realised things were very untoward indeed. He scrambled frantically for his phone and, fingers trembling, hit one fast-dial number after the next to alert the powers that be that the opposition weren't playing by the rules.

As the convoy of nine bicycles whipped past the excavator, they headed straight for the rear of a small car repair workshop located where the local suburban road joined the main urban clearway. The cyclists darted round the corner where they were out of view of prying eyes, jumped off their bikes and, working swiftly, first pulled off the cycles' homemade crossbars, immediately transforming them from men's into women's cycles. They then got to work stripping off all the bright metallic contact paper, completing the conversion into dull black or dark blue cycles. Only one rider ditched his trailer, for which he would have no need. Omar Obaidi had a task which he would be carrying out all on his own, and he wouldn't need the burden of a trailer. Before unhooking his trailer, however, he reached into it and pulled out a well-filled black backpack which he strapped over his shoulders and across his midriff. Everyone crumpled up their torn-off contact paper and dumped it into Omar's trailer, along with the makeshift crossbars, and heaved the entire trailer into a large wheelie-bin. Total time: just over one minute.

They returned to the cycle track in smaller groups. There were two reasons for this. For one thing, the authorities would be looking for nine brightly coloured men's cycles with trailers travelling in a group, but one or two people on dull black or dark blue women's bikes would not arouse immediate suspicion, especially if some of them weren't towing trailers. For another, they weren't actually all heading the same way.

One pair of cyclists – a man and a woman – swept down the left-hand cycle lane parallel to the dual carriageway heading towards Hjalmar Brantingsplatsen and Götaälv Bridge – the vertically opening drawbridge that connects the island of

Hisingen with mainland Gothenburg and the downtown commercial district. The first three police cars that left the police station in convoy headed towards them and screamed past without giving them a second glance. Only when a third lone cyclist towing a trailer appeared in their headlights, following in the trail of the first two, did the officer in the lead car make a possible connection and bark orders into his radio, telling everyone to turn around and follow the bikes.

Except this was a dual carriageway and there was no way of doing a U-turn and driving against oncoming traffic without endangering life and limb. So the drivers speeded up as much as they dared on the now icy roads, surging ahead to the next intersection where they could turn around and follow the three bicyclists. They were losing valuable time. But they had sighted the cyclists and knew what they were looking for, so they decided to stay with these three and alerted the other converging police and SÄPO units to continue on to Grumstad and intercept the remaining six cyclists.

Turning around at the intersection and fishtailing down the ice-blackened road back in the direction from which they had come, it didn’t take long for the convoy of three fast-moving police cars to catch up with the rear-most cyclist, and they could see the first two up ahead too. The problem was that although they were heading in the same direction as the bikers they were now on the wrong side of the dual carriageway with its four lanes of traffic – two in each direction – separating them from the cyclists, who also had the added protection of the sturdy waist-high metal crash barrier that kept road vehicles at a safe distance from the cycle path. With frustration building up all the police officers could do was to keep pace with the bikes and monitor their progress, one team driving swiftly ahead to the next junction to see if by any remote chance it offered their squad car access to the cycle path. It didn't – because by now the cyclists, moving fast under electric power, had already gained access to the incline leading up to the bridge. And this was definitely a one-way section of road without physical access from the other side.

Götaälv Bridge is a drawbridge that opens up in the middle to allow tall cargo ships to pass safely below, but the bridge isn't manned day and night. Tall vessels have to announce the time of their arrival at least twelve hours in advance, giving the bridge operators time to summon the engineer whose job it is to safely raise the structure, first closing off the roadway in both directions with automatic barriers that descend from vertical to horizontal, barring access to cars, buses and trams – and cycles.

But it was now past ten at night and no tall vessels were due for another two days. The cycles continued speeding up the curving approach road, heading for the brow of the bridge. Soon they would be past the bridge operator's control booth and then would come the descent into downtown Gothenburg, and who knew then which of the city's many vulnerable targets would be available to them.

But they didn't go past the top of the bridge. All three cyclists stopped beside the bridge engineer's control booth and got off their bikes, unpacking what looked like containers and bottles of explosives or inflammable substances.

The bridge! It was the bridge that was the target! Götaälv Bridge is one of just two bridge links between Gothenburg's industrial heartland of Hisingen, home to Volvo and countless other small and medium-sized manufacturing plants, and the city's commercial downtown district. There was also Tingstad Tunnel which passed below the Göta River and, much further to the north and east, Angeredbro Bridge, a tall, spindly structure that connected the city's eastern suburbs with Hisingen. If Götaälv Bridge was the target of the three cyclists headed this way, it was likely that the other vital links would also be targeted. The authorities had to move fast.

Relaying information back to HQ about the scene at the apex of Götaälv Bridge and agreeing on the likelihood of the other transit points being possible targets, the police received orders to shut down access to the bridge from both sides.

Traffic came to a standstill and backed up throughout the centre of town and out along the banks of the river leading to the Stena ferry terminals that carried passengers and freight trucks to Denmark and Germany and points south throughout Europe.

Other police cars and SÄPO operatives heading to Älvsborg Bridge and Tingstad Tunnel had strict orders to lock down all approaches to these vital communication links.

Gothenburg was in gridlock.

But not for cyclists, who have the privilege of their own traffic lights, their own road signs – and their very own cycle roads, separated from vehicular traffic by sturdy steel barriers.

Two cycles towing trailers had in the meantime headed along Stålhandskegatan out towards Älvsborg Bridge, the long suspension bridge that provides the most direct route from western Gothenburg to the Volvo production plants on Hisingen. Shadowing them was Omar Obaidi on his trailer-less bicycle. He was already on the approach to the bridge, its pylons rising majestically into the sky in front of him before the roadway snaked off to the right and spanned the river.

With the Gothenburg police force playing according to rules dictated by climate, all the force's motorcycles and mountain-bikes were by now safely in winter storage, awaiting their turn to be serviced and cleaned, ready to be pressed back into service in April the following year.

But Adan Hamati and his group weren't playing by Gothenburg's weather rules. They were on two wheels. Two wheels with powerful electric motors. And the police had no way of following them.

It is of course possible for motorised vehicles to access all cycle roads in Gothenburg – including those on the city's bridges. The Swedes are always meticulous in their planning, so of course cycle paths always had a combined width that allowed access to narrow-track construction and repair equipment, mechanical road sweepers and so on.

But not wide-track Volvo and Volkswagen police cars or Mercedes-Benz police vans. In rising frustration the police swiftly and efficiently set up road blocks at either end of Älvsborg Bridge, even placing vehicles across either end of the cycle roads leading up to the bride from either side. The result was that the whole of Gothenburg now came to a complete standstill. Two patrol cars approached the cyclists from either side up onto the bridge, two shadowing their progress and two driving on the wrong side of the carriageway, heading towards them.

There was nothing any of the policemen could do to stop them. Getting out of their patrol cars and pursuing them on foot was out of the question – the suspects were on bicycles, electrically-assisted at that so their speed would leave on-foot patrolmen in their wake. They could only keep pace with them in their cars.

The two police cars coming from the mainland, the opposite direction, arrived at the scene and stopped some way ahead of the cyclists and the other two oncoming patrol cars. The officer in the lead car used his loud-hailer to instruct the cyclists to halt, or else.

Or else what? This was Sweden – you couldn't shoot a bicyclist who hadn't even broken a road traffic regulation. The bikers didn't halt but continued pedalling doggedly onward. The officers had no choice but to engage reverse and shadow their progress, shouting warnings all the while.

The other two cars came up from behind the cyclists, following their colleagues, nose to nose at a steady 25 kilometres an hour.

Also travelling at a steady 25 kilometres an hour was Omar Obaidi, in the trail of his two colleagues up ahead. He had slipped up onto the south-going cycle track on the suspension bridge as the police were setting up their roadblock on the car roadway, and he had made sure nobody would be pursuing him in a hurry: jumping off his bike, he quickly unzipped his backpack and reaching in with his thickly gloved hand, pulled out handfuls of sharp, multi-pointed tyre-shredders, which Adan Hamati had spent so many hours making from lengths of stiff steel wire back in the lockup. He threw handfuls of the vicious multi-pronged spikes across all four lanes of the roadway, spreading them far and wide across a large expanse of tarmac. This was by no means a permanent solution, but it would slow down any pursuers and give him time enough to complete his main task.

He got back onto his bike and setting its battery assistance to maximum, cruised up the incline towards the apex of the bridge and his two colleagues.

At the crown of the bridge the two cyclists had already climbed off their bikes and, reaching into their covered trailers, whipped out bottles or containers – it was difficult to see clearly in the dimly lit patch between two street lights where they had stopped. Two minutes later Omar Obaidi joined them.

Impasse.

Chapter 51

Adan Hamati, Alina Murad and Jaffar Bargouti pedalled furiously along the cycle track heading towards the Volvo complex. Along this section of the newly built route, the cycle track was hidden, it was on a lower level than the road used by the cars and trucks that drove to and fro between Volvo and the outside world. Along this stretch, Adan Hamati and the operational core of his carefully selected team were not only out of sight of the road, they also had the protection of the usual steel barrier that shielded Gothenburg's bicyclists everywhere, as well as a steep bank of gravel leading off the dual carriageway's hard shoulder down to the cycle track.

They were effectively concealed as they headed out to execute their mission. Since Adan hadn't heard a single police siren or seen the reflection of any flashing blue lights from the safety of their submerged approach route, he assumed that his two-pronged ruse had worked. And if that part of his plan had worked, then the already overworked and undermanned police would doubtless also be heading out on a wild-goose chase to 'secure' Tingstad Tunnel and Angeredbro Bridge, where he had not deployed anyone at all. He felt sorry for the Swedish police – he had no bone to pick with them, but the job had to be done. And unless they tried to stop his mission, no Swedish police officers would be getting hurt – only their professional pride would take a bit of a bashing.

All Adan Hamati had ahead of him was Volvo's admittedly highly motivated and very professional, but totally unprepared and unarmed, security force.

Approaching a long downhill stretch, he switched off the electric motor to conserve battery power and alternately coasted and pedalled lightly ahead, knowing that his two companions would do exactly the same. They still had some way to go and a lot to get done.

***

Up on Götaälv Bridge, the three cyclists set swiftly to work. They had a blazing fire going – the cheap cotton clothing that Adan Hamati had purchased had already been pre-soaked in kerosene and was now quickly set alight. The fire was burning strongly and it looked spectacular, especially as the flames darted and reflected off the glass panorama windows of the bridge operator's control cab, which magnified and multiplied the appearance of the conflagration. It was laughable really, three people on cycles and a small fire had caused one of the main arteries in Sweden's second-largest city to come to a standstill, and nothing could be done about it because, with the police barricades at the foot of the bridge on either side and traffic backed up for kilometres, the fire engines couldn't get through. Not that they would need to really, because this fire wasn't going to do any damage. It wasn't intended to do any damage because it was designed to fizzle out and die all by itself – after a respectable interval.

They wanted publicity for their cause, they wanted to show the Swedes just how desperate they were for the world to sit up and take note of the situation in Palestine and for the world community to refocus its attention there instead of wasting time on Syria, Afghanistan and elsewhere. And a big fire was just the sort of thing to grab everyone's attention. Especially when it was combined with the banner that would proclaim what the mission was all about.

***

From one of the trailers Omar Obaidi retrieved a large but lightweight silk banner, weighted at one end and sporting the Palestinian national colours in the top two-thirds of the fabric and the legend 'FREE PALESTINE' in thick black lettering on the bottom third. Working quickly, Omar hooked the top of the banner onto the bridge's uppermost guard rail and unfurled the massive length of silk fabric, where it would be visible for the whole city of Gothenburg to see when the sun rose the following morning. His part of the operation was almost over and he hoped that his teammates on Götaälv Bridge had succeeded in doing the same there. All he had to do now was to continue on down the bridge towards Kungsten and meet at the predetermined rendezvous point. The colleagues he was leaving behind were already drawing attention to the massive banner by lighting a huge fire that would be visible to the entire city – nobody would fail to get the message. Especially when combined with the third – the main – part of the message that Adan Hamati and his operatives would be handling.

Omar Obaidi got back on his bike and pedalled off down the bridge, protected from the prowling police cars by the steel barrier that shielded cyclists from motorised traffic.

What he didn't count on was the changeable early-winter weather. Up near the top of the bridge, which perches 45 metres above the swirling inky waters of the river below, the winds howling in from the North Sea can in a matter of seconds transform any moisture on the tarmac into black ice – treacherous, invisible, deadly. During the daytime, when lots of cars, buses and trucks travel up and down the road in a steady stream of traffic, the friction from their tyres and constant blasts of hot exhaust gases tend to keep the blacktop clear. And of course in icy conditions the city grits and salts the road.

But now it was night, there was very little traffic on the roadway – especially after the police had set up their roadblocks at either end – and absolutely no movement on the cycle tracks on either side of the roadway. And this late at night, the municipality wasn't going to waste its meagre resources gritting or salting the cycle tracks – that would wait until early the next morning, if the remote-access weather station indicated it was necessary.

His eyes momentarily blinded by the strobe-like cascade of flashing blue lights awaiting him at the foot of the bridge, Omar lost his concentration for one crucial split-second as he involuntarily wrenched his handlebar slightly to the right and hit a slippery patch where moisture dripping off the suspension bridge's massive steel girders had pooled on the cycle track and frozen over in a thin film of invisible black ice. That was all it took for him to lose control of his bike and he ploughed straight into the steel barrier. The shock absorbers on the front wheel dipped their maximum of 10 centimetres upon impact with the barrier, shifting Omar's balance and weight forward on the bike and throwing him in a wide vertical arc over the handlebars and steel barrier and clear into the roadway. He wasn't wearing a helmet, and truth to tell even a cycle helmet probably wouldn't have helped, since the impact caused his neck to first compress, sandwiched between his head and torso, and then buckle sideways and snap.

Omar Obaidi died before he even registered what had happened.

At the summit of Älvsborg Bridge nobody saw any of this, there was too much happening. Here too there was now a big fire going. On this bridge there was no control booth, nothing to reflect and multiply the visible effects of a massive conflagration, but that too had been catered for. The tarps covering their bike trailers had been soaked in kerosene, the trailers themselves packed with wadding in the form of old clothes, anything that would burn. The advantage of being at the highest point of both bridges spanning the wide Göta River was that the entire city of Gothenburg would get a grandstand view of what was happening up there, with dramatic-looking flames reaching into the sky.

This was going to make big headlines.

Every time the flames started to die down, one or other of the Palestinians would pick up another bottle of fuel and hurl it into the fire. One smashed and burst open, spreading vicious tongues of flame in the direction of an approaching police officer. Startled by the fresh outbreak of fire in his direction and assuming he was being targeted with Molotov cocktails he pulled out his service weapon and shouted a warning in Swedish to his attacker. The Arab, a woman, not understanding the language and seeing a gun in the officer's hand, panicked and threw a second lit bottle directly at him. In one fluid motion a second officer drew his weapon and fired three rounds in quick succession, aiming squarely for the body of the attacker, bringing her to the ground where she lay twitching ever more slowly. Seeing this, the second assailant, a man, vaulted over the steel guard rail separating the cycle track from the roadway, heading towards the first police car with a lit bottle of fuel in either hand. Both police officers shouted to him to throw the bottles over the edge of the bridge into the river and get down on his knees.

He couldn't understand their Swedish commands – and in any case he had no intentions of allowing anyone to disrupt his mission.

Taking three steps back in quick succession the police officers commanded him to heed their instructions and do as he was told. He didn't. He kept approaching the police officers with both hands in the air. And with a lit Molotov cocktail in his either hand.

The Swedish police have a very restrictive gun use policy. Had it looked like the man was going to set fire to their half-million kronor patrol car, they would have kept backing away and waited for him to act before tackling him. But he was approaching them, never faltering in his pace.

They shot him, twice each, all squarely in the torso. No time for fancy leg shots to wing him – he had to be stopped before an officer of the law was torched.

He died before hitting the asphalt.

His wife, still squirming in agony on the ground, saw this and felt the disappointment well up inside her as her life ebbed out. This wasn't the way it was supposed to be.

The flames sputtered and died down as the light faded in her eyes and she lay there, cold and still. On a deserted, icy bridge in a far-off land to which she had travelled together with her husband to gain publicity for the plight of their land.

More death.

Chapter 52

When the action went down, Benny and Amira were in their borrowed apartment on Magnetgatan in Västra Frölunda, a five minute drive from the mainland side of Älvsborg Bridge. It was Marita Ohlsson who called Amira.

"Look, this is none of my business but I thought you should know – both main bridges are out of action, apparently there's some kind of terrorist activity going on there and all the approach roads in town are blocked. I'm pretty close to you, at my gym. Want me to swing by and pick you up? I expect you may want to liaise with uniform and SÄPO to find out if these are 'your' terrorists? You know, check it out? Interested?"

Amira was very interested. So was Benny, and not just in the terrorists. After all, he wasn't working, was he? No harm in spending a bit of time in the company of the delectable Ms Ohlsson.

Throwing on their jackets and locking the front door, they ran down the stairs and walked briskly to the head of the road leading to their apartment block – this was the only way in and out by car, Marita couldn't miss them.

She was driving so fast she almost did. Did a messy three-point turn and sped back up to pick them up.

As they headed towards the area of the bridge Marita Ohlsson was on her phone, speaking via her hands-free device to a variety of uniform and SÄPO officers to get clearance for access to the scene. This was her private car, so she had no lights or siren to clear traffic out of the way, but that wasn't her main problem. Neither was authorisation to access the site. The main problem was that the roads were snarled up with traffic. Only one option remained.

Radioing ahead her intentions and without waiting for acknowledgement or permission, she slipped off the main road and headed into a maze of hilly backstreets in the somewhat seedy – but nowadays increasingly gentrified – suburbs of Sandarna and Majorna, always with the spars of the suspension bridge floating up ahead of them, beckoning like an elusive mirage. Finally they emerged from under a viaduct and raced up a short hill, veered sharp left onto the pavement and bumped up onto a paved cycle track. The neat little blue sign showed a picture of a cycle and bore the legend "Älvsborg Bridge" and "Hisingen". Marita's little blue Toyota Aygo was showing its strength – its diminutive size meant it could go virtually anywhere a bicycle could.

Which it did. It sped along the narrow cycle track and up onto the bridge, whizzing past the police car that moved out of her way on instructions from control. She now had the bridge's perimeter steel parapet on her right side, with a 45 metre drop down to the inky black waters swirling far below, and the steel protective barrier on her left, with the car roadway beyond that. As she drew up to the apex of the bridge she saw the dying embers of what had apparently been a sizable fire, and several police cars. No ambulance or fire engine had been able to get through as yet – the police were having a difficult time clearing a path from either end of the bridge to give emergency vehicles access. And the scene still needed to be secured to ensure that neither the bodies nor the bikes and trailers were booby-trapped – who knew what might be in store for unwary officers?

With immense difficulty, Marita, Amira and Benny squeezed out of the car – there really wasn't much more than a letterbox of space on either side of the car to open the doors, so Benny reached back and opened the tailgate from inside, reclining the rear left passenger seat and crawling out backwards. The women followed his example, trying to look as though they did this sort of thing all the time.

Marita presented her warrant card and introduced her two companions, saying that Benny in particular may be in a position to identify the victims. If he was able to identify them, that was his contribution over, because if he recognised them as two of the Palestinians who had illegally entered using false Syrian documents, then Amira would have a pretty good idea of what their target might be.

Benny walked over to the first body. He recognised the face. Slowly, gently, he closed the dead woman's eyes and walked over to the second body. The man was lying face down, so Benny asked a policewoman to help him turn over the body.

He couldn't recall the name but yes, this one was also definitely on the list.

As he turned away to speak to Amira he realised with a shock that the two were likely husband and wife – he couldn't be quite sure yet but once the authorities got the bodies back to the morgue and he consulted his papers, he would be able to put names to faces. Most of the group were couples, he recalled, and he could see no reason for splitting up husband and wife in the execution of their mission – whatever that mission was. It was a sobering realisation to Benny, not for the first time, that the ongoing violence between Israel and her Palestinian Arab neighbours had immeasurably long tentacles covering time and space – and lives in far-off places.

Because although he couldn't quite see the connection, one thing was absolutely clear to Benny Hart: this was a Palestinian operation and if so, it definitely had an Israeli angle. But what?

After receiving confirmation from Benny that these were indeed two of the missing Palestinians, Amira immediately made a phone call to her office and asked a simple question: apart from the Nobel awards to which the Israeli ambassador would be invited together with all other ambassadors in Stockholm, what other events involving Israelis were planned for Sweden on the 9th, 10th or 11th of December?

Prominent Israeli public figures travelling overseas are encouraged to submit their travel plans to the relevant embassy and the Foreign Ministry. This is purely a precautionary measure. They receive advice – what not to do, where not to go, what not to wear to avoid attracting the wrong sort of attention. But it also means that anyone with a big enough name would be on that schedule.

Bingo! The importer of Volvo Cars into Israel, Daniel Nimrodi, was due to visit Volvo on the morning of the 10th of December for a photo-op at which he would take symbolic delivery of the keys to a large number of cars for Israeli government officials, including the very latest armoured vehicles for the country's top three ministers, most prominent among them being the Prime Minister.

Amira Hart glanced at her watch. It was nearing eleven-thirty at night, the meeting was due to take place at ten the next morning, at Volvo Cars HQ. That meant Nimrodi was probably already in the city, unless he was flying in early the next morning. No, the official at the other end of the phone didn't know exactly when Nimrodi would be arriving, or any details of his travel plans. He wasn't a government minister or anyone significant, for goodness sake, just some self-important businessman, so would Amira Hart please get off her high horse and stop making unreasonable demands. She thanked him tersely and flipped her phone shut.

A minute later it rang. Overseas call. It was the same official. He'd looked a bit further into the whole Volvo angle and found something that might interest her: the Israeli commercial attaché from the Stockholm embassy would also be in attendance at Volvo HQ. And no, he most certainly did *not* have the travel or any other bloody plans of Israeli foreign office bureaucrats who were on overseas tours of duty – did she think he was running a travel agency or something? What she could do, he informed her coldly, was to consult with the Stockholm embassy to get those details. He gave her the number and this time she remembered to thank him politely for his assistance. Having the Israeli commercial attaché on site was an added complication – it was certainly a matter for the Swedish security agency to deal with and with a bit of leeway it could also be said to fall within her responsibility since she was on site and able to liaise between her outfit at home, uniform on the ground at Volvo and SÄPO both at HQ in Stockholm and locally in Gothenburg. If – and this was a very big if – they saw fit to accept her involvement. She would have to be as discreet and low-key as possible, and she would have to keep Benny entirely out of it – he wasn't even here in any official capacity.

Amira Hart walked back to Marita Ohlsson, who was in animated conversation with Benny.

In as few words as possible because she was convinced time was of the essence, Amira explained the situation and asked Marita Ohlsson if she could take them on to Volvo. She wanted to scout around, just wanted to see what the place looked like, what possible points of entry there could be. It was almost midnight so nothing was going to happen now, she reckoned, but if something was going down the following morning they had to quickly see the lie of the land for themselves – two potentially high-profile Israeli targets were involved, one of them a serving diplomat in Sweden, which meant that it was very much both a SÄPO and uniform police concern.

Marita made a couple of calls, explaining what they were doing and saying she would get back with information on the security status of the Volvo factory as soon as she had anything to report. She also suggested that both uniform and SÄPO send units to Volvo to liaise with Volvo's own security personnel as soon as the backed-up traffic was sufficiently dislodged to allow cars to move freely.

As they crawled back into the tiny Toyota Aygo the way they had exited it, through the still-open glass hatchback at the rear, the first emergency vehicles began to trickle through the backed-up traffic jam at the Hisingen end of the bridge approach road. Marita Ohlsson started her car engine and drove along the narrow cycle track. She had to stop as she hit the tangled mess of by now burned-out bicycles and other paraphernalia blocking her way. She powered down her window and surveyed the carnage. Bomb squad be damned, the mess had to be cleared out of the way so she could make her way through. Extremely warily, and extremely unwillingly, a couple of uniform officers dragged off the bulk of the obstruction into the roadway, slipped in under the massive steel girders separating the cycle track from the roadway. Marita Ohlsson gunned the tiny engine of her little car and headed for Hisingen and the Volvo Cars production plant.

Chapter 53

Adan Hamati and his two assistants made swift and uninterrupted progress all the way to the traffic lights where the approach road to the Volvo complex veered off to the left, with the main road heading on towards Säve Airport and all points east and north.

The cycle track rose to road elevation at the traffic lights, and the three cyclists crossed the junction and headed past the massive high-rise automated Volvo warehouse on their right. In the distance was the red bubble of the Volvo Cars Exhibition Centre where on the following day the Israeli Volvo importer would ceremoniously accept the keys to the latest batch of armoured cars for the protection of the Zionist occupiers of Palestine.

Adan Hamati glanced at the digital readout on his cycle handlebar. Apart from displaying battery status and other data, it also showed the time. Correction: not the following day, but today. It was already half past midnight.

The red dome of the Volvo Cars Exhibition Centre gleamed in the half moon as the cyclists approached. What a tantalising thought! Taking out the Zionist lackey as he proudly accepted the keys of the vehicles that would symbolise the continued oppression of the Palestinian people!

But neither Adan nor his two team members were going to do anything of the sort, much though they would have loved to. This was a mission to gain publicity. And goodwill. The Swedes were already massively sympathetic to the Palestinian cause, they weren't going to jeopardise that by killing people – if they could help it.

What Adan was going to do was create a win-win situation. The Palestinian Resistance was going to win some much-needed publicity. And Volvo was going to win a big new order for cars – only they didn't yet know it. A big new order for cars meant job security for factory workers in an industry that was chronically nervous about where the next order was coming from, how many workers were going to be laid off if more cars weren't bought to keep people in jobs.

Because Adan Hamati was going to destroy all ninety-eight new Volvos currently waiting to be shipped to Israel. That would gain the Palestinian Resistance all the publicity they needed. And because the cars could not be delivered, an order would have to be placed for ninety-eight new replacements – good news for Swedish jobs.

With an almost audible sigh of regret Adan Hamati pedalled past the exhibition centre and at the bottom of the road turned right, then left, heading towards a brightly lit, securely fenced-off open yard. Thank you Yousep Yonan – his extorted information had proved correct.

In the brightly illuminated yard were parked rows upon rows of brand-new white Volvo S60 and S80 sedans – as well as three gleaming black long-wheelbase Volvo S80 limousines. Although considerably heavier than their sedan stablemates, they sat taller off the ground – the significantly greater weight of the added armour was offset by the far sturdier suspension with which these cars were fitted.

Adan's target was in sight.

***

Marita Ohlsson's little blue Toyota Aygo pulled up at the gate of the Volvo high-rise warehouse, the first part of the huge Volvo Cars complex that she encountered after entering the premises from the public road. She got out of the car and approached the guard inside his security booth, who slid open the glass window as he eyed her. She pulled out her warrant card and showed it to him, asking him if he had noticed anything untoward that evening.

He chose not to answer her. Instead, he picked up the phone and called a number. He wanted to verify the identity of someone who claimed she was from SÄPO, who had turned up unannounced in the middle of the night, asking probing questions about security. And there were two suspicious-looking characters who were sitting in her remarkably non-official-looking car, furnishing no evidence of their identity.

Valuable minutes ticked by before the verification he needed came in. He slid open the glass window and handed back her ID card. “Sorry about that,” he said. “Can’t be too careful. So what’s this about then?”

“I’d like to ask the questions, if you don’t mind, and we don’t have a whole lot of time. Tomorrow…” she glanced at her watch, “or rather today you will be hosting a visit by some Israelis who are taking delivery of a number of cars. Where is this going to take place?”

The guard looked into the distance, towards the top of the red dome which could just be seen above the roof of the Engineering Office off to his right. “Well, it’s not here, that much I can tell you. Here we only deal with warehousing and components stocks, that kind of internal stuff. My guess is it will be down at the Volvo Cars Exhibition Centre, that’s the red bubble-shaped building behind there,” he jerked his thumb over his shoulder. “There’s nobody there right now, but if you want I can call in one of our mobile security units to meet you there if you want to check it out.”

That was exactly what Marita Ohlsson wanted. She thanked the guard for his assistance and got back into her car, following his instructions and the top of the dome that seemed to float above everything else, visible, it seemed from just about everywhere within the Volvo complex.

Waiting for them in the deserted parking lot was a Volvo XC70 station wagon equipped exactly like a police patrol vehicle, but with the words 'Volvo Security' painted on the side instead of 'Police'.

The building and its surroundings were quiet, nothing untoward had been reported either that night or the day before. Yes, this was where the handover ceremony would take place, inside that glassed-in part there where there was a permanent display of some classic Volvo models from the 1960s interspersed with cutaway sections of the company's very latest engines and transmissions. Old meets new. It was the sort of environment that visiting dignitaries loved, it gave them a feeling of heritage, of history, of doing business with a company at the cutting edge of technological development today, but with a solid background in engineering and design excellence going back seven decades or more.

The security supervisor's radio crackled. Some movement had been observed near one of the open lots where new pre-delivery cars were stored prior to shipping. Would he go have a look and report back to base?

Excusing himself, he started making his way back to his car when Benny whispered a few words to Amira who in turn spoke rapidly to Marita.

Marita called out to the security supervisor. "Mind if we tag along? We won't get in your way, it's just that we have an idea that this may be relevant to what we're working on." He shrugged and got into his car.

***

Adan Hamati sensed a car approaching, saw its flashing blue strobe lights before he heard its engine. He urged his two companions to speed up. Reaching into their trailers they each pulled out a lightweight nylon rope ladder with hooks at one end. Working swiftly they threw them over the top of the security fence and tugged on them to ensure they had fastened properly. Adan climbed up and over, pulling the ladder over to his side of the fence as he did so and waiting on the ground on the inside of the fence. Jaffar Bargouti climbed up and held his position at the top, pulling his ladder onto the other side too, while Alina Murad started handing up the equipment to Jaffar on top, who in turn relayed it down to Adan on the inside. Plastic bottles of kerosene and denatured alcohol plugged with fabric wicks. Six-pack sets of cheap but sharp steak knives with serrated edges. Several disposable lighters in a plastic bag. Sturdy straight-edge screwdrivers and hefty hammers. Three small handheld gas torches used by chefs to char meat or by keen DIY enthusiasts to strip paint off old cars or motorbikes.

The cars destined for Israel were not going to be vandalised. They were going to be destroyed. Totally. Nothing was to be salvageable. Volvo Cars would gain ninety-eight new orders. The Zionist regime would not get their cars on schedule. And the world would sit up and take notice. Already Sweden's second-largest city had come to a complete standstill. That generated publicity. This was all going to plan.

Except it wasn't. Adan Hamati didn't know it, but the mission had already cost lives up on the two bridges, and with Volvo security already on to him, there was always the risk of personal injury in any ensuing scuffle here. He shouted to Alina to reach into his cycle trailer and pull out the three powerful industrial staple-guns. If they needed to keep security at bay through physical resistance while they went about their mission, so be it.

As a showpiece for Volvo's Police Special, the company's own security vehicles are identical to the cars issued to the Swedish police from the viewpoint of technical specification. The security supervisor floored the accelerator as he saw the first intruder scale the fence and sounded both the car's siren and its bull-horn. At the same time he hit the red emergency button retro-fitted to the dash of his car that automatically alerted Volvo Security HQ via a GPS transmitter and equally automatically fed the car's precise coordinates to the system's computer. Over the built-in hands-free system he shouted to his base that intruders were penetrating the new-car compound and that all mobile security units as well as Gothenburg Police were to be alerted. This was a full-scale alert, repeat a full-scale alert, not an exercise.

Heavily laden with three adults, Marita Ohlsson's little three-cylinder Aygo struggled to keep the powerful XC70 in sight. She watched in frustration as the big station wagon surged ahead, speeding up to the perimeter fence where it looked like two or three people were in the process of entering the supposedly secure complex.

The big Volvo XC70 ploughed straight into the three cycles. Whether deliberately or because the driver had lost control was something that would never be clarified. From the other side of the fence, Adan Hamati shouted to the security supervisor in English, telling him to back off and nobody would get hurt. As Marita Ohlsson skidded to a halt mere inches away from the fence, the rear door of her car was already open and Benny Hart was leaping out of the rear seat, ready to provide assistance should the Volvo security man need any. Perched on top of the fence, Jaffar Bargouti aimed his staple gun and fired off a series of murderously sharp C-shaped steel barbs in the general direction of the two cars. He wanted to cause enough of a distraction to give Alina Murad on the outside time to scramble up the last ladder and over to the relative safety of the other side, where they would have time to execute their plan.

But Benny was a large, although inadvertent, target. First one, then another steel staple hit him with surprising force. The first tore through the shoulder of his jacket and sent a sharp spike of pain shooting down his left arm, the second barely pricked the side of his neck just below his ear. Strangely enough, this second one didn't really hurt all that much but it caused a lot of blood to gush from his neck. It was a superficial wound but it looked a lot more serious than it really was.

Seeing her brother's neck slashed once again by Palestinian terrorists, something snapped in Amira Hart. She whipped off first her woollen hat and then Marita's and held them tight against the wound in Benny's neck. She took his right hand and held it firmly against the improvised wadding and led him round to the back of the big Volvo, seating him on the ground away from the action. He protested that he didn't need looking after, told her to get out there and bring Marita to safety.

Marita had pulled out her phone and was issuing crisp instructions to whoever was on the other end, directions, current status and assessment of the danger.

The security officer got back into his car, shouting to Benny to get in the back. He stuck the automatic transmission in reverse and backed off the now mangled bikes, away from the scene of immediate danger. His job was to protect Volvo property – including the lives of anyone on Volvo property. But he wasn't going to play Hollywood hero when there wasn't a hope in hell of single-handedly tackling three opponents who seemed to be prepared for any eventuality.

He watched in horror while a brand-new white Volvo S60 went up in flames as Adan Hamati lit a Molotov cocktail and placed it under the area where he knew the car's reinforced plastic fuel tank was located. The security officer didn't know the specification of the cars parked in the compound – if they had petrol engines, they'd explode in a fireball. If they were diesels, the fuel itself was difficult to ignite but there was plenty of other stuff inside and under the car that would burn much more easily. Either way, a fire would destroy any car irrespective of its specification.

Amira pulled Marita aside and jumped into the Aygo's driving seat. Weighing less than 1000 kilograms and seemingly made of more plastic than metal, this was never going to make much of a battering ram but something was always better than nothing. With its tiny one-litre engine rasping and popping and its studded front tyres scrambling for grip on the now icy road surface, Amira banged the car into first gear and lunged for the fence. She needed to shake the assailant off the rope ladder she was climbing, before she reached the other side.

The car hit the fence full-front, causing Alina to lose her grip and slide down the ladder, entangling her right leg between two of the rope rungs. Clinging on tenaciously with her left arm she swung her right arm in Amira's direction, her right hand holding the vicious-looking staple gun.

Amira ducked below the dash panel as a dozen or more steel staples rattled against the car's windscreen, causing a maze of cracks to spider all across the glass. Amira waited until the sound abated and in one fluid movement opened the driver's door and dived out through the opening, tucking her head in and to the left in a tight somersault. The ground was hard and stony and she winced in pain as the sharp granite chips that were loosely spread along the verge beside the tarmac dug into her back, tearing through the scanty protection offered by her jacket.

Unfolding onto her feet in the same motion that had ejected her out of the car, Amira took three quick steps forward, approaching Alina Murad from her blind side, the left. With a bone-jarring strike she smashed the entire weight of her right forearm down onto Alina's right arm, dislodging the staple gun. Before her right arm had come to a standstill at the bottom of its downward arc, her left knee jerked up and struck the helplessly dangling Alina in the small of her back.

Alina Murad screamed in pain and her left hand involuntarily lost its grip on the ladder. Her upper body arched back and down, the weight of her head adding to the momentum of the pendulum effect.

There was a resounding crack and she hung there, eyes open in surprise. Awake, aware, but unmoving.

Quickly assessing the new situation, Amira reckoned the woman was going to need immediate emergency medical assistance if she wasn't to suffer permanent spinal damage. Meantime, there were still two assailants inside. Damage to property on Swedish soil – even if it was Israeli property – was none of her business. The Swedish police were more than capable of looking after their own interests. But a civilian – her brother no less – had been attacked with a potentially lethal weapon, and a serving SÄPO officer and a Volvo security official had also both been threatened and attacked. And so, of course, had she.

Amira Hart wasn't sure what domestic Swedish law said about protecting oneself in a situation of perceived danger, although she was very aware of what would apply in Israel. This wasn't Israel, however, so she couldn't act in a manner that may offend her hosts.

As things turned out, the matter was decided for her. Jaffar Bargouti, who had been waiting at the top of the fence handing down the materials to Adan and who had rapidly descended onto the inside while the two women were engaged in their battle, apparently decided that enough was enough. He didn't know who the black woman was but she had come in the company of the other woman and the blond giant, the one who was bleeding inside the Volvo security car. So she was obviously there to stop him.

It was at this moment that Adan Hamati paused between igniting his second and third car, speaking rapidly in Arabic to Jaffar and informing him that the blond man was from Shabak and that he suspected the woman was with him. They needed to be taken out.

The Palestinian couldn't fire his staple gun from behind the fence, so he climbed agilely back up the ladder to get himself into position. He needed to get up there anyway – the third ladder was still on the outside, with the wounded – or was she dead? – Alina still dangling upside-down from it, her head almost touching the ground. Jaffar Bargouti needed to cut away the ladder to deny the Zionists access to the compound.

In the distance they could all hear the wail of approaching sirens. Marita's instructions had apparently gotten through. Spurred on by the urgency of the situation, the Palestinian perched himself on the top and aimed at the black woman. The blond Israeli was out of his reach, hidden behind the bulk of the Volvo security car. But the black woman, also apparently Israeli, was in sight.

Amira dived behind the Volvo as a hail of razor-sharp metal darts spattered against the bodywork and glass. She risked a look from behind and below the rear bumper. Her attacker was apparently out of staples and needed to reload. He was reaching into a tote bag slung from his shoulder. His gloved hand came out with a handful of gleaming, evil-looking spikes which he flung out into the roadway. Dipping his hand with robotic efficiency in and out of the bag, he came up with fistfuls of spikes that he threw onto the road in every direction. Any vehicle that moved in any direction within a radius of thirty metres was going to have its tyres shredded. And anyone on foot who slipped, would meet a gruesome end.

As the sound of sirens drew ever closer, Amira shouted to the security officer and Marita to warn the oncoming emergency services not to approach in their vehicles and to be careful on foot too. As they picked their way gingerly in the direction of the sirens, watching out for the barbs that seemed to have landed everywhere, the first three police cars and two Volvo security vehicles came screaming up, diesel engines roaring powerfully.

And overlaid over it all was the sound of hissing as one tyre after another deflated and the front of each car – in the case of two of them the rear too – sank down onto its aluminium rims. Marita shouted to the officers as they opened their doors to be careful of the sharp spikes and to warn any other oncoming vehicles.

Amira wasn't particularly concerned about the torching of the cars that was proceeding apace on the other side of the fence – they were mere lumps of metal and plastic and rubber and they could always be replaced, as far as she was concerned. She was more interested in human lives, and on this side of the fence there was a woman who was still hanging upside down, eyes open but disconcertingly not making a single sound or moving. She was definitely breathing though. She had to be laid flat before her awkward position made her condition any worse. And Benny was bleeding profusely from at least one wound. And anyone moving on this side of the fence was liable to slip or tread on any of the hundreds of sharp spikes and cause themselves serious, possibly fatal, injury.

"Listen!" Amira called out in Arabic to Jaffar Bargouti. "You back away from the fence and let me bring down your friend here – she's badly injured and if we don't get her some urgent medical attention I don't know what her chances of survival will be."

While Adan Hamati continued on his macabre mission, setting fire to cars and slashing tyres and melting anything within sight with his gas-powered torch, Jaffar Bargouti replied to Amira.

"We're *shahids*, life or death doesn't matter to us so you stay where you are or there's more of this coming your way!"

"OK, die if you want," responded Amira, "but does your friend have to die in agony? Can't she die a respectable death instead of hanging upside-down, trussed up like a chicken ready for slaughter?

"All I want is to clear the area near her of these sharp spikes, then cut her down and place her on the ground so the blood doesn't continue rushing to her head. That's all. She's gasping for breath already!" Amira shouted through the fence above the noise of more police sirens approaching from two different directions.

"OK," Jaffar replied, "but that's all. You make one move towards the fence after she's down and I'll pepper you full of holes!"

Amira called over Marita and the security officer, who were closer to her than the officers in their stricken cars. They walked over carefully, looking carefully where they put each step. "We're going to bring this woman out of the ladder and lay her on the ground. I reckon she might have some serious back injury, so we shouldn't really move her, but if we don't she's going to die a horrible death asphyxiating under the pressure of her own bodily fluids."

Under the watchful eye of the Palestinian on the other side of the fence, they struggled with the injured woman's dead weight as they tried to extricate her from the tangled ladder. As soon as they touched Alina she started screaming in agony, her body arching this way and that. Above the cacophony Amira felt a sense of relief flood over her – it wasn't her back after all. Alina screamed to them in Arabic to leave her shoulder be. A dislocation. OK, incredibly painful, but not serious. Amira didn't feel she had to be too mild with Alina after all – serve her right for the mayhem she and her partners had caused. After they placed Alina on the bare ground, the security officer went back to his car and returned with a couple of stout black cable ties, industrial strength. He bound the woman's feet with one and was reaching for her wrists when Amira put a hand on his shoulder and told him to stop – Alina Murad had a dislocated shoulder and it would be agony for her to have her hands wrenched together in makeshift handcuffs. Reluctantly the security officer agreed and backed away.

More police cars were arriving, parking well away from the scene. Seeing two bodies on the ground – one lying flat and the other leaning out of the Volvo security car and bleeding profusely, some of the officers drew their weapons and held them in readiness. Seeing this the Palestinian on the inside reached into his bag to reload his staple gun. When the officers shouted to him to stop and raise his hands in the air, he ignored them and continued, pulling out a black plastic cylinder pre-packed with staples. It looked for all the world like the barrel of a handgun and the officers didn't hesitate. One dropped to her knee and took aim, while her male colleague fired two rounds in the direction of, but not directly at, the suspect. Amira shouted to him in Arabic that the police wanted him to freeze, put his hands in the air.

But either he was beyond caring, or he couldn't discern who was saying what in the noise and confusion and the flashing strobe lights and the never-ending wail of sirens. Whatever the reason, he continued to load his staple gun and when he was finished he swept it from left to right in the direction of the assembled officers.

The policewoman fired two rounds from her handgun, one missing its mark but the other hitting him in the fleshy part of the thigh. It must have hit a major blood vessel because even through his multiple layers of clothing it was easy to see a huge deep red, almost black, spread of blood spilling down along his leg and onto the frosty ground. He dropped to the ground, leaning on his uninjured knee, then toppled over and lay still.

Shouting to Marita to explain who she was and for the police to hold fire, Amira clambered up the remaining rope ladder and made her way to the flickering image of Adan Hamati as he leapt nimbly from one conflagration to another, alternating Molotov cocktails with knives plunged into tyres and gas-torching plastic panels as he went.

At the top of the fence she shouted to Marita to get Volvo Security to open up the gate for vehicular access to the compound, but that nobody should enter yet – the danger was too great with Hamati still on the loose. She yanked the ladder up and over onto the inside of the fence and shinned down it.

Seeing Adan Hamati at work in the middle distance, she made her way towards him. By now about ten or twelve cars were burning furiously, and he was working swiftly and efficiently. Damage to property be damned, this was now personal. Her brother had been targeted, and she had distinctly heard Adan order both Benny and herself killed. His partners were out of the equation, but Adan Hamati was still very much in control and if he weren't stopped there was every reason to believe that both she and Benny were at personal risk. Surely even the Swedish authorities would recognise that the man represented a clear and imminent danger to the two Israelis – while they were on Swedish soil.

Amira Hart went after Adan Hamati.

Chapter 54

The security gate leading into the compound of delivery-ready cars was finally unlocked and both Volvo Security and police personnel poured in, staying just inside the gate while waiting for the fire service to arrive. Like many large industrial concerns, Volvo has its own fire service, but it is only equipped to serve as a first-response unit while the municipality of Gothenburg's fire engines make their way out to the large, sprawling Volvo complex.

Accordingly, the Volvo fire truck was first on the scene and, ignoring the burning cars nearest the fence because there was nowhere for those fires to spread except the empty open road, turned its hoses on the heart of the conflagration, where Adan Hamati was still at work setting fire to one car after another.

As luck would have it the first blast of the high-pressure jet knocked him off his feet and washed him out into an aisle between two rows of parked cars. Amira darted quickly in his direction and was relieved to see that the stream of extinguishing foam had swung away from Hamati and was now being trained on a group of cars burning next to a row of untouched vehicles. Prevention was apparently the name of the game for the fire crew.

Amira raced up to Hamati as he was lying on the ground, spitting out mouthfuls of bubbly white foam, and without breaking stride gave him a hard kick in the groin, then danced around to his left and planted a heavy kick into his ribs.

As he lay writhing on the ground she put all her weight behind her right knee and dropped it like an axe squarely into his abdomen. Even Amira could see that his face had gone deathly white from the force of the blow, the breath totally knocked out of his body. This wasn't going to last, of course – he would soon regain his breath and he was a bigger and heavier, and probably also far stronger – fighter than she was. So she quickly bundled him flat onto his stomach and, making sure his right arm was pinned uselessly under his own body, she placed one knee into the small of his back and dug it in. At the same time, she grabbed hold of his left hand and twisted his arm back up towards the back of his head.

He wasn't going anywhere. But that didn't mean he wasn't going to try. He bucked and shoved as much as his trussed-up position would allow, but that only meant his arm hurt indescribably. He decided to suffer in patience the humiliation of being attacked and overcome by a woman. Not just any woman, but a Jewish one and, to make matters worse, a black woman.

Amira wasn't sure how long she'd be able to keep Adan Hamati subdued, but she decided she'd keep his mind occupied in the meantime, until the police arrived to relieve her. Problem was, they were on the ground in one of several dozen rows of parked cars, and unless someone walked into their particular row, they would remain concealed. And there was scarcely any point in shouting, what with the throb of the fire truck's diesel engine and the roar of its pumps and compressors, and the chaotic wail of police and other sirens.

Amira Hart leaned close to Adan Hamati's and spoke. "Why?" she asked. "Why all this mayhem? You want to destroy a few cars? You don't get your fill destroying cars by throwing rocks at them in Jerusalem?"
"Bitch!" he hissed back at her. "This is nothing to do with cars. This is to draw the world's attention to what you pigs do to us in our homeland. Palestine is ours. Ours!" he shouted. "What business do you have to be there? Go back to Russia and America and Germany and Lithuania!" he was fairly screaming now. "You don't belong in Palestine. Look at you – you come from Ethiopia. Go home!"

Amira had heard it all before. Most Israelis had heard reasoning of this kind, specious arguments that had little to do with fact. She reckoned a short history lesson wouldn't be amiss, even though the classroom more resembled a scene from the Apocalypse as fires raged all around them and the wails of police and fire service sirens lent an other-worldly aura to the proceedings.

"Listen to me instead of speaking nonsense," she said. "What's your name? Hamati. Do you even know where your name comes from? Hama. The city of Hama. Hama is in Syria. Your father's folks came from Syria. No," she raised her

voice. "Don't interrupt me, you know it's true. If we Jews don't belong in our country because we once came from other countries, then nor do you or anyone else in your family – your family of Hama émigrés. And how about that poor woman out there?" she continued. "No, she's fine, it's only a dislocated shoulder. Her married name is Murad. That indicates her husband's family originated in the Yemen – that's a thousand kilometres away across the sands of Arabia, for heaven's sake! And look at Gaza – half the families there are called al-Masri. Come on, surely you know Arabic well enough to know al-Masri is Arabic for 'the Egyptian'? And Hamid al-Masri is a minister in your Hamas government there. You too are a nation of émigrés, yet you point the finger at us."
"Garbage!" he raged back at her. "We are Arabs, we were the original occupiers of Palestine."

"Garbage yourself," she hurled back at him. "There – you used the word correctly for once in your lifetime: you *occupied* Palestine, throwing out the indigenous Jewish population and clearing it for the Muslims. Today this is called ethnic cleansing, yet that is the term you use for us – even though twenty percent of the population of our Jewish state consists of Arabs, both Christian and Muslim. How many Jews do you have in your Palestine? I'll tell you: not a single one. And you're chasing out all the Christians too. Your religion is only 1400 hundred years old, ours is more than 3000 years old – are you so bad at mathematics that you can't see that if anyone came, displaced and occupied Palestine, it's you? You people occupied the Jewish provinces of Judea and Samaria, which you called the West Bank, and ethnically cleansed us from there – you killed hundreds of civilian Jews in places like Hebron and Safed as long ago as 1927 – was that because you could predict that forty years in the future, in 1967, we'd take back the two Jewish provinces from your illegal occupation and put our people back in their own homes – the homes you stole from us with Jordan's help in the 1948 war? We take back what was ours – even by UN charter and by the League of Nations charter before that – and you have the cheek to call *us* 'occupiers'? You're not even logical!" she barked at him.

"Logic?" he shouted up at her. "You want to talk logic? How logical is it that you build walls to keep us at bay? What do you think we are, dogs?"

"Typical!" she snarled back at him. "Beautiful, just keep going – reversing cause and effect. We didn't build walls or fences without reason. We built them to keep you from your favourite hobby – blowing up children, pensioners, shoppers, buses, cars. In Tel Aviv, Jerusalem, Haifa. *Haifa*, for God's sake!" she yelled at him. "Half the population of Haifa is Arab Muslim, and still you blow up civilians in restaurants and buses in Haifa. You no longer know what you're doing, it's violence for the sheer pleasure of violence, it's your drug!"

"We wouldn't have to blow up anything if you just left our homeland and went back to your homes in Ethiopia and Latvia and Germany and America. You don't belong here!" Adan Hamati grunted back at her.

Amira Hart wasn't prepared to give an inch of ground, this was idiotic reasoning. "This is our home. It was our home 2000 years before Islam was even invented – in a desert a thousand kilometres away in Arabia. And in modern times, just 100 years ago, the world community recognised our claim to our homeland. And in even more modern times, not even 70 years ago, the UN – your sacred cow which gives you billions of dollars year in, year out! – officially recognised the Jewish homeland of Israel. Your problem is that it is the homeland of the Jews. You hate Jews, you're nothing but a simple, primitive racist, and that goes for every one of your people who refuse to recognise the Jewish state of Israel within any – ANY – boundaries. Because that's what this is about. It's not about land, it's about racism. Your Arab racism against Jews, and against black Jews like me in particular. We know what you do to black African Muslims who seek asylum in Egypt – your lovely Muslim Egyptians rape and murder them by the thousands."

"You reckon we are racists?" he hurled back at her. "In all wars throughout history the victors have always raped the vanquished, but the Zionist army is so racist it won't even touch, let alone rape, our Palestinian women. I've seen a PhD thesis that said exactly the same thing."

"You're mad!" exclaimed Amira. Who in their right minds got upset because their womenfolk *weren't* raped? This was reverse logic in absurdum!

"That's idiotic," she spat out. "As usual you people just look for any excuse to perpetuate the conflict, no matter how ridiculous your reasoning! For you, the non-existence of rape is evidence of racism? Do me a favour!

"The truth is," she went on, "and you know this yourself, that you simply need to keep the conflict going because you see that wherever we Jews went we were welcomed, we worked hard, we studied, we integrated, we contributed. But you people, you contribute nothing, you are hated by your own Arab brethren, who want nothing to do with you. Because you're lazy, you sit around expecting US and UN and EU handouts. That's why seven decades have passed since the date on which we got our independence and you idiotically declined to have your own independence alongside us on exactly the same date. You didn't want Arab Palestine as long as there were Jews in the region – that's why your people are still in refugee camps in Arab countries all over the Arab world. In Lebanon Palestinians are not even allowed to have certain jobs or own property. Now *THAT's* racism! But you don't talk about that, do you? It's an inconvenient truth. You're still in camps in Lebanon, and in Syria, and in Jordan, and in Egypt, even in the Palestinian Authority territory. The only – the *ONLY* – country in the region where there are no Arab refugees, only Arab citizens with full voting rights, is Israel. The Jewish state. We spend our time building our society and our people and our country, whereas you spend your time and the resources donated by the rest of the world trying to destroy us and keeping yourselves in abject misery into the bargain. We travel the world selling our high-tech products, you travel the world trying to persuade people to boycott our high-tech products – the products that keep the Western world ticking, from computers to agriculture to medical devices to clean water. How about actually producing something positive instead?"

Amira Hart leaned harder into Adan Hamati's back and spoke slowly and clearly into his ear, enunciating every single word as though her life depended on getting it right. Perhaps in a way she felt that she needed to give a voice to so many decades of frustration with a people who just didn't seem to be able to listen, and right now she had literally a captive audience. "You need the conflict to continue so the world will keep funding the refugee camps; this UN-funded reservoir of resentment and indoctrination and 'martyrs' and hatred and racism. 600,000 Arab refugees in 1949 – from the war *you* started – have become five million today. While 850,000 Jewish refugees from Arab countries, kicked out as punishment for the creation of the State of Israel, have become zero today. We haven't had refugee camps for Jews in Israel since the 1970s, when the last few were torn down and everyone was housed in proper homes. Our only refugee camps today are for the black African Muslims who are fleeing Arab-on-Black-Muslim pogroms, people making their way to the only country in the region that will give them asylum – the Jewish state of Israel. You know – the country you accuse of being an 'apartheid' state! Stop fooling yourself – you *need* this conflict, you can't afford to let it die down."

It was as she finished speaking that Adan Hamati caught her by surprise, turning into rather than away from the direction in which she was twisting his arm and bucking her off his back. As he scrambled to his feet he half-turned, landing her a massive blow to the side of her head that knocked her out cold. When she finally came to she was seeing double, and she felt that the top of her head was being wrenched off the rest of her body. Gasping with the most pain she had ever felt in her life, Amira Hart sat still, her entire body trembling both from the shock and the pain, waiting for her focus to return to normal.

One thing she was already sure of, however. She was seeing two of everything, but she couldn't even see one of Adan Hamati.

He had vanished into thin air.

Chapter 55

As Amira Hart stumbled to her feet and made her way to the nearest police officers, she saw Marita and Benny talking frantically to a group of people who were not in uniform. Obviously some of Marita's SÄPO colleagues. The traffic backlogs leading to the bridges were obviously clearing. Marita redirected her steps towards them. Benny ran to her, wincing with every step. "How are you, where's Hamati?" demanded Benny.

"First things first," answered Amira. "How are your injuries?" She looked at his neck.

"This looks way worse than it is," he said, gingerly fingering his neck. "It was just a nick really but they've put a first-aid dressing on it. The shoulder is going to need some proper treatment. Nothing serious, but they want to clean it up and check on my tetanus jabs. I'll go in later. *Nuuu*, where's Hamati, did you see him?"

Amira Hart explained what had happened. Marita immediately got onto her phone and issued an alert.

Amira turned to look at Alina, who was now sitting in the rear of an open ambulance, her wrists together and placed in her lap. The medics had apparently popped her shoulder joint back into place. It couldn't have been very pleasant at all, but she looked OK. "I want to talk to Alina Murad," Amira said to Marita. "Can you square it with the cops?"

Marita went off and returned a minute later, nodding. Amira set off in the direction of the ambulance, and Benny walked at her side.

"Where do you think you're going?" she stopped and looked at her brother.

"I want to question her role in this," replied Benny.

"First, you're not entitled to do so. This is Sweden. Second, as far as she's concerned you killed her husband – she won't say a word with you present. You'll be lucky if she doesn't scratch your eyes out. I'll go alone. She doesn't know who I am and I don't look anything like you." And with that she turned on her heel and walked off. Benny sighed – his sister was very irritating when she was right.

He brightened immediately. At least that gave him some time in the company of the highly appealing Marita Ohlsson.

Amira climbed into the ambulance. Alina Murad eyed her coldly.

"What?" she demanded.

"Nothing really," replied Amira. She was tired. Physically tired, tired of the constant death-dance that seemed to be the unchanging lot of the symbiotic Israeli-Palestinian relationship. "When does all this end?" she asked, more to herself than in the expectation of any answer from the Palestinian woman.

"When your people stop pursuing my people," came the prompt answer. "And when your people stop occupying my people's land."

What was the point, thought Amira to herself. She had been through all this so many times – most recently just a few minutes ago with a Palestinian who seemed to have vanished off the face of the planet. Surely Alina herself understood the significance of her married name – logically it meant that she and her people too didn't belong in Palestine, which meant that either everyone had a rightful place there, or nobody did. Either it was home to everyone who called it home, however or whenever they had arrived there, or it was not home to anybody and was therefore destined to be fought over for all eternity, each side denying the right of the other to the privilege of a life lived in peace and harmony – or at least the permanent absence of war. Even that would be better than the current, everlasting low-level war of attrition that periodically exploded into intifadas, incursions, terrorism, wars, occupation – there were as many names for it as there were points of view.

And that perhaps was the whole point, thought Amira. There were so many points of view because the land represented the hopes, the aspirations, the cultures and religions of so many disparate narratives.

She shook her head despondently. "That's rubbish and you know it. We have our land. It was legally agreed by the UN – quite apart from the fact that it is our age-old historic home and the home of our religion. The UN also granted you your own country alongside ours – alongside ours, not instead of ours – on the very same date in 1948. But your people refused – you didn't want your Arab Muslim country if it meant accepting the existence of a Jewish country. That's your problem, not ours. Stop the violence, the indoctrination, the hatred, and we'll each have a country. But continue it and the death-dance continues. We both know the steps, we both dance to the same music, we both know what the other will do, what the other wants, and yet we continue as before, hoping that somehow the result will be different. Isn't it a sign of madness – doing the same thing over and over again and expecting a different result?"

Alina Murad looked at Amira with a faint smile of amusement. "You think this is a dance? For us it is a matter of liberty and destiny, and you think it's a dance? You Zionists have a funny idea of what makes good entertainment." She snorted derisively.

"You know exactly what I mean," retorted Amira, stung by the tone of the Palestinian's voice. Alina Murad was right, in a way. Not in terms of content – no, the Israelis and Palestinians were indeed locked in a macabre death-dance and something needed to be done to break the stalemate. That was up to the politicians, she was merely a lowly law-enforcement officer. But in terms of the way each saw the problem, the way each verbalised the running sore that was the Palestinian-Israeli conflict. Israelis were by and large pragmatic, realistic. You had a problem, you identified it, and you went to work to solve it in the most resource-efficient way possible.

The Palestinians had a far more emotive perspective. Like most people in the Arab world, for them symbolism was everything, truth was less important. This didn't mean they were congenital liars. But for them symbolism was a more important commodity than whether you kept to what you promised. There was no value judgement involved – you could agree to attend a meeting and simply not turn up, and nobody would think the worse of you. But woe betide the person who issued a public insult that offended someone's status.

And to denigrate the life-and-death struggle for hegemony in the part of Mandate Palestine that both Arabs and Jews regarded as theirs by referring to that struggle as a dance, well, that could be seen as insulting. Amira bit her lip. Alina was right. It was an offensive choice of words. Although not in terms of content.

"You know very well what I mean. We do the same things time and time again, and we make no progress. You are aided by massive UN and EU propaganda and financing that you exploit mercilessly," she said.

"And you are aided by massive US propaganda and financing that you exploit mercilessly," replied Alina.

"The difference is that we are always ready to compromise," said Amira, "whereas all we get from you is increased intransigence."

"Really?" responded Alina. "Defending our national rights is not intransigence, it is pride in our heritage."

"Oh yeah? And where does that heritage come from, Alina?" replied Amira. "Your own husband's family's 'heritage' is Yemen, your friend Adan Hamati's 'heritage' is Syrian – and there are Palestinian family names that trace clear routes to Iraq, what is today Saudi Arabia, Jordan, Egypt, Somalia. So just why is it that you're OK with all these Arab foreigners flooding into the region over the past few decades, but when Jews move to the same region, home to Israel which the UN itself ratified, they have no rights?"

"Not Israel. Palestine," replied Alina.

"Whatever you and I want to call it, eventually we are going to have to agree to live side by side. You're there. We're there. We're OK for you to be there. But you don't agree for us to be there," said Amira. "That's the whole problem. There simply has to be a future without never-ending violence. Ultimately both you and I know it has to end with an accommodation of some kind – for the sake of the next generation or the one after that. It has to end some time."

"It'll end when you leave and give us back our land," replied a sullen Alina.

"And there we are again, back once again at the starting-point," said a despondent Amira. She paused for a long while. Then said: "You'll be sent back now".

"Sent back? To what?" Alina hurled back scornfully. "To another so-called 'questioning' by the police that will somehow mysteriously end with me in a body-bag while in custody in a police station, and nobody to take the blame? That's what you want to send me back to face? No thanks." And with that she hurled herself at Amira, flailing punches at Amira's face before pushing her backwards out of the ambulance where Amira Hart fell hard onto her back.

Even as she was falling backwards, spreading her hands to her rear to try and cushion her fall as Alina Murad shot out of the rear of the ambulance, Amira registered in shock that the Palestinian woman hadn't been secured, she was not handcuffed! Just because her hands had been held closely together in her lap after the medics popped her dislocated shoulder back into place, Amira had assumed that she had been restrained. The sheer incompetence of the Swedish police! This was mind-boggling!

Amira didn't have time to think of anything else before she landed with a painful thud on her back and rolled immediately to her right to absorb the fall and utilise the momentum of her motion to get back onto her feet.

Alina was running fast in the direction of a group of police officers shouting at them in Arabic. As she reached the first one she lunged for his sidearm. Failing to release it smoothly from its holster she struggled before freeing it and gave the surprised policeman a hard kick in the shin that doubled him over.

Feeling frantically with her index finger for the safety catch of the unfamiliar weapon she waved the pistol in the direction of the officers, shouting all the while in Arabic.

A SÄPO officer off to one side unholstered his pistol and pointed it at Alina, ordering her to drop the gun. She spun round in his direction, her gun hand still at chest height. The agent hesitated only a split-second and squeezed off three rounds, advancing as he fired. The first round hit Alina in the shoulder and spun her round, the second missed as she was turning.

It was the third bullet that did the fatal damage. By the time it hit home Alina Murad had been spun forty-five degrees by the impact of the first round so she was now fully facing the SÄPO security agent. His third round punctured her lung and she staggered back, blood bubbling up between her lips. In frightening slow motion her gun arm dropped, she fell symmetrically to both knees, swayed, and then toppled over onto her back, her legs tucked unnaturally behind her back.

Amira screamed as she rushed up. “Don’t shoot! Don’t shoot!” She ran up, prised the gun out of Alina’s hand and threw it away so no over-eager officer would be tempted to shoot.

Bloody froth was bubbling out of Alina’s mouth and her face had turned a ghostly white. Her right hand was trembling as she tried vainly to grasp Amira’s coat, hand, anything.

“Shh, don’t say anything,” said Amira. “I’m going to move your legs so you’re more comfortable.” She slipped both her arms under the surprisingly light torso of Alina Murad and gently slid her right arm under her, straightening the woman’s legs out from under her. Amira laid her back down on the ground.

Turning her head she called out “Blankets! Get me some blankets! And paramedics, where are the paramedics”? she yelled.

Alina was trying to speak. Her eyes were searching out Amira’s. “No more dancing,” she whispered, barely audibly.

The faintest of smiles flitted across her face, replaced immediately by a look of horror. Amira knew what was coming. The Israelis and Palestinians had been locked in their mutual death embrace for so many decades now that they were both intimately conscious of each other's innermost thoughts and fears.

And Alina Murad was afraid of dying in a far-off country, far from the land of her forefathers, buried in a grave that her children would never be able to visit.

Amira Hart squeezed Alina's hand gently, seeking out what little light there still remained in her eyes. "I give you my word you will go home. You will be buried beside Haydar. Your children will be able to go to your grave – if I have to pay for it myself. I promise."

Alina winced, perhaps she had heard, had understood. It was impossible to tell. Amira leaned closer and whispered quietly into her ear. "Your children will be safe. They will come to no harm. Nobody in Israel will target them. May Allah protect them and grant them long and happy lives. Go in peace sister!"

And with that Alina Murad closed her eyes, sighed, and was no more.

Chapter 56

The aftermath was surprisingly anticlimactic. The first police car to make its way up Älvsborg Bridge from the Hisingen side hit the bed of tyre-shredders and came to an ignominious halt. The police spent valuable time and resources they could ill afford clearing up the treacherous spikes. Their irritation was reaching bursting-point.

If the aim of the coup had been to win over more Swedish sympathy through the use of 'soft tactics' it had failed abysmally: the police and SÄPO did not appreciate the disruption to the city's routine. They already had their hands full dealing with the increasing radicalisation of Muslim extremists living in Gothenburg and elsewhere in Sweden. So the import – illegally, at that – of even more troublemakers simply got their collective backs up. The already negative attitudes of many police officers, fire crews and ambulance paramedics were further entrenched by this incident. In many parts of Sweden's high-immigrant-density suburbs the emergency services were routinely subjected to stone-throwing attacks and this simply cemented their conviction that it wasn't social deprivation among Muslim immigrants that was the problem, it was the religion they followed that was the heart of the matter. These ten were Muslims who had come from Palestine to spread chaos in faraway Sweden. There was no other way to see it. What they all had in common was their religion.

SÄPO in particular was angered beyond anything the intelligence service had experienced since the assassination of Sweden's Foreign Minister Anna Lindh a decade earlier. SÄPO had ultimate responsibility for security at the Nobel awards ceremony and their resources and patience were already stretched thin. Having to divert scarce time and manpower to counter the lunatic antics of a bunch of Arab hoodlums didn't exactly earn the Palestinian cause any brownie points in Sweden's security establishment.

Truth to tell, Sweden's security establishment was staunchly pro-Israel. Not officially, of course. And it was definitely nothing the political elite would sign off on. But the country's politicians knew nothing of real life, in the eyes of the police and SÄPO. They didn't have to deal with the raging epidemic of rapes and violence and drug wars and car thefts and arson that somehow always seemed to take place in areas with high concentrations of immigrants. Or "Muslim-adjacent ghettos" as one police old-timer drily observed.

SÄPO decided to clamp a lid on the whole sorry incident.

The gutted cars were quietly hauled away by Volvo. The banner was quickly hauled off Älvsborg Bridge – the banner intended for Götaälv Bridge had never even been deployed – and the fires there and on Götaälv Bridge were quickly extinguished. The tangle of cycles and trailers was carted off in a panel truck and dumped in the Högsbo metal recycling station as soon as it opened at seven the following morning, and the bodies of the dead Palestinians were swiftly removed to the morgue at Sahlgrenska University Hospital, listed for administrative purposes as John Doe 1, 2, 3 and 4 and Jane Doe 1, 2, 3, 4 and 5. Not even a name to their credit. Well, they had entered on false papers, and SÄPO only had the Israeli Mossad agent and her Shin Bet brother's word regarding their claimed real identities.

The roads were cleared, the news media informed that an electrical fault had by strange coincidence caused fires to break out almost simultaneously in the new lightning conductors recently attached to the base grounding-plates of both bridges. Perhaps they had been incorrectly fitted. An investigation would be initiated and a report would be issued in the fullness of time.

Volvo Cars put out a press release early the following morning to the effect that an electrical fault in a security camera guarding the perimeter fence around its delivery-ready cars had caused a short-circuit and unfortunately set a small number of cars alight. New build orders had already been entered into the computerised production system and the relevant cars were scheduled for manufacture three weeks hence, just after the automaker's short Christmas and New Year production break. The ninety-eight cars were not due to be shipped to Israel until the twenty-eighth of January in any case – the CEO of AutoSwed was only visiting Sweden and Volvo Cars HQ for a publicity shot during which he would symbolically receive the keys of one of the cars to be delivered the following month. This sort of PR event happened all the time with importers and dealers large and small from all over the world.

The world media that had gathered in Stockholm, just 550 tantalising kilometres away to the east, never even got wind of the Palestinian angle. All the domestic Swedish media reported on the traffic-jams that had been caused by the fires on the two bridges and in City Hall there were calls for city engineers to participate in a conference (oh what a surprise) at which the exact workings of the lightning conductors could be explained.

The planned Palestinian PR coup died before it was born. Violence as a tool for publicity – even 'soft' violence – had failed. Abysmally.

Behind the scenes – and totally off the record – the Director-General of the Swedish Migration Board was summoned to a conference.

No, not another one of these interminable time-consuming conferences for which Swedes had such a penchant.

This conference had just three participants, and nobody was there to take the minutes. Not even a digital recording, audio or otherwise, was made or kept of the meeting.

The Swedish Prime Minister, the Director-General of Swedish Security Service SÄPO, and the Director-General of the Swedish Migration Board.

The meeting was short, it was acrimonious, and it left the head of Sweden's immigration organisation wondering whether this wouldn't be a good time to look for a new job. Preferably overseas. She left the conference room after six minutes, heading for the ladies' restroom where she repeatedly threw up into a toilet bowl.

The gist of that meeting was really very simple. The Swedish Migration Board was an absolute waste of money and would soon lose its entire funding and all its staff – that's how disgracefully it was run. The only thing that kept the PM from closing it down immediately was the political backlash that would undoubtedly ensue from making so many people unemployed overnight.

The PM had it on good authority that ten Palestinian terrorists had entered Sweden on false Syrian papers. That they were false was something even a child ought to have been able to see, let alone the massively funded, useless state-run organisation that was the Migration Board. The Migration Board, the PM went on, had surprised not only the Swedish government but also the entire Syrian nation, which was in the throes of breakup as that country descended ever further into the anarchy of civil war, by announcing that anyone who could show Syrian refugee status at a Swedish border would be granted not just temporary asylum but permanent residency. With immigrant-dense suburbs in Stockholm, Gothenburg, Malmö and elsewhere increasingly resembling Dante's Inferno as bouts of arson repeatedly seared into the public consciousness, just how many more potential troublemakers was the Director-General planning to import? Where were they going to live? Who was going to finance them? Where were they going to work? And where was the money going to come from to keep an eye on potential subversives?

Which was where the Director-General of SÄPO weighed in. Exactly what kind of checks did the Migration Board have on incoming asylum-seekers? Even the SÄPO chief's 80-year-old über-Swedish Aunt Dora knew there was a difference in vocabulary, in cadence, in accent, in style between Syrian Arabic and West Bank Palestinian Arabic – how on earth could the Migration Board not run so elementary a check as this before admitting into the country people who claimed to be Syrians? How many other potential terrorists had Madam Director-General admitted into Sweden for his agents to follow up and track down? How many from al-Qaeda? From Islamic Jihad? From Hezbollah? From Hamas? Could he count on her to divert fifty percent of her annual budget to his department so he could attend to the job of cleaning up the mess she had caused through her sheer incompetence? And what of the political fallout of removing unwanted immigrants after the Migration Board had already generously assured them they could stay – not only they but their dependents too?

The PM re-entered the dressing-down: the political cost was ultimately going to have to be his, as Prime Minister. But he was going to make sure that unless this mess was sorted out quickly – and at source – he was going to be looking for a new Director-General for the Swedish Migration Board. By the end of next week.

With a curt nod in the stunned woman's direction, both men pushed back their chairs, got up and strode out of the room. Their respective bodyguards had not been allowed into the conference room, they were waiting attentively outside.

The Director-General of the Swedish Migration Board had not yet uttered a single word since entering the conference room apart from a muted "Good morning".

She only just made it to the lavatory before she retched up her breakfast.

Chapter 57

If there is one chink in Israel's armour that makes the country truly vulnerable, at least in terms of its psyche, it is bureaucracy.

Sweden wanted to repatriate the bodies of the dead Palestinians. The Swedish Foreign Minister, one of the Palestinian Authority's staunchest supporters in Europe, insisted they be returned "home to Palestine where they could be given a decent burial as was befitting their proper status". The term "proper status" raised more than a few eyebrows in Swedish law enforcement circles, which had had to deal with the events of the 9th and 10th of December that had resulted in several deaths and the total meltdown of Sweden's second-largest city. Indeed, the running joke in some SÄPO circles was that the wrong Swedish Foreign Minister had been assassinated – an oblique reference to the tragic murder of Foreign Minister Anna Lindh back in 2003 by a deranged Serb immigrant to Sweden.

The Jordanians refused to allow the coffins to be flown to Amman because the deceased were not Jordanian citizens. The Palestinian Authority was not keen on pressurising the Jordanian monarch on this issue, either, because the PA did not want it to look as though it had been in any way involved in the mission in Sweden. Sweden was one of the Palestinian Authority's foremost diplomatic and financial allies and had a documented history of overt animosity towards Israel, despite the excellent industrial, commercial, academic, cultural, military and security/intelligence relations between Stockholm and Jerusalem. Especially the security and intelligence aspect – the single most important reason why Sweden had not yet officially succumbed to the immense pressure of Islamisation that was sweeping throughout the Scandinavian country. The Palestinian President was not about to jeopardise Sweden's goodwill.

The Hamas regime in Gaza said they would be happy to give the deceased state funerals with full military honours, but Egypt, facing its own immense security problems with the radical Islamist regime in the Gaza Strip, wasn't about to help them gain the symbolic upper hand over the Palestinian Authority in the West Bank.

So it was up to Israel to overcome its bureaucratic hurdles and admit the coffins and transit them quickly and quietly to Ramallah for the Palestinian President to give them decent burials.

The Israelis were very reluctant to have any part of this. It wasn't their pigeon and never had been, not from the start and not at the end. The deceased had not even committed any crime in Israel, so it was none of their business. They could stay in Sweden for all they cared. But the Jewish state was also extremely susceptible to the horrors of non-closure – not having bodies to bury when violence overtook fighting men and women. Israel still had several soldiers and airmen missing in action and some of its Arab neighbours dangled the possibility of their lives, deaths, corpses or even just information about their fates as bargaining chips. The Jewish state would not engage or be seen to engage in this kind of depraved trade.

So Jerusalem authorised the entry of the coffins, provided the Swedish state paid for their delivery to Israel. Israel would pay for their transfer to the Palestinian Authority – there was little hope of persuading the PA to pay for the transport of its dead citizens when it wouldn't even pay its own electricity and other utility bills, which were several years in arrears and running up a debt to Israel in the hundreds of millions of shekels.

There was one proviso: the Palestinian Authority had to conduct low-key burials, no state-wide propaganda exercises.

Nothing could be closer to the PA's heart so for once the two uneasy neighbours actually found something on which they could agree.

One coffin that did not return, however, was that of Adan Hamati. Because no body had ever been found. He had disappeared.

Disappeared, that is, in Sweden. He turned up suddenly several months later in Gaza, courtesy of one of the myriad tunnels that the Hamas terrorist organisation had excavated under the sands south into Egypt and east into Israel. If Adan

Hamati was able to get into Gaza from Egypt, he was probably also able to surface in Israel via one of the many subterranean 'toll roads' as the tunnels were caustically referred to by the Israeli security establishment, since they carried people and goods at high speed and were taxed according to a set tariff by the Hamas government.

Hamas gave Adan Hamati a hero's welcome and congratulated him on a "glorious victory" that had echoed in the media and political echelon the world over.

"Some 'glorious victory'," commented Amira Hart caustically to her brother and parents as they sat drinking coffee on the patio one balmy spring afternoon. "This is another 'glorious victory' beautifully disguised as an abysmal failure, just like the 'glorious victory' of the 1973 Yom Kippur war in which our forces decimated both Syria and Egypt and were finally forced by the UN – under threat of war by the Soviet Union – to halt just 100 kilometres from Cairo and a mere 40 km from Damascus. When are our neighbours going to stop their constant hyperbole and start getting real?"

It wasn't a question anyone felt able to answer. Sarah and Dov Hart sat comfortably in their lawn chairs, and Benny was too preoccupied with his mobile phone to get involved.

"So," he said casually. "I'm having a long weekend in Eilat next week." Sarah and Dov looked at each other. They never knew if such information meant their son was on a training course, a mission or just hanging out with his friends. If either of the first two, they knew better than to ask. And if it was the last reason, they knew better than to pry into his personal life.

Amira had no such qualms however. She looked up at her brother's reddening face. "You dog!" she exclaimed. "Who is it? Anyone I have even the remotest chance of liking? What's she do? Where does she live? How much money does her father have?"

"What?" she exclaimed as both Sarah and Dov looked at her in amused alarm. "If you're happy to fail in your parental duty that's your problem, but it's my duty to get information out of unwilling suspects. *Nuuu*?" she turned her interrogative skills back on her brother. "Who is it? Out with it. I have ways of making you talk..."

"Apparently," said Benny "there's some sort of public holiday in Sweden next Wednesday and if you take a couple of days from your annual holiday and use them on the Thursday and Friday, you can have a long time off work. Did you know they actually have five weeks of paid vacation in Sweden? Six in some government jobs?" He shook his head in wonder.

"Well, say hi to Marita from me," said his sister slyly, and added: "And tell her to look after you – I'm fed up of having to come to your rescue."

"Unless," she went on hopefully, "you feel the need for a bodyguard and are willing to pay for my hotel room in Eilat.

No? Ah well, you can't blame me for trying – nothing ventured, nothing gained."

Benny smiled. "Marita says she has heard that Israel is a lot calmer and safer and less violent than Gothenburg – she could do with a spot of relaxation. And that means no prying nosy-parkers. But thanks for your kind offer anyway."

Chapter 58

Despite all the hype from the Hamas regime's posturing, Adan Hamati was a spent force. He even felt like a spent force. He had tried the softer approach that Fatah and the Palestinian Authority said they supported – publicity instead of lethal violence – even though in his experience Fatah and the PA were themselves always very keen to support lethal violence, in Arabic at least, if not in English.

Yes, a few cars had been torched, that symbolism was strong. Unfortunately not the three most heavily armoured Volvo limousines for the Zionist entity's top government ministers, but still, it was an achievement.

But then what? They had set out on a PR mission but returned in coffins. The struggle for a liberated Palestine had claimed yet more martyrs, had created yet more orphans.

Hamas, Hezbollah, al-Qaeda, al-Shabab – these were the organisations that knew how to get things done properly. When they were done, the coffins were always those of the infidels.

He pondered. True, his 'soft terrorism' had almost worked. His operation had brought an entire city to a standstill. The operation had cost peanuts – and in fact had been financed by the intended victims themselves. There was poetic justice there somewhere.

And it had all been carried out by a bunch of moms and dads without any weapons and little real training, at least not in the conventional military sense. It had almost achieved its aims.

So did this soft approach work? Or did one go along with Hamas, Islamic Jihad and their ilk – spectacular raids that caused the enemy's blood to flow?

A tricky question.

Not so many kilometres north of Adan Hamati, Amira Hart was pondering over exactly the same question in Ashdod. Hard or soft tactics, which approach was best? Because ultimately, the two sides had to come to a settlement.

Funny how that simple word 'settlement' had been stripped of its original meaning, hijacked by the Palestinian Arabs and twisted beyond all recognition.

Hijacked. Like so much else.

END

Author's note

Bridges Going Nowhere is a work of fiction. The characters, plot and action are all figments of my imagination.

That does not mean everything in the book has been made up. The countries, cities and even the names of some suburbs and roads are real. This is because it is this element of authenticity that gives any work of fiction a grounding in reality. If I have managed to convey a genuine sense of the societies, institutions and countries depicted in this novel, I'll be delighted. Equally, any errors or inconsistencies are also entirely my own doing and mine alone.

The art of the thriller writer is to inject so much fiction that the story does not reveal any confidential truths, while at the same time keeping the tenor so realistic that the story could conceivably be regarded as a hand-on-heart documentary of actual events. The fiction has to be sufficiently believable to be virtually indistinguishable from the truth, at the same time as the truth around which the story is based should not shine through as though this were actually a documentary. A thriller is thus something of a fictional truth – believable, yet not factually true. It is my hope that I have in some small measure succeeded in uniting these mutually incompatible strains on the writer's skill.

To the best of my knowledge no Palestinian terrorist activity has ever taken place in Gothenburg or indeed anywhere else in Sweden. Having said that, the depiction in *Bridges Going Nowhere* of the often violent Palestinian Arab mind-set has been frequently – and publicly – documented in the international media and is entirely accurate. There is little doubt that there are other, more moderate, Palestinian Arab voices that would gladly strike a different note. But as in so many autocratic societies, freedom of expression is actively, and often lethally, discouraged both in the Palestinian Authority and in the Gaza Strip – two Palestinian territories each governed by a separate and rival faction, Fatah and the terrorist Hamas organisation respectively, bitter enemies that vie with each other.

I wish to make it clear that I have not offered an insider's representation of the inner workings of the various organisations – the Mossad, Shin Bet, SÄPO, the Swedish Police, the Swedish Migration Board or Volvo – that to varying degrees tangent this story. That such organisations and companies exist is well-known, but the way in which they operate, the degree to which Swedes are electronically monitored via their banking system, whether in fact any Swedish car manufacturer has ever sold cars to Israeli government ministries – all this is purely conjectural. Some of these details may by sheer coincidence turn out to be somewhere near the truth, others not at all.

What is not in dispute, however, is that Sweden is already a largely cashless society, so it is not beyond the realms of the plausible that even relatively minor cash purchases would be as traceable as online and in-store credit-card purchases already are.

What is also not in dispute is that Sweden has a remarkably generous – some would say foolhardy – policy of asylum and immigration. One need only look at the political turmoil across large swathes of the Arab world to appreciate that there are hundreds of thousands of hapless civilians – children especially – who are caught up in a violent upsurge fed by religious, tribal, sectarian, ethnic, political and other rivalries. Civilians who want nothing of the chaos that is engulfing them, decimating their families and demolishing their livelihoods and homes. A world community that does not do its utmost to alleviate this terrible suffering is truly a world community that does not care.

Sweden is a country that does care, immensely. The problem is that by and large, Sweden is also a country ruled by bureaucrats whose foremost allegiance is to the national religion of Political Correctness rather than reality. As such, Sweden is fast developing into a safe haven for all manner of subversives, extremists, religious fanatics and avid proponents of every actively anti-democratic Islamist movement in the world today. Not for nothing is the country's right-wing Sweden Democratic party, previously considered a fringe political movement, gaining increasing grassroots support with each succeeding national election.

Anyone who has spent time in Sweden and has taken the time to study the Swedish psyche will be struck by the two main traits of its people: a manic dedication to perceived fair-mindedness, cost what it may, and a naïveté bordering on national suicide.

Sweden's fair-mindedness takes the form of a constant drive towards consensus; where in most other societies a businessman or lawyer would be concerned first and foremost with his or her client's best interests, Swedes have a penchant for ensuring that their counterpart doesn't feel hard done by. This means half of any profit – monetary or otherwise – has already been mentally given away before negotiations begin. Looking out for the other is an admirable trait, but it tarnishes Sweden with the second trait that characterises its national psyche; suicidal naïveté.

Because the fact is that everyone in Sweden understands the problem of unfettered and often inadequately monitored immigration, but nobody wants to be the first to point out the elephant in the room. Immigration is healthy, granting asylum to the needy defines the humanity of the nation; but unchecked segregation, the continued non-integration of ever-increasing numbers of people from diametrically different societies who never get the chance to blend into their new host society – all this merely stores up trouble for the future.

And that future seems to be approaching at a rapid pace. It is a future that the country's mainstream media have historically avoided spotlighting. It is the nation's bloggers who have finally succeeded in forcing Sweden's media and politicians, kicking and screaming in protest, to finally acknowledge the problem that they have spent so many years building up and ignoring:

For all its wonderful beauty, its remarkable achievements, its heart bigger than that of just about any other nation on Earth, Sweden has made some dreadful mistakes in the non-integration of its half a million strong Muslim immigrants. In an ironic twist, Sweden is now seeking the expertise of the one country that has had the most intensive experience of, and the best results from, large-scale immigration and subsequent integration: Israel.

Israel: the country that so many Swedish journalists and so many Swedish politicians love to hate. Yet these are the very people who created Sweden's current problem in the first place.

September 2014

Acknowledgements

I would not have been able to write this novel without the untiring encouragement, support and enthusiasm of Rachel, my wife, my companion, my best friend – and my most unforgiving critic. If this book is well-received, it is thanks mainly to her clarity of thought and her dedication.

They are not aware of it, but much of the inspiration for this book comes from the four people who have been the greatest blessing in my adult life and the source of my inspiration. My children Talia, Tamir, Navit and Nadav are all in here somewhere – in their mannerisms, their approach to life, their achievements, their skills and, in the case of my daughters, the way in which two diminutive slips of girls have always managed to whip their huge, muscular brothers into line.

Made in the USA
Charleston, SC
07 October 2015